THE MYSTERY
OF THE
PERFECT PROPERTY

*Private detectives go around the houses
to solve a murder*

Book #5 in the Quentin Cadbury Investigations

Christine McHaines

Published by The Book Folks

London, 2025

ISBN 978-1-80462-324-4

www.thebookfolks.com

THE MYSTERY OF THE PERFECT PROPERTY is the fifth standalone cozy mystery novel in this series by Christine McHaines. Details about the other books can be found at the back.

Prologue

April 2008

The dead of the night took on a new meaning that spring. The trouble was, what was dead in the night was still dead in the day.

Quentin Cadbury discovered this when he stumbled on the unknown man's body one April morning. As he made his early run through the Greenwich streets, a loud whimpering from a side alley made him slow. He glanced sideways, sensing a movement rather than seeing it. Halfway along the alley were some tall waste bins, and by them a dog lay, its body contorting as though in pain. It moved aside just long enough for Quentin to glimpse a human foot. If it hadn't been encased in a white trainer, he might have missed it.

Stopping in his stride, he stood trying get his breath back and wondering if he'd been seeing things. No, it was definitely a foot. Tentatively, he stepped into the alley towards the dog. The animal tried to stagger to its feet then collapsed again, and Quentin guessed it was injured. He approached it cautiously, calling to it with comforting words. No collar, he noticed as he drew nearer. A gaping cut showed just above one of its ears and a hind leg lay at a peculiar angle.

Behind it, another leg lay in a strange position; the human body it was attached to was slumped against the wall between two bins. Quentin involuntarily recoiled, almost tripping over the dog and lurching against the wall behind to stop from falling. Steadying himself, he forced his gaze frontwards. The man was slim, casually dressed and looked fortyish, with receding mousy hair. From the bottom of his T-shirt sleeve, the faded blue markings of a tattoo were visible. He looked, Quentin thought, exactly like any other man in the street. Except for the dark red stain that covered part of his chest and the liquid which had pooled on the concrete beside him.

The blood still glistened in the early morning half-light, so Quentin surmised the body hadn't been there too long. The man had died sometime in the night.

His detective instinct coming into play, he took his mobile from the waistband of his running shorts and photographed the scene, including the dog, from all angles. After he'd rung 999 and explained the situation, all he wanted was to be away from the body, but he didn't want to leave the dog in pain and he didn't want to move it in case he caused more damage. Also, he knew the police would want to see the scene exactly as he'd found it. Kneeling to comfort the dog, he settled down to wait.

Chapter One

Quentin sat on the Scillonian ferry fighting nausea and wishing it would go faster. He looked up at the slender, blonde-haired woman standing in front of him, and followed her gaze through the sea-sprayed window. Wanda Merrydrew, Quentin's partner and the other half of their London-based detective agency, displayed no visible reaction to the constant rolling of the boat as it ploughed through the choppy Atlantic waters.

I must be mad, travelling nearly three hundred miles to run round an island when the London Marathon is on my doorstep, Quentin thought. He'd taken part in the London Marathon before, but after being in Cornwall on a case, they'd wanted to return and explore the area at a more leisurely pace. So, three days after finding a body in Greenwich, here he was, combining a prearranged holiday with the Tresco marathon in the Isles of Scilly.

The duration of the trip was estimated at two hours forty-five minutes, but it seemed a long time since they'd left Penzance. Quentin couldn't wait to get to St Mary's, the largest of the islands, where they would spend some time before taking the boat to Tresco. All he knew about the Scilly Isles was that they were located off the coast of Cornwall and that there were very few cars on the islands. Transport consisted mainly of buses, bicycles, taxis and roadworthy golf buggies.

A disgruntled bark disturbed his reverie, and he reached down and patted the white West Highland terrier that nestled against Wanda's legs.

'All right, Mozart, not much longer,' he said.

'You two make a right pair,' Wanda told him, turning from the window. 'Why don't we go on deck for some fresh air?'

The thought of trying to walk against the rise and fall of the boat made Quentin feel queasier than ever.

'No thanks. You go with Mozart. I'll stay here with Victor.'

He bent and stroked the silky coat of the golden retriever sprawled at his feet, careful to avoid the area around the top of the splint that supported its hind leg. A plastic cone encircled its neck, protecting the wound that Quentin guessed had been caused by its collar being cut off. The dog twisted its head awkwardly to look at Quentin with soulful eyes.

Wanda picked up her own dog's lead and stepped into the aisle. Mozart followed, trotting into the path of a man who pulled up short and grabbed the back of Wanda's empty seat too late to stop himself from stumbling, almost falling headlong onto his front. A yelp came from the dog at Quentin's feet as it struggled onto its three uninjured legs, the cone wedging itself between Quentin's legs and the seat opposite.

'It's all right, Victor,' Quentin murmured, shifting his legs and easing the cone free.

The man righted himself and glared angrily at both dogs, then at Wanda when she turned to apologise. Whirling round, he went back the way he had come. Catching Quentin's eye, Wanda pulled a face, shrugged, then made her way on to the deck, Mozart at her heels.

What's the matter with him? Quentin thought. Most people felt sorry for injured animals, and many fell instantly in love with Mozart; and, in Quentin's experience, very few men were impervious to Wanda's china-blue eyes and low-pitched, seductive voice. Older than Quentin by almost fifteen years, and with her fortieth birthday behind her, Wanda still drew the attention of a good proportion of the male population.

Dismissing the man from his mind, Quentin waited for Victor to settle down. He shook his head, unable to believe he'd been stupid enough to bring a dog he hadn't known existed until a few days ago on a three-hundred-mile journey. He wasn't particularly a dog person, his attachment to Magpie, his black and white cat, taking precedence in his affection. Of course he was fond of Mozart, because Mozart was part of Wanda. But when Victor had drawn his attention to his dead master, and then had no one to take care of him, those soulful eyes had melted Quentin's heart. How anyone could leave an animal wounded and bleeding was beyond Quentin. But then, the person who had left Victor in that state had left his owner in an even worse state.

Quentin couldn't get the image of the man he'd found out of his mind. The police were still trying to trace his next of kin. He'd had no identification on him, no mobile phone. With no collar and no microchip, the dog had no identification either, and had been named Victor by the police. Quentin had thought that, after he had been treated by the veterinary surgeon, Victor would have been kept with the working police dogs, at least for a while, but this wasn't encouraged; hence Quentin's offer to give him a temporary home.

'It's too windy out there.' Wanda plumped into the seat opposite Quentin, her fair hair blown over her face.

Mozart settled himself at her feet, keeping as much distance as possible from Victor. Whether it was the splint and cone collar that spooked him, or whether Mozart was jealous of any attention Wanda gave Victor, Quentin wasn't sure. The two of them looked quite comical together, one large and encumbered with medical aids, one small and agile but obviously resentful of another dog being anywhere near his mistress. Victor shifted his position and Mozart growled.

'Stop it, Mozart,' Wanda scolded. 'Cheer up, Quentin. We'll soon be there.' She reached over and touched his arm. 'I know it's not just seasickness,' she said softly. 'You're still thinking about the guy you found.'

Quentin nodded and fingered the heart-shaped mole by his right ear.

'Just think,' he said, turning hazel eyes on Wanda. 'If I hadn't been training for this marathon, and if I'd waited for the park gates to open instead of running round the streets, I wouldn't have found him.'

'No. And if it wasn't for Steve Philmore, you might be a suspect.'

Quentin knew that sometimes the person to find a possible murder victim was considered a suspect until the details of the case were known. When he had given his statement, he'd mentioned that he'd previously worked with Detective Chief Inspector Steve Philmore of the Metropolitan Police, a fact that was substantiated by the DCI.

He remembered the subsequent phone call he'd had from Philmore.

'Don't think because you found the body it gives you a right to get involved,' he'd warned. 'Let us do our job. As far as we know, it's just a random attack.'

Random attack or not, the guy's still dead, Quentin had thought. It was still murder, or at least manslaughter.

'They still don't know if it was a random killing or something more,' Quentin mused, aloud now.

Wanda nodded. 'It's quite common for someone to be mugged for their phone; why take everything else, even his keys?'

The boat lurched and Quentin gripped the rim of the chair, swallowing hard and praying that he wouldn't be seeing his breakfast for the second time. As the vessel steadied and his nausea receded, he chided himself for even being on the boat. He'd been warned that the crossing was often rough. On the way back they'd fly, and damn the expense.

Wanda's voice filtered through his thoughts. 'He must have put up a fight, that's why they stabbed him.'

Realizing she was repeating what they'd already discussed to take his mind away from his seasickness, he tried to concentrate on her reasoning.

'But do muggers usually carry knives?' Wanda continued. 'And what a strange time to be out looking for someone to mug. Not many people are about at that time of night. Unless he interrupted something or... unless he was deliberately targeted.'

They had considered these scenarios as possibilities. Quentin knew Wanda felt the same as him – that the man's death needed investigating. Of course, the police would conduct their own enquiries, but until he was identified, their investigation was limited to the householders who lived near the alley where he was found. As far as Quentin knew, no one had heard or seen anything.

'Plus,' Wanda was saying, 'muggers don't often pick on people with big dogs.'

Quentin's gaze strayed to the retriever by his feet. Perhaps Victor had tried to come to his master's rescue. Was that why his leg was broken? Or had he been attacked first to keep him from intervening?

Quentin's thoughts turned to the upcoming marathon. He enjoyed running, not only as a way to keep fit, but because he found it therapeutic. If he had a problem, going for a run often provided an answer.

He was grateful when St Mary's came into view and the boat entered the calmer waters of the harbour, even more grateful when he and Wanda joined the queue to disembark. He kept Victor on a short lead, his injured leg close so it wouldn't be bumped by a swinging bag or a wheeled suitcase. Although the dog seemed to be coping on three legs, Quentin could see it was difficult for him.

They were halfway along the gangplank when Quentin noticed a man staring at him from the jetty, but by the time they got to the jetty he'd disappeared, swallowed by the surging crowd.

'What's up?' Wanda asked as Quentin swept his gaze around.

'Probably nothing,' he told her. 'That bloke, the one who nearly tripped over Mozart, he was looking at us, that's all.'

'So? He's allowed to look at people. It's a free country.'

'Yeah. Well, lots of guys look at you, but not many are interested in me.'

Wanda's mouth twitched. 'There you are then. He must have been looking at me. Perhaps he thinks I'm a glamorous film star, incognito.'

'You wish,' Quentin quipped, though Wanda had been compared to a film actress before.

'No, I don't. I can't think of anything worse than being recognized all the time. Come on. Let's get to the guest house.'

Wanda had pre-booked a taxi, and they piled into it with their luggage and the two dogs. As they drove away, Quentin glanced back towards the harbour. Standing with his hand shading his eyes, staring after them, was the man from the boat.

Chapter Two

The guest house was picturesque, set on a hillside surrounded by trees and shrubs. It was quite small, with an intimate feel and superb views over the countryside. Away to the right, the sea glistened silver, belying its ability to toss ships around like corks. They were welcomed enthusiastically by the owners, Mr and Mrs Allen, who fussed over Mozart and showed concern for Victor.

'He was in an accident,' Quentin said, not wanting to give a lengthy explanation.

'Poor thing,' exclaimed Mrs Allen. 'How upsetting for you. Well, they're both welcome, but as I told you, I don't allow dogs in the bedrooms, so there are some baskets and food bowls in the conservatory. And you're here for the marathon, you said on the phone.'

'Yes,' Wanda answered. 'Quentin's running, so we thought we'd make the most of it and stay here a while before heading to Tresco.'

Their en suite room was attractive and comfortable, with a TV and a king-sized bed.

'Perfect!' Wanda said.

Quentin grunted, pleased to be on dry land but unable to stop thinking about the man on the boat. He'd looked ordinary enough – possibly late thirties, deep-set eyes, close-cropped red-brown hair and a reddish stubble, a black leather jacket and a definite paunch showing over blue jeans. When he'd seen him staring at them though, Quentin had felt uneasy. Oh well, he thought, I expect I'm making mountains out of molehills. Tired after the journey, he shook off his shoes and flopped onto the bed.

* * *

He was awakened by the door opening as Wanda came in. Sitting up and swinging his long legs off the bed, he saw it was nearly one o'clock.

'Hello, sleepyhead,' Wanda said. 'Have you recovered enough to have lunch or do you want to wait till tonight?'

'I can manage lunch,' he said.

'Good. I've been exploring.' She moved over to the window and looked out. 'I like it here. There's a lovely view.'

Yes, Quentin thought, his eyes lingering on the apple-green top that hugged her figure and feeling the beginnings of a tingle. A beautiful view. A view he wished he could see every morning when he woke up. But despite their three-year romance and spending much of their time together, Wanda adamantly refused to move in with him. True, she only lived next door, but she wouldn't make that final commitment.

'The age gap is too big,' she'd told him many times. 'One day you'll meet someone your own age. Let's make the most of what we've got while we can.'

'On the other hand,' he ventured now, holding out his hand, 'we could forget lunch and have a lazy afternoon.'

She swung round, amusement on her face. 'You can't afford a lazy afternoon. You've got to keep training. You're used to running on the flat, or up the slope in Greenwich Park. It's hillier here. You need to practice, not slack off.'

'Some chance of slacking off with you around,' he complained. 'Anyway, there's plenty of time. That's why we came early, to get used to the terrain.'

'I'll be on dog duty,' she reminded him. 'We can't leave them here all day, and there're lots of places to walk them. Not that we'll be able to walk far with Victor. Maybe we should have left him with Colin. He offered to have him.'

At the thought of Colin, Wanda's long-term friend who sometimes assisted with their enquiries, Quentin felt a stab of jealousy. When Wanda's husband had died, Colin had made no secret of the fact that he wanted to marry her. Quentin's resentment of Colin had lessened over the years, and Colin, who was much nearer Wanda's age, seemed to have accepted that Wanda wouldn't end her relationship with Quentin to be with him.

'I didn't think it was fair to palm poor Victor off on someone else after what he's been through,' Quentin said.

'I suppose you're right. Well, it's not far to Old Town. There's a nice café just on the edge, apparently. We could hire bikes too. I could get one with a basket – Mozart would fit in one.'

'Victor wouldn't,' Quentin said, picturing Victor balanced precariously across a basket and handlebars, the plastic cone blocking Quentin's vision. 'He'll be all right on the bus, or we could hire one of those golf buggies we saw advertised. Golf carts, they call them, and you can drive them all over the island.'

'Hmm. Mrs Allen said we can leave Victor here if he's not up to going far,' Wanda told him. 'We'll take him with us as much as we can but he can stay here today. I've already taken him out. We'll walk to Old Town. It'll limber you up.'

'What about you? You've already walked Victor, you said.'

'I'll be fine. Hurry up.'

The April day was cool, but Quentin knew he'd be hot if he decided to run part of the way. Finding his shorts and a vest top, he put on his running shoes and tied a sweatshirt round his waist.

'Come on then,' he said. 'Let's go.'

* * *

Although there were no big hills to conquer, Quentin found the terrain far more challenging than the flat ground he was used to in London. He was glad he'd given himself time to acclimatize before the marathon. He knew there were hills on the Tresco route, and although the circuit was only 3.6 miles, he'd have to complete seven and a half laps to make the full marathon. He ran half the way to the café, stopping several times to wait for Wanda, who panted with exertion when she caught him up.

'I should have got the bus and met you there,' she puffed.

As soon as he arrived at the café, Quentin ordered a bottle of water and collapsed onto an outside seat to wait for Wanda. His mobile rang, and he answered.

'Is that Quentin Cadbury?' The female voice was high-pitched.

'Yes.'

'Hello, Mr Cadbury, my name's Lorna West. I'm a journalist with the *London Herald*. I understand it's you who found a body in Greenwich a few days ago.'

Surprised, Quentin straightened up. How did she know that? Quentin had been told he would only be described as "a member of the public" in the police report, which was what he'd read in the local paper when the headline had appeared.

'How did you get my number?' he asked.

'I told you, I'm a journalist,' she said, as if that were explanation enough. 'I was wondering if we could meet, or I could come to you if that's more convenient.'

'I can't tell you much,' Quentin said, thinking that a three-hundred-mile trip was hardly convenient. 'I was out for a run. I found him and called the police. That's it.'

'I'd still like to meet you, if you don't mind.'

'I'm away at the moment,' Quentin told her.

'Where are you?'

'The Scilly Isles. I'm taking part in the Tresco marathon.'

'Right,' Lorna West said, after a pause. 'I suppose I can justify that. Where are you staying?'

Bloody hell, Quentin thought, amazed that a journalist was willing to travel so far to talk to him.

'Can't we just talk on the phone? Now?' he asked. From the ensuing silence, he surmised that she was thinking about what questions to ask him.

'No,' she replied at length, 'I don't think so. Tell me where you're staying and I'll be there as soon as I can.'

Quentin gave the guest house address, waving to Wanda as she and Mozart came into view.

'Thanks. I'll ring to arrange a time.'

The call ended just as Wanda flopped down opposite him and fanned her face with her hand.

'Phew, that was a marathon in itself,' she panted. 'Was that Colin?'

Quentin shook his head. 'It was a journalist from the *London Herald*. She's coming over to talk to me about the dead guy.'

Wanda's eyebrows lifted. 'Coming from where? Not London? How did she find out it was you?'

Quentin shrugged. 'Don't know, but I get the feeling she knows something, something she didn't want to say on the phone.'

'Really? Why does she think you can tell her anything?'

'No idea,' Quentin said with another shrug. 'I guess we'll find out when she gets here. Let's get some food, I'm starving.'

* * *

When they'd eaten, they wandered around the town, believed to be the oldest settlement on the island, imagining it as it would have been in bygone times and taking in the view of the old harbour and slipway, and across to the airport on one side and the medieval Ennor Castle on the other. In the shopping area, Wanda was able to buy some dog food and treats for Mozart and Victor.

After his meal and his sleep earlier, Quentin felt refreshed enough to walk back to the guest house.

'You go on,' Wanda said. 'I'm not walking back with this dog food. I'll wait for the bus with Mozart.'

As if he was grateful not to have to walk, Mozart barked and wagged his tail furiously.

'We can tell you're a city dog,' Quentin said, laughing. 'See you back there, Wanda.'

Jogging through the old roads, Quentin tried to fathom why Lorna West was prepared to travel so far to see him. Had she found out who the dead man was? Even if she had, why would she want to meet him rather than talk on the phone?

As he left the town for the open road, a golf cart overtook him, not exactly speedily but fast enough to leave Quentin behind. Quentin gave it a cursory glance, registering only that it was a two-seater with a single occupant. It wasn't until it was well past him that he realized who the driver was. Or who he thought it was. The man from the boat.

So what? he thought. It's a small island. He jogged on at a steady pace, trying to put it out of his mind, and succeeding until he was almost back at the guest house. A flash of light shone from a clump of bushes on the hillside, like the sun reflecting from glass.

A mirror, perhaps, or… binoculars?

Chapter Three

Lorna West arrived the next morning. She rang to ask if Quentin could meet her in Hugh Town, the island's capital. Unlike Quentin and Wanda, she'd flown to Newquay, then taken the helicopter from Penzance, making her journey time much shorter. Quentin wondered whether she could claim her travel expenses from the newspaper.

'OK,' Quentin said when he, Wanda, the two dogs and the journalist were settled at a corner table in a pub. 'What's so urgent you couldn't ask me on the phone?'

He looked at Lorna curiously. He judged her to be in her late twenties. She had copper-coloured skin, soft brown eyes and bright-red lipstick that matched her nails. Her shoulder-length hair, held back with a band decorated with red flowers, was a mass of tight curls that hinted at African or Caribbean origins. Definitely attractive, Quentin decided. And as different from Wanda as any woman could be.

Lorna leaned forward and lowered her voice. 'Sorry to be so cloak and dagger,' she said. 'But the man you found – can you tell me exactly what happened?'

When Quentin had relayed the story, she asked, 'Was there anything there, a notebook or maybe a flash drive, something like that, anywhere near him?'

'Not that I saw. I'd already contaminated the scene by being there. I didn't want to disturb anything, and I certainly didn't touch him. I took photos, and I passed them on to the police, but there was nothing to see except the body and the dog.'

'Why do you want to know if Quentin found something?' Wanda said. 'Did you know him?'

Lorna hesitated. Then, as if making up her mind, she said, 'I think it might be someone I was supposed to meet. A man contacted me and said he had information I'd find interesting.'

Quentin exchanged a look with Wanda.

'Interesting how?' Wanda asked.

'He said he wanted to tell me something about the company he worked for. Something he'd found out about them.'

'A whistle-blower,' Wanda said.

'Call him that if you like. He said it was something big, and that he had proof and could provide me with evidence. I arranged to meet him early, six-thirty that morning, but he didn't show. If your dead guy is him… well, I just wondered if he might have had the information on him. When I found out it was you who discovered him—'

'How did you find out?'

Lorna shook her head, making the tight curls bounce.

'I can't reveal my source,' she said, in a practised way that told Quentin she was used to saying this. 'I checked up on you. You're a private investigator, so I figured, you know, more inquisitive, maybe a bit more observant than some people. You might have noticed something before the police got there.'

'If I had, the police would have it now.'

Lorna made a face. 'Hmm. It's just… I've known private investigators who've kept things to themselves.'

Quentin shifted in his seat. He and Wanda had acted off their own bat on occasions, but they'd never withheld evidence and they'd never handled a murder case.

'Sorry to disappoint you, but there was nothing to see. They covered their tracks pretty well. They'd even cut his dog's collar off. This is him, by the way.' Quentin nodded towards Victor, sitting quietly by the table. 'And this is Mozart.'

Mozart's ears pricked up when he heard his name.

'The only thing was scuff marks on the concrete,' Quentin went on. 'They could have been there before. The police had forensics onto them, onto the whole scene. They might have got some fingerprints or DNA from the bins, but that won't help if the attackers are not on their database.'

Lorna looked at him with something Quentin liked to think was respect. 'You know a bit about police procedure, then.'

Quentin was tempted to boast about previous cases, the ones over and above the mundane jobs that usually landed on their desk. The ones where they had collaborated with DCI Steve Philmore and helped stop the activities of an international criminal gang more than once; where DCI Philmore had admitted that their input had been invaluable. But he didn't, because while some members of those gangs were behind bars, the mastermind behind many of these crimes was still at large; a man Quentin called Cultured Voice because of his distinctive way of speaking, who had a personal grudge against Quentin.

Before he could say anything, Wanda spoke.

'Yes, we've worked with the police a few times. So, if this *is* the guy you arranged to meet, do you think he was killed because of what he knew?'

Lorna nodded. 'It seems strange that he didn't turn up. He sounded genuine on the phone – really keen to expose what was going on.'

'You didn't tell him to go to the police, then?' Wanda persisted. 'You wanted an exclusive story?'

'Of course I did. That's my job. Anyway, I couldn't tell him to go to the police until I knew his whole story. He might just have been some nutter trying it on.'

'Did he ask for money?' Quentin asked.

'No, he didn't mention money and neither did I. I don't think getting paid was his motivation.'

'In that case, why didn't he go straight to the police instead of coming to you?'

'He said he'd read some of my stuff, and he thought the police would be too slow on the uptake. I agreed to hand whatever he had over to the police as soon as the story was in print. We made arrangements to meet and he said he'd ring me if he needed to change them. His phone number didn't show when he rang, so I had no way of contacting him.'

'Did he give a name?' Quentin asked.

'Dave; Dave Brown, he said. It mightn't be his real name, and even if it is, it mightn't help much. It's a common name. My colleague on the crime desk liaises with the police press office. As of yesterday afternoon, they still knew nothing about the dead man. He had a tattoo, an old one, but that didn't tell them anything. They're trying dental records. Still, I'll have to tell them he contacted me. If the guy's dead, so is my story.'

'You should have told them your suspicions before now.' Quentin cringed a little under Wanda's reproving gaze, knowing she was thinking of the times they had tried to solve mysteries, or at least gained some useful leads, before contacting the police.

'I only put the two things together yesterday,' Lorna said, looking at him defiantly. 'I'll ring them, but I'll buy you both lunch first if you haven't already eaten. I only had a sandwich on the plane.'

Over his fish and chips, Quentin eyed Wanda's salad and knew he should have ordered the same. He wouldn't be able to run until this evening now, after his food had been digested. He couldn't help feeling sorry for Lorna. She'd travelled a long way to gain nothing in return.

'It's par for the course,' she answered when he said as much.

They were on their coffee when Lorna's mobile rang. As she listened, she turned to a blank page in her notebook and jotted something down. Her conversation ended after a few minutes, and she looked from Quentin to Wanda, a knowing look on her face.

'That was my colleague on the crime desk,' she told them. 'I asked him to let me have any updates. They think they've identified your man.'

Chapter Four

'Well, come on then,' Quentin said. 'Who is he and how did they find out?'

'Someone's been reported missing,' Lorna said. 'He didn't turn up for work for three days and didn't answer his phone. A work colleague went to his house and got no reply, so she told the police. She gave a description that matched their John Doe. They're checking with his company to see what details they hold for him.'

'Could be your Dave Brown, then. Which company is it?' Wanda asked.

'The police haven't said yet. They wouldn't even give his name. They probably want to trace any family before they release too many details.'

'Right.' Quentin was beginning to think coming to the Scilly Isles had been a mistake. He still couldn't get the image of the dead man out of his head, and the more he thought about it, the more he was convinced that the man had been deliberately murdered.

Lorna's voice interrupted his thoughts. 'Well, I need to get back. I've booked a seat on the next helicopter. I might be able to salvage at least part of my story. After all, if it is him, he came to me first. Thanks for seeing me. It was good to meet you, Quentin, and you, Wanda.'

Quentin cleared his throat. 'Hold on a minute—' He stopped, casting a glance at Wanda.

'We *are* private investigators and Quentin did find the body,' Wanda said smoothly, as if reading his mind. 'So… if you find out anything, could you let us know? And vice versa, of course.'

'Vice versa?' Lorna surveyed them, a sceptical look on her face. 'You mean if you remember something else about when you found him, Quentin?'

Is that what they meant? Quentin felt the irrepressible urge luring him towards what he knew he should have done the moment he'd discovered the body: forgotten the marathon and made investigations. Don't get involved, Philmore had warned. They knew the DCI well enough to call him by his first name when they met, but Philmore was still a police detective who tended to regard private investigators as interfering amateurs. But since when had that stopped them?

'OK,' Lorna said, as though tired of waiting for a reply. She produced a business card and handed it to him. 'You scratch my back and I'll scratch yours. The police have their resources and they do a great job, but there's no reason we can't give them a bit of help on the quiet, is there? After all, they often appeal to the public for information.'

Quentin nodded, pocketed the card and watched as Lorna rose, picked up her coat and bag, flashed them a smile and walked away.

'Well,' said Wanda when she'd gone. 'How does she think she can salvage her story? She said herself it was dead. Whatever this Dave Brown – if it is him – wanted to tell her, she won't be the first to know now.'

'No, but… she seems quite a determined lady. She won't give it up without a fight.'

'*We're* not giving anything up,' Wanda said, as though trying to justify their decision to come to the Scilly Isles. 'We never got started on the case, and you've been training for this run for months. Anyway, by the time we go and get our things, we'll miss the next flight.'

For a long moment, they gazed at each other, the import of these last words hanging between them.

Quentin grimaced. 'I know.'

They spent the next few hours wandering through the streets and down to the harbour, then up to the Garrison overlooking the town, mostly in silence, each wrapped in their own thoughts. When Quentin thought of the upcoming marathon, his heart beat fast. When he thought of the mystery unfolding back in London, it beat faster. Stupid, he told himself. If he withdrew from the race, he could get to London and find the case all wound up. Even if it wasn't, what could they do? It wasn't as if they had a client, someone who'd pay them to find the killer. But then they hadn't been paid for solving their three biggest and most important cases either. The excitement and satisfaction had been enough.

The whirr and beat of a helicopter's rotor blades sounded above them, and they looked up to see it flying over the town and disappearing into the distance.

'I'm getting the bus back,' Wanda said when the noise had faded. 'I'll have to go with Victor. You take Mozart if you want to walk, and I'll buy some pasties and scones for later.'

'OK.'

Quentin headed back the way they had come, Mozart at his heels. When he'd left the town behind, he unfastened the dog's lead, clipped it to his shorts and wound it round his middle, tucking the end under his elastic waistband. Initially he walked, giving his lunch time to settle. Mozart trotted obediently beside him, speeding up when Quentin did and breaking into a run when Quentin decided to take the last mile at speed. He stopped on the final incline, taking in the beauty of the place and marvelling at the shrubs and flowers that bordered the path, some of which he'd never seen on the mainland.

As he resumed his journey, a flash of light caught his eye. It came from the same clump of bushes as before, ideally placed to observe both the road and the guest house. A birdwatcher? A twitcher, in the exact same spot as before?

Pulling his gaze back to the road ahead, Quentin walked on. He hadn't mentioned seeing the flash to Wanda, dismissing it as unlikely to be anything untoward, even thinking he'd imagined it. But now he knew he hadn't. Someone *was* there.

High enough to conceal anyone in its midst, the clump of bushes was about fifteen feet to the right of the path. Quentin walked quickly as he approached, keeping his eyes to the front. When he was parallel with the bushes, he suddenly swerved, broke into a run and dashed towards them, reaching them in seconds. Sweeping the branches aside, he gasped when a startled face appeared and recognition washed over him. It was the boat man.

Chapter Five

The man instantly turned and tried to get away, dropping the binoculars he'd been holding as he did so. Quentin reached out, grabbed the collar of his jacket and yanked him back. Seconds later, he cursed as the jacket went limp in his hand and the man pushed his way out of the bushes and began to run. Flinging down the jacket, Quentin sidestepped the shrubs and sprinted after him. His quarry's efforts didn't match Quentin's running prowess, and Quentin felled him in a few easy strides. His opponent was strong though, and he wrestled with Quentin until he was able to break free and stand. Once he had broken loose of Quentin's flailing grasp, he ran. He'd only gone a few feet when he fell again. Quentin heard the thump as he hit the ground. Thinking the man must have tripped on a stone, Quentin leapt forward, intending to straddle him to keep him down. Instead, something pulled taut at his legs, and he tumbled headlong on top of the other man, his nose connecting with the back of the man's head. Dazed, he manoeuvred his way onto his knees, the constriction on his legs tightening.

Bloody hell, he thought groggily, looking down to see that Mozart's lead had unwound and wrapped itself round Boatman's leg, while the other end was still clipped to Quentin's shorts.

Mozart, barking excitedly throughout the escapade, now stood over Boatman, growling each time he tried to get up.

'What's going on?' Wanda's voice resounded as she came up from the bus stop at the bottom of the road.

Covering his nose with one hand, Quentin struggled to his feet. Then, with bloodied fingers, he clutched at his shorts as they were pulled down to his knees by the dog lead. Cursing, he unclipped it and let it drop.

'Who's this?' Wanda asked as she came up beside the felled man.

Mozart, his front paws on Boatman's back, looked up at her as though in triumph. "Look what we've got," Quentin could see written on his face. Mozart's demeanour changed as soon as Victor limped up to them. He yapped and hovered over his prize possessively. Ignoring him, Victor padded uncertainly up to Quentin and stood by him, growling softly.

'That's what I'd like to know,' Quentin grunted, taking the tissue Wanda proffered and dabbing at his nose. 'He's the guy from the ferry – he's been spying on us.'

'Has he indeed.' Wanda moved along so she could see the man's face. 'It's all right, Mozart, you can let him up now.'

Mozart retreated, padded over to Victor and gave a single bark. "You might be bigger than me," he seemed to say, "but I can do anything you can do."

Quentin watched as Boatman got to his knees and swivelled into a sitting position. Rounding on him, Wanda said calmly, 'OK, who are you and why are you following us?'

Boatman glowered at them but said nothing.

'You might as well tell us,' Quentin said. 'We'll find out anyway.'

Still nothing.

'Look, is this to do with the bloke I found?'

'It's none of your business,' Boatman snarled.

'I think we're entitled to know why someone is spying on us,' Wanda replied coolly.

'Perhaps we should phone the police, Wanda,' Quentin suggested, wondering how she could keep so calm. 'We could lodge a harassment complaint.' He had no idea if such a complaint could be made, but it didn't matter. The mention of police was enough to change Boatman's expression to one of alarm.

'That won't stick,' he said. 'All I've done is watch you.'

'What for?' Quentin demanded. 'You don't know us. Why would you need to watch us?'

Boatman resumed his glaring but still didn't answer.

Wanda whipped out her phone, and before Boatman realized what was happening, took a photo.

'Good thinking, Wanda,' Quentin said. 'That'll help the police when we report this.'

'Look,' Boatman said. 'I was hired to follow you, and before you ask, I don't know who by.'

Quentin snorted, then wished he hadn't, his hand going to his nose.

'Hired!' he spluttered. 'Don't tell me you're a private investigator.'

Boatman's glare seemed to be a permanent facial expression. The look he gave Quentin left no doubt as to his opinion of private investigators.

'I think what he means,' Wanda put in, 'is he's been told to watch what we're doing, in case we find out something we shouldn't. They should have picked someone a bit more discreet.'

The glare switched to Wanda. Instead of answering, Boatman stood up and began walking towards where his jacket lay. Mozart growled, but Wanda grasped his collar.

'Look,' she said, 'we won't call the police if you tell us who sent you.'

'I told you, I don't know.'

'You must know who to contact with any information.'

'I don't. They're going to contact me.'

'Yeah, right,' Quentin scoffed. 'You must be getting a nice big handout to take a job without knowing who's paying you.'

Boatman scooped up the black leather jacket and shrugged it on.

'I'm off,' he said. 'If you try to stop me, I'll have you up for assault.' Looking at Mozart, he added, 'And I'll report that mutt as a dangerous dog.'

As Wanda gasped, he whirled away and started to run to where a track wound up the hill, past the guest house and out of sight. Quentin made to go after him, but was stopped by Wanda's restraining hand.

'We can't make him talk,' she said. 'And he's right. He hasn't actually done anything except watch us and we can't prove that.'

'We've got the photo, though that doesn't prove anything, and we've got these,' Quentin countered, rummaging through the bushes until he found the binoculars.

Wanda nodded. 'That's another thing. He could say we attacked him and stole his binoculars.'

'I didn't attack him,' Quentin protested.

'Tell that to a copper when your nose is bleeding. Come on, let's go and get you cleaned up.'

Quentin saw her point. Victor padded up to him and licked his leg. 'Thanks for your help,' Quentin said. 'No wonder your master got stabbed if all you did was growl and lick him.'

'That's not fair,' Wanda objected. 'The poor thing's probably still traumatized. Come to think of it, I haven't heard him bark at all since we've had him.'

They made their way back to the guest house. They'd nearly reached it when they heard the whine of an electric engine, and a golf cart went past within yards of them as Boatman drove away.

'Bloody hell!' Quentin exclaimed. 'Where did he hide that? And what sort of spy follows people in a golf cart?'

'His sort,' Wanda said, shading her eyes to see the retreating buggy. 'Still, it blends in here perfectly. Honestly, you can run faster than that thing.'

Quentin was tempted to do just that.

'Don't bother,' Wanda warned, guessing his thoughts. 'We've already said we can't make him talk. Come on, let's get back.'

* * *

'We didn't even get his name,' Quentin grumbled when Wanda had washed the blood from his nose.

'No, but I got the registration. We just need to contact the hire company and find out who hired that cart.'

Wanda picked up a brochure from the dressing table and found the number. 'Let's hope they're still open.'

Almost as soon as she'd punched the number into her mobile, the call was answered.

'Hello,' she said. 'I wonder if you can help me. I was out today and I saw a man get into one of your carts and drive off. The thing is, he left his binoculars behind. They look like good ones so I'd like to return them. If I give you the registration, can you tell me his name and contact details?'

There was a pause, where Quentin assumed the person at the cart rental firm was checking the details.

'Nick Crawford,' Wanda said. 'The Blue Lodge, Hugh Town. Do you have a mainland address, or a telephone number, in case we don't get there before he leaves? ... No telephone number. Home address? ... Oh, all right, never mind. How long did he hire the cart for? ... A week. Yes, of course, we'll have time to return them. Thank you. That's very helpful.'

Quentin put down the pen he'd used to note down the details.

'They wouldn't give you his home address?' he asked. 'He must have shown his driving licence, some ID with his address on.'

Wanda shrugged. 'The address may not be right anyway. I forgot to change the address on mine for months when I moved. Anyway, they wouldn't give it to me. They said to contact him at the hotel he's staying at. He's hired the cart for a week so I'm guessing he wasn't planning on leaving the island till we did.'

Quentin drew a deep breath before saying what had been on his mind since his encounter with Boatman.

'Talking of leaving the island...' He left the sentence unfinished, knowing there was no need.

'What about the race?' Wanda asked. 'All that training? You don't need to go back. I could go, start enquiries. Colin would help.'

'Colin!'

Wanda flashed him an impatient look. 'Don't start that, Quentin. Colin's been helpful and you know he'll do as much as he can.'

The thought of his rival for Wanda's affection stealing his thunder made Quentin more determined to return to London.

'I can't just stay here running round an island while you're working. This guy who's been following us may be an amateur, but whoever killed Dave Brown isn't. Dave was about to reveal something, something bad enough to get him killed.'

'But we could get back and find the police have already found who did it, and then you'll have given up the race for nothing. Anyway, I thought Philmore told you to leave it alone.'

The voice of reason, Quentin thought. Yet when he looked into Wanda's eyes, he saw the excitement there, and he knew she shared his need to get to the bottom of things. A tacit understanding lay between them. Before either of them could speak, Quentin had a call from Lorna West.

'Thought I'd let you know the dead guy *is* my Dave Brown,' she said. 'My source has just confirmed it. Mum's the word, though. We can't print anything until his next of kin IDs the body, but that's the name the work colleague who reported him missing gave.'

'OK, Lorna, thanks,' Quentin said, thinking that Lorna's source must be someone connected to the police force – someone who could well be fired for leaking information.

'All right,' Wanda conceded when Quentin repeated the information. 'We'll go in the morning. But we should check out this Nick Crawford first.'

'How? I mean, it's pointless without knowing more about him. We could ring the hotel he's staying at in Hugh Town, but if he's still there, how could we ask for his home address? They'd probably ask for our number and get him to ring us, maybe take a message or say go there to see him. It's not as if it's a million miles away.'

'You're right. It's no good going there to confront him. He's already threatened to have you up for assault. What a cheek, saying he'll report Mozart as a dangerous dog! No one would believe that.'

'No,' Quentin said with a shake of his head. 'It wouldn't stick, any more than the assault charge would, but it's the hassle, and the time it would take to sort it out.'

'Yes, that would be a hassle. Still, seeing him confirms one thing, Quentin – he wasn't there when your man was killed. He didn't recognize Victor and Victor didn't recognize him. So if there's no more we can do here, what are we going to do for the rest of the evening?'

Indicating towards a box on the dressing table, she continued, 'After our pasties and scones, that is.'

Quentin gave a meaningful grin. 'Well, there's always television.'

'So there is. It's a bit decadent, lazing around, eating scones and then watching TV in bed.'

'Well, there are other things to do in bed.'

Wanda shook a finger at him, trying to look stern. 'You're a very naughty boy.' Unable to stop her mouth from twitching, she continued, 'Still, I suppose we've got to work off the pasties and scones somehow.'

Chapter Six

Having left his car in Penzance, Quentin resisted the temptation to fly from St Mary's to Land's End, and they made the return journey on the Scillonian. To Quentin's relief, the crossing was reasonably calm.

They used the drive back to try to make sense of things. Knowing that Dave Brown was a whistle-blower deepened the mystery. From what Lorna had said, it didn't seem as though the man had wanted money for the information he held – information he'd likely been killed for.

This stirred Quentin's sense of justice. The man may have been a totally unsavoury character for all he knew, but no one deserved to die because they'd discovered something someone didn't want them to know. Whatever he'd been, Dave Brown's death felt personal to Quentin. He could still picture his body, slumped against the wall between the bins. If he was deliberately murdered, as now seemed the likeliest scenario, then Quentin felt he owed it to him to find the murderer.

'The question is,' he mused aloud while Wanda was driving, 'if he had proof of wrongdoing which he was going to give to Lorna, where is it? I mean, he was blowing the whistle on the company he worked for, so if the powers that be knew Dave had proof of illegal dealings, they'd have wanted to erase any evidence. If he had it on him when he was attacked, they would have taken it, so why send someone after me?'

'Why would he have had it on him?' Wanda said, taking her eyes from the road to cast a glance at him. 'He wasn't meeting Lorna till the next morning.'

'Hmm. If he didn't have it on him, maybe they tried to make him say where it was and things got nasty.'

'But they wouldn't kill him until they'd found it, would they? The company would have his address, so if they couldn't get it from him, they could get someone to break in and search his house. It has been known.'

'Yeah, you could say that,' Quentin said drily, recalling the time he'd been broken into. 'Well, now the police know who he is, they'll probably check his place, if they haven't already, especially if Lorna's told them what she knows.'

Pulling in at a service station, Wanda parked Quentin's aging BMW and took Victor and Mozart for a walk around the edge of the car park. When she returned, she located a bottle of water and gave the dogs a drink.

'Come on,' she said. 'We'll go in for a break. I'm desperate for a coffee.'

'You know,' Quentin said when they were in the service building, 'if Lorna's contacted the police, it'll help their investigation.'

'Yes. And your point is?'

Quentin fingered the mole by his ear. 'Well…'

'Don't even think about it, Quentin. Philmore's told you to stay out of it. We can't ask him anything.'

'Why not? We've given him enough information in the past.'

Wanda looked at him over the rim of her cup. 'We'd be better to ring Lorna, see if she's found out anything else. Not yet though. Give her a chance.'

'Yeah. Right, let's get going then. We're wasting time.'

* * *

The first thing Quentin saw when he opened his front door was Magpie. The black and white cat was sitting at the bottom of the stairs, his back arched and his tail high.

'It's only me, boy. It's all right – Victor's staying with Mozart tonight.'

Magpie eyed him disdainfully. Quentin knew it would be a while before he was forgiven for his absence. He hadn't been forgiven for bringing Victor home either, which was why Wanda had offered to have Victor tonight.

Leaving his suitcase in the hall, Quentin went to the kitchen, made tea and carried it into the lounge. The familiarity of the house relaxed him. He loved its simplicity; one big room – originally two – a bathroom and kitchen downstairs, two bedrooms upstairs, a small forecourt, and an easy-maintenance courtyard garden. No garage, but his rented lock-up was just a few streets away. He loved the location of the house too. Right next door to Wanda's, close to shops, buses, trains, and Greenwich Park. "Compact and convenient," he supposed an estate agent's description would be, although he hadn't had to deal with an estate agent himself. Strictly it was his mother's property, left to her by her sister, Quentin's Aunt Josie.

Quentin reached into his pocket and took out his wallet and mobile phone. Feeling something else there, he drew out Lorna West's card. He glanced at the clock. Almost seven. Late, but he guessed journalists didn't work standard hours. After all, Lorna had planned to meet Dave Brown at six-thirty in the morning.

Fighting the urge to ignore Wanda's advice and ring her, he went back to the kitchen and opened a fresh pouch of cat food for Magpie.

'Here you are, boy,' he said as he placed a bowl in front of the cat. 'The automatic feeder's all right, but I expect you're fed up with dried food.'

Magpie sniffed at the food, and as usual when Quentin had been away, ignored it and stalked imperiously out of the room.

Quentin rolled his eyes and went back to the lounge. His gaze rested on his mobile, and Lorna West's card. Unable to resist, he snatched up the phone and punched the keypad.

'Lorna? It's Quentin Cadbury. Sorry to disturb your evening – I just wondered if you'd found out anything more.'

'Not really,' she replied. 'I've told the police what Dave Brown said, so now they've got a motive for his death. That should help.'

'Have they told you what company he worked for?'

'No, but I'm working on it. Do you know how many Dave Browns there are in London?'

'Thousands, I should think.' Quentin paused before continuing. 'Any idea who's handling the case in CID?'

'I spoke to a Detective Sergeant Turner. Who did you see after you found him?'

Not who I wanted to, Quentin thought. 'Just the duty officer. I wondered if you had a name, that's all.'

'Well, they won't thank us for going direct to whoever's got the case unless we've got something substantial to tell them, and they certainly won't share information with us. My source will only go so far.'

Lorna spoke as though she'd been taken to task for pestering the police herself, and Quentin had no intention of mentioning Philmore's name. Although Philmore had warned him off when he'd learned that Quentin had found the body, as far as Quentin knew the case hadn't been assigned to Philmore.

'So nothing new then?' he asked.

Lorna's slight hesitation alerted him instantly. 'What is it? Come on, I thought we had an arrangement.'

'It's probably nothing,' she said. 'It's just – when I left the pub yesterday in St Mary's, I saw someone outside. I think he followed me. I got a taxi so I lost him.'

'What did he look like?'

'I didn't get a proper look at him, but he was wearing a black leather jacket.'

'Boatman!'

'What?'

'A bloke in a black leather jacket followed us,' Quentin explained. 'He was on the boat when we went to the Scilly Isles, so we've nicknamed him Boatman. He's been watching us. I caught up with him and confronted him. All he said was he was told to watch us.'

There was small silence.

'OK,' Lorna said eventually. 'So someone doesn't want us poking around. I'm guessing it's the people Dave Brown was going to expose.'

'His name's Nick Crawford,' Quentin said. 'The guy who's been watching us.'

'Nick Crawford? How did you find out?'

'He was using one of those golf carts, so we got the registration and phoned the cart hire company.'

'Neat. So, if this guy reported seeing us together, they'll know it's me Dave was going to spill the beans to.'

'Not necessarily,' Quentin said, wishing he hadn't admitted to confronting Boatman. Lorna would be worried that she'd be watched all the time now. Why would anyone want to watch her? Were they afraid Dave Brown had already given her some information? Another thought came to him – if the killer had taken Dave's phone, they could have checked the outgoing calls and traced Lorna that way.

'Look, Lorna, this Nick Crawford and whoever's hired him don't know why we met. You could have just wanted to interview me about finding the body.'

'The paper's already covered the unknown body story,' she told him. 'And you weren't named.'

'Of course I wasn't. So how did they find out it was me? Maybe the same way you did?'

'No,' Lorna said immediately. 'And before you ask, I can't reveal my source. The thing is, Dave said he had proof of what was going on, which he was going to give me. That's why I asked if you found anything at the scene. You didn't, and the police couldn't have done or they would have identified the body sooner, so what did Dave do with it? If someone from the company killed him for it, they can't have it, otherwise they wouldn't be following us.'

Quentin had thought this himself. If the killer had found out it was Lorna who Dave was going to whistle-blow to, and they hadn't found the so-called proof he was planning to give her, she could be in danger.

'There's always police protection,' he suggested, though he knew they would need more than Lorna's one sighting to warrant that.

'I'll be careful,' Lorna said.

'Well, don't take any risks. If you need to go somewhere, meet anyone, I'd be happy to tag along. Safety in numbers and all that.'

'Thanks. You shouldn't be taking risks either, or your partner.'

'We'll be careful too. OK, Lorna. Call me if you learn anything.'

When he'd rung off, he went to the cabinet – a legacy from his Aunt Josie, as was most of his furniture – and located the whisky bottle. After pouring himself a measure, he flopped onto the settee, watching Magpie as he strutted in. He caught a whiff of chicken on the cat's breath.

'You decided to eat it after all then, eh boy?'

Magpie ignored him and began to clean himself, lifting a paw to brush any pieces of food from his whiskers. Quentin leaned back, cradling his whisky and trying not to think about Dave Brown, but it was no good. He was convinced Dave had been murdered for what he knew; and murder, it seemed, couldn't be ignored.

Chapter Seven

The trill of his mobile woke him the next morning. Having suspended their current cases – all three of them mundane – until after the marathon, he had allowed himself the luxury of a lie-in. He was shocked to see that, after hours of restlessness and sporadic dozes, he'd slept until nine-thirty. He snatched up the phone and pressed the green button.

'Quentin? Quentin Cadbury?'

Quentin frowned, unable to place the feminine voice. 'Yes,' he croaked.

'Good morning, Quentin, it's Debbie Francis, DS Francis.'

Quentin swung his legs over the edge of the bed and sat up. He hadn't spoken to the detective sergeant since working with her and Philmore on a previous case.

'Debbie. This is a surprise.'

'DCI Philmore asked me to ring you.' Although she'd used his first name and given hers, DS Francis kept up an official tone. 'A relative of the man you found has been traced and has identified the victim. We haven't told her who you are, but she's expressed a wish to meet you.'

Fully awake now, Quentin's eyebrows shot up. 'Has she? Did she say why?'

'Only that she wants to thank you personally for looking after the dog.'

Quentin's mind raced. If he met this person, perhaps he would at least find out what sort of man Dave Brown had been.

'Well, it's OK with me. Where and when does she want to meet?'

There was a pause, as if the detective sergeant was deciding what to say. 'I suggested you came here, but the chief said you're away–'

'Actually, Debbie, we're back now, so any time will be all right.'

'Are you? Well, anyway, she didn't want to meet you here. She asked for your number, but I said I'd check with you first.'

'Right. You can give her my number, that's fine. What's her name?'

'Anne Roberts. She's his sister.'

'Right,' said Quentin again. 'So… does this mean you're handling the case now? Is Philmore the senior investigating officer?'

'Yes.' The word was clipped, sharp, as though Francis thought she shouldn't be talking to him about the case. Although she and Quentin got on well enough, she'd never made any attempt to hide her disapproval of private investigators. 'But that doesn't mean–'

'I know,' Quentin interrupted. 'I won't ask for any favours. After all, it's not my case.'

'Good. Well, as long as that's clear.'

Message received and understood, Quentin thought. In spite of all the help they'd given in the past, it was clear that Debbie Francis still resented what she considered "interference" from a member of the public. Contrarily, Philmore had once told Quentin that, if he could learn to follow the rules, he wouldn't make a bad copper.

'Perhaps you'll get back to us when you've seen her,' Francis went on. 'Let us know what she says in case she tells you something she forgot to tell us. She was pretty upset when we spoke to her.'

When the call ended, Quentin went downstairs to shower. Then he made tea and toast, turned on the radio and fed Magpie. It was ten-thirty before he heard a key grating in the front door lock. Realizing he hadn't unbolted it, he walked though and pulled back the bolt.

'Morning,' Wanda greeted. 'I knocked at nine but you were obviously still asleep.'

'Sorry, I didn't hear you. I kept waking up in the night. Tea?'

'Yes please. Why did you keep waking up?'

Quentin relayed his conversations with Lorna the night before and Debbie Francis that morning.

'His sister wants to see you?' Wanda sounded surprised. 'What for?'

'She says she wants to thank me for looking after Victor. Maybe she'll take him.'

'Yes, maybe. How did they trace her, did Debbie say?'

'No, and I didn't ask. She had her official hat on. Or do I mean officious?'

Wanda gave a half-laugh. 'She's all right, really. Just trying to do her job.'

Quentin nodded. 'Yeah, I suppose. Well, we'll see what this sister has to say, and take it from there.'

* * *

Anne Roberts had her brother's mousy hair and fairish skin, but as far as Quentin could remember, she didn't look like him. He felt slightly guilty that, although he kept picturing Dave's body as he'd seen it – the glassy, unseeing eyes, the bloodstains – his features were beginning to fade.

Anne was dressed in well-cut grey trousers, a blue jumper and a dark-blue jacket. There was a daffodil badge pinned to her lapel. Quentin wondered if she'd known anyone who'd died of cancer or whether she just supported Marie Curie. He found her sitting alone in the foyer of the small hotel where they'd arranged to meet. Although she looked like she'd been crying, she managed a weak smile as Quentin approached her.

'Mrs Roberts?'

'Anne, please. You're Quentin.' Her voice was flat, with no trace of a question in it. 'Can I get you a drink?'

'Tea, please,' he said, eyeing the teapot and two cups already on the low table beside her.

'They've just brought this,' she told him, 'and I asked for two cups, but order something else if you prefer.'

'Tea's fine,' he said, taking a seat opposite her. When she'd poured the tea, she leaned forward, her eyes watery.

'The police told me you sat with Goldie after you… after you found Dave.'

'Goldie? Oh, you mean Victor. Sorry, we didn't know his name. The police named him Victor so we called him that as well. Yes, well, the poor thing was injured.'

Anne picked up a serviette from the tea tray and dabbed at her eyes, smudging her mascara.

'Dave and I were close until he moved down here,' she sniffed. 'I suppose we still are – were – close, but, you know, it's a long way to Newcastle. Dave hasn't been home much lately. Our mum died last year and, well, you don't want to know our family history. In a way I'm glad she's gone. Losing Dave would have killed her.'

'I'm sorry,' Quentin said, feeling inadequate.

'It's not just that he died,' Anne went on as though she hadn't heard him. 'It's the way he died. Knifed down in the street. Murdered. You see it on the news, but you never think it will happen to you or anyone you know.'

Quentin waited. He felt sorry for this woman, so obviously distraught, but it was apparent he wasn't going to find out anything about her brother unless he asked.

'Anne, when did you last speak to your brother?'

'Two weeks ago. Why? The police asked me that.'

'I expect they think he might have said something to give them a clue as to why he was killed. What did he say when you spoke to him?' Seeing the question on her face, he continued, 'It was quite a shock, finding him like that. I'd like to know why he was killed as much as you would. I'd like to find who did it, too.'

'You would?'

'Yes.' Quentin leaned forward and lowered his voice. 'The thing is, Anne, I'm a private investigator. I know the police do a good job but they're stretched.'

Anne nodded. 'So what are you saying? You'll investigate Dave's murder? I haven't got much money.'

Quentin spread his hands. 'I don't want money, Anne. I want to see the people who killed Dave behind bars.'

'That's good of you,' Anne said, looking surprised. 'I don't think I'll be much help though. Like I said, since he moved to London, we only spoke on the phone.'

'What sort of person was he? Was he married, children?'

'No. He had a partner for years but she ended up marrying someone else. That upset him. That's why he moved from Newcastle, plus he was made redundant. He was a kind man – loved animals, wouldn't hurt a fly. I remember when he was a teenager, he saw someone mistreating a dog and told them to back off. He got a black eye. After that, he stopped tackling people and reported them instead. He wasn't really built for fighting.'

A picture of the dead man was taking shape in Quentin's mind. Kind, animal-loving, but more, he sounded like the type of person who didn't look the other way when he saw something he thought was wrong. Which bore out what Lorna had said – that he wasn't interested in money, just in stopping whatever was going on in his company.

'Did he tell you about his job down here?'

'Oh yes, he was thrilled when he landed that job. He said they're a top-notch estate agent, you know, they find posh properties for people, some in the UK but mainly abroad.'

'So he was an estate agent then?'

'Not really. I mean, he did some work on that side of things, but it was his IT skills they employed him for. He was a whizz on the computer.'

'What was the company called, do you know?'

Anne's forehead wrinkled. 'I told the police. Something like Perfect Properties. Apparently it's quite upmarket.'

Pulling a pen and a notebook from his jacket pocket, Quentin wrote down the name. He was pleased to be getting this insight into Dave Brown. Now he knew a little about him, he felt even more compelled to investigate his death.

'So, as far as you know, there was nothing on his mind when you last spoke? He seemed the same as usual?'

Anne's frown deepened. 'Well… I must admit he was a bit distant. I thought maybe he was worried about work — you know, too much to do and not enough time. I asked him and he said not to worry, he'd sort it out.'

'He'd sort it out? He didn't tell you what it was?'

'No. He started talking about his dog. That was it, really.'

Disappointment flooded Quentin. So now he knew what Dave had been like, but he was no nearer to finding out what he wanted to expose.

'About the dog,' Anne said. 'I'd like to take him, but I don't think my husband would agree. He's not too good with dogs. I'll ask my son though. He might have him.'

'It's OK, Anne, I can keep him for the time being. If you remember anything else Dave said, anything you think might help, would you ring me?' Quentin produced a card and passed it to her.

'Of course. I'll be going back to Newcastle tomorrow. The police say the coroner might not release Dave's body yet, so there's no point staying here. I'll come back when I can make arrangements.'

'Did the police say how they traced you?' Quentin asked.

'They got his address from the person who reported him missing – someone he worked with, apparently – and went to his house. They found me in his address book. I asked if I could take some things – you know, photos, family stuff, but–' Anne stopped and looked away.

'But?' Quentin urged.

'They said unless there was anything I needed to take urgently then would I mind waiting. I asked what else they wanted to do there but they said they couldn't tell me at the moment.'

'I see,' Quentin said, though he didn't. His understanding was that once a property had been checked, then relatives were able to go in and remove any items they wanted – unless it was still being treated as a crime scene, which Dave's house surely wasn't. Why should it be, when he'd been killed in an alley away from the house?

'Where did he live?' Quentin continued. 'I mean, I know where I found him, but I don't know his actual address. Can you give it to me, and your number?'

When he'd taken the details, he finished his tea, then stood up to leave. Anne looked ashen, bereft.

'Don't worry,' Quentin said, putting a sympathetic hand on her shoulder, 'we'll get them.'

And as he left her there, he wished he felt as confident as he hoped he sounded.

Chapter Eight

Quentin went straight back to Wanda's and repeated everything Anne Roberts had told him.

'Perfect Properties?' Wanda mused. She went to her computer and typed in the name.

'Nothing,' she said. 'Oh, there's a Property Perfections. "Exclusive properties just for you, at home and abroad." Maybe that's it.'

She jotted down the address and telephone number, and handed the information to Quentin.

'Must be,' he decided. 'Shouldn't think there'd be two estate agents in London with a name like that. Looks like our first lead.'

He met Wanda's gaze and saw the same excitement there that was rising in his stomach.

'OK,' she said. 'So Property Perfections is the place to start.'

'Yes... but what about Anne not being allowed to get things from her brother's house?'

'Well, I suppose they haven't finished there yet.'

Quentin frowned. 'Why not? He wasn't killed there. My theory is they attacked him in the street and he ran down the alley to try to get away, then they clobbered him by the bins, so the only reason the police should have needed to go to his house was to find his next of kin and–'

'See if the evidence Dave was going to give Lorna was there,' Wanda finished.

They gazed at each other for a long moment.

'And, of course,' Wanda resumed, 'that's exactly what the company would do if they suspected that Dave was going to blow the whistle on their little game, whatever it is.'

'You mean, if Dave didn't have what they wanted on him, they might have forced him to tell them where it was, killed him, either purposely or accidently, then broke in to look for the incriminating evidence?'

'That's it, unless he didn't tell them where the evidence was and they broke into his house in case it was there. Either way, if the house has been done over, it's connected to a major crime, so the police are keeping it under wraps for a bit.' Wanda paused, letting this idea settle before continuing. 'Anyway, we should go to this Property Perfections and get the feel of the place.'

Quentin looked at her. 'There's only one problem with that. If Boatman has reported what happened in Scilly and given our descriptions to someone in the company, they'll rumble us.'

'Hmm. Do you think he works for them?'

'I hope not. I shouldn't think he's capable of persuading anyone to buy an expensive property, unless he glares them into it. I don't think he's got the perfect sales pitch.'

'I didn't mean as an agent; I meant, I don't know, as a handyman or something? Or do you think they advertised, you know, "part-time spy wanted, must be able to follow people undetected"?'

'Ha ha. Seriously, we can't risk them realizing who we are.'

'Well,' Wanda said, 'as I see it, we've got two options: either go in disguise or get someone else to go.'

'Disguise? That didn't go too well last time, as I remember.'

'I could do it.' She ran her hand over her blonde hair. 'I quite fancy a change. I've got that wig I had for Emma's fancy dress party, and some of those sparkly glasses.'

Emma was Colin's daughter, and Quentin recalled the party with chagrin. He had gone as Robin Hood, which had been fine until a toy arrow had caught on his green tights. He'd tugged at it and the material had ripped, the resultant hole extending up to the crotch.

'Or we could ask Colin to go,' Wanda suggested, sensing his misgiving.

'I think you'd be more convincing,' Quentin said. 'Colin doesn't look like the type who could afford an exclusive property.'

'Do *I* then?'

'Yes. You're elegant and sophisticated, and a widow. Your husband could have left you a fortune.'

'Don't you think they'll check?'

'Don't give them your details. Just make a general enquiry.'

Wanda shook her head. 'I can tell you haven't had much experience of estate agents. They won't let me out of the place without my name and contact details.'

'Give a false name and address then.'

Wanda fell silent and chewed at her bottom lip, something Quentin knew she did when she was either worried or trying to work something out.

'What are you thinking?' he asked.

'It seems daft just going on the off chance that I'll find something out. I think we should do something that will bring results.'

'Go on,' Quentin urged.

'I could probably get away with a false name, but I'll have to give contact details. How about we set up an email address to go with my fake name? We need to keep in touch with them if we're going to learn anything about them.'

'Yes, Wanda, good idea.'

They spent the next hour creating a new email address, using the name Eleanor King.

'It's got a nice ring to it,' Wanda said. 'I hope we get something from it.'

'Yeah. Well, we've got to start somewhere and so far we've done nothing constructive.'

Wanda stood up. 'OK, I'll go to see them. Make some coffee while I look for that wig.'

* * *

Property Perfections was located in Southwark, discreetly positioned just off the main road next to a florist. Quentin had already strolled past the premises several times. Other than the smart fascia, there was nothing to distinguish it from any other property agents. The small car park at the rear sported a couple of expensive cars, one a vibrant red. It looked like a Maserati.

'Looks pretty average, except for the cars in the car park,' he said when he was back in his BMW where Wanda was waiting for him. 'Give as little information as possible, and don't forget you're Eleanor King, the widow of a wealthy antiques dealer.'

Wanda rolled her eyes. 'I have done this before, you know. Anyway, it's not so far from the truth, apart from the wealthy bit.' She climbed out of the car and stood beside the open door. 'How do I look?'

Bloody gorgeous, Quentin wanted to say. 'Every inch the lady,' he said instead, and meant it. Wanda had some nice clothes, including a Versace handbag and a pair of Jimmy Choos, though she rarely used them. The brown wig, glasses and darkened eyebrows transformed her face, yet there was no disguising how striking she was. He watched as she walked away, the understated but stylish oyster-coloured outfit doing nothing to hide the tantalizing swing of her hips.

Thoughts of Wanda and what she was about to do were interrupted when his mobile rang.

When he answered, he was surprised to hear his sister's voice.

'Hi, Quentin.'

'Shelagh? Anything wrong?'

'No, why? Does something have to be wrong for me to phone my brother?'

'No, but you normally email.'

'I wanted to tell you personally. We're coming over. Me, Howard and the children.'

'That's brilliant news, Shelagh.'

Quentin pictured his sister, five years his senior, her Australian husband, Howard, and their young son, Michael, whom he and Wanda had spent some time with in Sydney. He hadn't yet seen their baby daughter, Megan, born after he'd returned to the UK.

The conversation ran on. Quentin could tell that his sister was excited about coming home. It would be lovely to see her, but he knew he'd have to be finished with this present case before he could concentrate on her visit.

The call ended and Quentin sat waiting for Wanda. Why was she taking so long? Should he go and make sure she was all right? What if—

His thoughts stopped when Wanda came into view. She walked slowly, opened the door and plumped into the passenger seat, letting out a long moan and kicking off the Jimmy Choos.

'Ouch! I remember now why I stopped wearing high heels.'

'Well?' Quentin demanded. 'Did you find out anything?'

'Not much,' she said, settling back in the seat. 'It's not your usual run-of-the-mill estate agents. It's very comfortable inside, more like somebody's lounge than an office. There aren't many photos of properties for sale. The ones there are didn't show prices, but they look as though they're worth several million. There was only one staff member there when I went in, though I could hear movement and talking in the next room.'

'Hmm. I don't suppose they need many people up front,' Quentin speculated. 'It doesn't sound as though their clientele comes from the average man in the street. Was the person you saw a woman?'

'Yes, why?'

'Well, Lorna said it was a woman who reported Dave Brown missing. I don't suppose you gleaned any info from her?'

'No. I made general enquiries, kept it as vague as I could. It might not have been her who reported Dave missing, and I didn't want to arouse suspicion. I told her I'd recently lost my husband and was looking into buying a place away from the humdrum. I didn't want to rush, it was too soon for that. I just needed to know if they could find me something in the UK when I was ready. I hinted that money wasn't a problem. She said she hadn't been there long and wanted to bring someone in from the back room, one of their top agents, but he was on the phone and would be with me in a few minutes. I said I couldn't wait, but I gave my fake name and email, took their business card and left.'

'Is that all?' Quentin was disappointed. He'd expected more.

'Not quite.' Wanda turned to him, a mischievous glint in her eyes. 'When she said she'd get their top agent to see me, she called him Philip Chandler.'

'Philip Chandler,' Quentin repeated. 'Well, I suppose that's something.'

'And,' Wanda continued, 'as I was leaving, I looked back and saw a man coming out of the back office.'

Quentin straightened. 'Was it Philip Chandler?'

'Well, she called him Phil. She called me back but I was through the door by then. I pretended I hadn't heard and carried on.'

'Right. So what did he look like?'

Quentin found his notebook and began writing as Wanda spoke, anxious to record her description of the man.

'About five feet ten, good-looking, dark hair, glasses, quite tanned, grey suit. That's as much as I could take in.'

'Good,' Quentin said when she'd finished. He closed the notebook and returned it to his pocket, glad that he'd listened to Wanda about keeping proper notes instead of the random pieces of paper he'd used when they'd first opened their agency. Wanda, he knew, sometimes made notes on her phone, but Quentin didn't. Phones were too easily lost or stolen.

Back at Quentin's house, Wanda googled Philip Chandler.

"'Senior partner at Property Perfections,'" she read aloud. 'He's a bit more than an estate agent, then. Perhaps that Maserati you saw belongs to him.'

She read on. "'Established 1998. Guaranteed to satisfy the most discerning of tastes. Exclusive, private properties in desirable locations at home or abroad. Quick, efficient and discreet service." Discreet? What do you think they mean by that?'

'Your guess is as good as mine,' Quentin replied. 'Does it say anything else about his background?'

'No, and there's no photo. There's one of the shopfront but not of him. Not that there has to be, but usually companies show photos of their people.'

'Well, at least we've made a start,' Quentin said, trying to sound positive.

Victor came up to him, his neck cone scraping against Quentin's leg. Reaching inside the cone, Quentin stroked the fur above his nose.

'Missing your master, eh Victor?' he said softly, forgetting that Anne Roberts had said his name was Goldie.

The dog whined, and once again the image of it lying injured by Dave Brown's body came to him, reinforcing his determination to find the killer. Determination, coupled with a tinge of hopelessness. Yes, they'd made a start, but where could they go from here?

Chapter Nine

It was Lorna West who influenced their next decision. She rang Quentin that evening, a note of anxiety in her voice.

'I think I saw that bloke from the Scilly Isles today,' she said. 'It was just a glimpse, but it looked like him.'

'Really?' Once again, the seriousness of the situation impressed itself on Quentin. He thought of all the cases where they'd kept information to themselves and followed leads that had led to successful conclusions, but this was a murder enquiry.

'Lorna,' he went on, 'you should tell the police. These people, whoever they are, have already killed someone they thought could shop them.'

'Well, the police know why Dave contacted me, and I can't be absolutely sure it was this Nick Crawford I saw. I ran a check on him but nothing came up. Anyway, if I tell the police, I'll have to mention you. You're the one who had an altercation with him.'

'Yeah.' Quentin thought for a moment. He knew he'd be in trouble if he admitted to catching the man spying on them and not reporting it, especially now Philmore was on the case. He could always say there was nothing to tie Nick Crawford to Dave Brown's murder – he could have been sent to spy by anyone – but he knew Philmore wouldn't swallow that.

'Well,' he continued, 'if you're still being watched then I imagine we will be too. I mean, I found the body, you were going to help Dave expose the company, and we've been seen together, so we'll both be on their radar. I don't really see why though. I mean, if you'd had the info from Dave, you'd have printed it by now, so why are they on your back? It'd be too late to do anything once it was out. And I didn't know Dave from Adam.'

'Maybe they didn't get the evidence back when they killed Dave, or maybe they think he passed it on or kept a copy. The company he worked for looks legit–'

'You've found out which company it is then?' Quentin asked, realizing he hadn't shared this with her.

'Yes, from my source. It's called Property Perfections. As I say, it looks legit, but I'll do some more digging, see what I can find out.'

'Perhaps you shouldn't. If you leave it alone, they might decide you don't know anything and leave it at that. Either forget it or go to the police.'

'What can the police do? They're already investigating the murder. I'll sleep on it, and maybe call them in the morning.'

As she rang off, Wanda appeared from the kitchen. Quentin repeated the conversation, and Wanda looked concerned.

'They must think she knows something,' she concluded. 'We should report what happened on Scilly. It's not just us this time, Quentin. I know we've taken risks before but someone else might be in danger now. Lorna probably wants to get to the bottom of this herself, like we do, but I think we'll have to concede and tell Philmore. I'm going to ring her back.'

Quentin nodded. 'OK, but I didn't tell her about going to Property Perfections, and I don't think we need to tell Philmore. We haven't done anything wrong, or encroached on their investigation, so there's no need. You never know, something might come of it – we can carry on with that ourselves.'

'All right. Have you got her number there?'

'She doesn't want to go to the police,' Quentin said, 'but maybe she'll listen to you more than me.' He brought up Lorna's number then passed the phone to Wanda.

'No answer,' Wanda said, lowering it. 'I'll try again later.' She entered the number into her own mobile.

'I hope she's all right,' she said, two more unanswered calls later.

'Probably having an early night,' Quentin countered, checking the time. Nine-thirty. Their first call had been at eight-thirty. 'People do have early nights,' he continued, more to assure himself than Wanda. 'Or maybe she's gone out, switched her mobile off or left it behind.'

'Left her mobile? She's a journalist.'

'Even journalists need time off,' Quentin argued. Then seeing Wanda's impatient look, he said, 'All right, so she wouldn't go out without her phone, especially now. But she's probably got a personal phone as well as a work one. She could have taken that. Still, it does seem odd that I spoke to her and now we can't contact her.'

'We don't know where she lives,' Wanda said, 'but her paper will. I'm sure the news desk doesn't close at five. They could send someone round, see if she's all right.'

'Ring them? I suppose we could but… I don't know, it seems like we're being a bit hasty. After all, I only spoke to her at eight. Not much could have happened in that time.'

Wanda sent him an incredulous look. 'Really? You've got a short memory if you've forgotten what happened an hour after I left here that time when we first met.'

Quentin hadn't forgotten. 'That was different,' he said. 'For a start, I knew for sure what had happened. As far as we know, nothing's happened to Lorna.'

'Let's hope not,' Wanda said tersely. 'But what happened to me was because someone thought I knew something.'

She didn't need to say any more. The implication stared Quentin in the face.

'All right, all right,' he said, sighing, 'but we'll look like idiots if she's just having an early night.'

The person Wanda spoke to at the paper wouldn't give Lorna's personal number, but said they would ring her and get back to them if they couldn't reach her.

Quentin's phone rang five minutes later and he snatched it up, half expecting it to be Lorna. He grimaced when he heard a familiar male voice.

'Quentin? Is Wanda with you? I can't get through on her phone.'

'Colin. Yes, she's here. She was making a call.'

'Oh. Well, how's it going over there? All set for the race?'

With a pang of guilt, Quentin realized they hadn't told their friend they were back in Greenwich.

'Er, not exactly, Colin. Something came up and we had to come back.'

The line was silent for a few moments. Quentin waited for Colin's response.

'Something came up? Must be a pretty big something to make you give up the race,' Colin said, a trace of annoyance in his voice. 'Is it a case?'

'Yes,' Quentin admitted. Although he never wanted to involve Colin in their cases, Colin always managed to inveigle his way into them.

'Really? So soon after finding that body? Or is it connected with that?'

'Yes,' Quentin said again. It was pointless denying it.

'Well?' Colin barked. 'Tell me then.'

'I'll let Wanda tell you,' Quentin said, passing her the phone.

'Why don't you come over tomorrow, Colin,' he heard her say after a brief explanation. 'Then we'll tell you all about it.'

As the call ended, Quentin clicked his tongue, turning away so that Wanda didn't see his irked expression. If she did, she would remind him that Colin had been helpful on previous cases and that Quentin had no need to be jealous of him.

Before either he or Wanda had a chance to say anything, Quentin's phone rang again. Exchanging a look with Wanda, he answered it and was relieved to hear Lorna's voice.

'Hi, Quentin. John at the paper called me. Thanks for worrying about me but I'm OK. My phone was in the kitchen and I didn't hear it with the TV on.'

'OK, Lorna, we were just checking. If it was Boatman – Nick Crawford you saw – well, you know, better safe than sorry. You should report it.'

'That's what John said, and I rang my editor and he said the same, so I will. You should too.'

'Yeah, we will,' Quentin told her, though he didn't relish the reprimand he knew Philmore would give him.

'Right. I've usually got my work phone with me, Quentin, but do you want to take my personal mobile number as well?'

When he'd taken the number, Quentin ended the call and turned to Wanda. 'There,' he said. 'I told you we'd look like idiots, didn't I?'

'I'm sure Lorna didn't think that,' Wanda said with a toss of her head. 'How do you think you'd feel if we'd done nothing and something happened to her?'

'Terrible. We did the right thing.'

'Of course we did. Well, I don't know about you, but I could do with an early night.'

'Me too,' Quentin said. 'We could have a lie-in tomorrow. We're still supposed to be on holiday.'

Wanda stood up and held out her hand. 'So we are. Perhaps we should make the most of it then. You never know what may happen tomorrow.'

No, Quentin thought, taking her hand, you never know. And at that moment he didn't want to know.

Chapter Ten

Colin arrived at Wanda's the following morning before Quentin was dressed. He saw him through the window, going through Wanda's gate and ringing her doorbell.

Wanda had woken at seven, taken Mozart and gone home, leaving Victor with Quentin, much to Magpie's disgust. When Quentin went down to the bathroom, he found the cat biffing a paw at Victor's cone, which Quentin had removed overnight so the dog could sleep more comfortably.

'Hey, leave that, Magpie, it's not a toy. Here, Victor, you'd better put it on.'

He fastened the cone around the dog's neck, wondering how much longer he'd need it. The wound seemed to be healing well and Victor had stopped trying to scratch it.

He made tea and had just put some bread in the toaster when he heard a key in the front door. Wanda had his key and he had hers, an arrangement they'd set up during their first case. She came in, followed by a thin, balding man with dark-rimmed glasses.

'Hello, Colin,' he said, noting the other man's usual attire of casual trousers overhung by a short-sleeved shirt. 'You're bright and early.'

'Not like you then,' Colin replied, eyeing Quentin's dressing gown.

'Just going to have breakfast,' Quentin said, ignoring his comment. 'Do you want some toast?'

'No thanks.'

'Nor me,' Wanda said. 'I was just telling Colin why we came home—'

'Yes,' Colin interrupted. 'And I was saying you should tell the police what happened. If someone's following you, they're not doing it for fun. If it's connected to the body you found, then it's serious.'

'We realize that, Colin, and we are going to report it,' Quentin told him.

'When?' Colin barked. 'After someone's had another go at you? What if he has a go at Wanda too?'

'Calm down, Colin,' Wanda said. 'It was Quentin who had a go at him, not the other way round. He was watching us, that's all.'

'That's all? Isn't that enough? Going all the way to the Scilly Isles just to keep tabs on you? What if he'd been armed?'

'He wasn't,' Quentin assured him.

'But he could have been,' Colin persisted. 'I'd have pretended I hadn't spotted him.'

'Would you, Colin?' Wanda asked. 'I seem to remember you clobbering someone when they were running away from a crime scene.'

'That was different, and I called the police immediately after.'

'All right, Colin, you've made your point,' Quentin snapped. 'We've already decided to call Philmore. He's handling the case.'

'There you are then.' Colin sounded pleased. 'All the more reason to tell him what's going on. And when you've done that, you can tell me what I can do to help.'

Quentin sent him a quizzical look. 'What do you mean? Once we've told Philmore, that'll be the end of it.'

'Yeah, right,' Colin sneered, shaking his head. 'When's the last time you stopped investigating something because the police were handling it?'

'This time,' Quentin protested. 'After I found the body, I was quite happy to leave it to the police. That's why I went away.'

'Yes, all the time you had nothing to go on. Now you have, and this journalist's involved. Don't tell me you'll stop investigating, cos I won't believe you.'

Quentin looked at Wanda. Apparently she'd decided not to tell Colin everything, which he appreciated. At a nod from her, though, and knowing they could trust Colin, he sighed.

'You're right, Colin,' he said. 'We'll tell Philmore about the guy following us, but we'll make our own enquiries too. Discreetly, of course. Nothing obvious.'

'OK, so what can I do?' Colin asked, taking off his glasses and polishing them with the hem of his shirt, a habitual action Quentin was used to seeing.

'Nothing yet,' Wanda said. 'We haven't really got a plan of action, but we'll let you know if there's anything you can do.'

'Right. Look, I know I always say you take too many risks, and you do. After all, the police are paid to uphold the law. That doesn't mean I think they're always right. It's OK to do our own thing as long as we don't tread on their toes or put ourselves in danger. I mean what I say – I want to help. I'll tell you if I think you're in the wrong or if I don't want to do something.'

'Fair enough,' Wanda said. 'Agreed, Quentin?'

'Agreed.'

Colin looked pleased. 'Right. So when are you going to ring Philmore?'

'As soon as I've had my breakfast,' Quentin told him.

He didn't have to wait that long. He was halfway through his toast when his phone rang. Swallowing, he pressed the answer button and flinched as Philmore's angry voice sounded in his ear.

'Why didn't you tell me what happened in the Scilly Isles?' the DCI demanded. Not waiting for a reply, he ploughed on. 'These people are dangerous, Quentin. You need to stay away from them, so does Wanda.'

'Hold on a minute,' Quentin rasped. 'The guy was following us. It wasn't us that made the first move.'

Sounding calmer, Philmore continued. 'All right, I get that, but you should have reported it, especially after finding the body.'

'We didn't know if it was connected. He could have been anyone.'

'And talking to a reporter about a police matter. May I remind you–'

'She came to us, we didn't go to her.'

Philmore harrumphed. 'She should know better too. We have a press office to handle information.'

Quentin knew the police press office only gave limited information during an active investigation, to avoid anything compromising the case.

'Well,' he said drily, 'now you know, what are you going to do about it?'

This seemed to stump Philmore. 'Lorna's told us about this Nick Crawford,' he said after a few silent seconds. 'He's a small-time crook, no violence or weapons recorded. Not very efficient either, if you and Lorna West both spotted him. I'm surprised–' He broke off, as though deciding he'd revealed enough.

'You're surprised anyone's employing him for surveillance? He's not working off his own bat, that's for sure.'

'No,' Philmore snapped. 'And neither should you be, unless you want to wind up like Dave Brown.'

'I've got a photo of Nick Crawford, Steve, if it will help, but if he's got a record, you've probably got a mugshot.'

'We have. We've checked, and he's not at his last known address. Listen, Quentin, I know you're a PI and I know you like to help, but this is murder, so don't do anything stupid.'

'All right, but can you at least tell me if you've got any idea who killed Dave?'

'Not yet, but we're working on it.'

'What about the person who reported him missing? Can't you tell me her name? That can't do any harm.'

'You've met the sister, Anne Roberts. I'm guessing she told you where he worked, so you could easily find out anyway. It's Tina Patterson. She hasn't been there very long and she's still learning the ropes. She liked Dave and sometimes they took their lunch together.'

'Thanks. I appreciate it.'

'And I'll appreciate you not causing me any problems. And don't forget what I've said.'

Taking a risk and playing on previous experiences with Philmore, Quentin tried a more informal approach.

'OK, Steve. I know you're only trying to protect us. We'll stay safe and ring you if we need to.'

'Right,' Philmore said, mollified. 'Well, keep your heads down and stay out of trouble. I take it you've still got that other mobile?'

'Yes, I have,' Quentin said, thinking of his second phone, bought for emergency contact with Philmore during their first case. 'Thanks, Steve. Bye.'

Quentin ended the call and turned to Wanda and Colin. 'Happy now?'

Wanda nodded.

'Oh well, looks like Philmore's got his work cut out,' Colin said. 'Right, if you haven't got anything for me to do, I'm off. Call me when you've got a plan, or I'll call you if I have a brainwave.'

In Quentin's experience, Colin wasn't given to brainwaves, but he thanked him and watched him kiss Wanda on the cheek before letting himself out.

Giving up on his cold toast, he searched his mind for a brainwave of his own, but found nothing. As it happened, it didn't matter, because not long gone after Wanda had gone back next door, she rang Quentin.

'Come in here,' she said, excitement in her voice. 'I've had an email from Property Perfections!'

Chapter Eleven

'Bloody hell, they don't let the grass grow under their feet,' Quentin remarked as he peered over Wanda's shoulder. 'They don't even know what kind of property Eleanor King is looking for, except it has to be in the UK.'

'I said I wanted to be away from the rat race,' Wanda said, 'and they advertise exclusive places. They haven't mentioned prices in this email.'

Leaning in closer, Quentin read:

Dear Mrs King,

I understand you have recently lost your husband, so may I offer my sincere condolences. I believe you may soon be seeking a property, and while I completely understand that it's early days to be thinking about such things, I wouldn't want you to miss out on two properties that have recently come on the market. The first is a period cottage, with an olde worlde appearance but fully modernised inside, and the other is a house, quite separate from neighbours but with easy access to local amenities. Both are very private, with mature gardens which are not overlooked.

Thank you for registering your interest, and I look forward to answering any enquiries when you are in a position to proceed.

With kind regards,

Philip Chandler

Senior agent and partner

'Crikey!' Quentin said. 'He's very chummy considering he's never even met you.'

'Like I said before, once they get their teeth into you, they don't let go, especially if there's a lot of money involved.' Wanda clicked on one of the attachments. 'Look at this place.'

The picture showed a modern-looking house with wrought-iron gates at the end of a wide driveway. The description boasted a swimming pool complete with changing rooms and a bar and barbecue area, five bedrooms and three bathrooms. The price was given as 1.75 million.

'Bloody hell!' Quentin said, trying to compare his modest terraced house with this mansion. 'You'd need some mortgage to afford that.'

Wanda screwed her face up. 'Too big. I like this one better.'

Opening the second attachment she revealed a charming, thatched cottage with roses climbing the walls. It was smaller than the house but looked cosier, with an inglenook fireplace and a separate studio in the garden, half hidden by wisteria.

'This one's only a million,' Wanda said. 'That's the one I'd choose if I had the money. Imagine sitting by that fire with a nice glass of wine on a winter's night.'

'Wine? I should think anyone who could afford that would have champagne, not your everyday plonk.'

Wanda sighed. 'We can't afford champagne or the cottage, so it's purely academic.'

'Yeah, but they don't know that. You could reply, say you really like the cottage,' Quentin suggested. 'At least find out where it is. Doesn't it tell you where it is?'

'It just says "Quiet location in Devon". I could register my interest, but that won't help me find out anything. I need to meet someone who works there, preferably this Philip Chandler, and the woman who reported Dave missing, see if I can suss anything out. Hmm. Senior agent and partner. Could you be a partner in a business and not know something dodgy was going on?'

'Unlikely,' Quentin replied. 'And you're right – we need to talk to Philip Chandler face to face if we can.'

'Well, you're the one who found Dave's body,' Wanda said. 'You'd better stay in the background for now. I'll make an appointment to see Philip Chandler.'

'He might try and talk you into going to see it, you know, think you'll fall in love with it and go for it straight away.'

'That's all right, I can handle that.'

Quentin hesitated. 'I'm not sure you should go alone. I mean, he may know nothing about what Dave found out or he could be in the thick of it. If he rumbles you, you'll be in trouble.'

'So I won't go alone.'

'But you just said I should stay in the background, so who–' Quentin broke off, enlightenment showing on his face. 'Oh no, not Colin.'

'Why not? I think I'd take a friend with me if I was recently bereaved and looking at a possible house move or a second property. It would make sense to take a man. They'd be less likely to try to talk me into things.'

'I suppose,' Quentin said reluctantly. 'But I won't just sit here while you go. I'll come separately, be on hand just in case.'

Wanda shook her head. 'We haven't even got an appointment yet. Let's see how it works out, shall we?'

She clicked on the reply button and began typing.

> *Dear Mr Chandler,*
> *Thank you for your condolences and for sending me these properties. The cottage looks enchanting. Could you give me its exact location so I can check out the area?*
> *Many thanks*
> *Eleanor King*

'We'll start casually,' Wanda said, turning from the computer. 'We don't want to look too keen.'

A reply came shortly after lunch.

> *Dear Mrs King,*
> *The cottage is a few miles outside Bovey Tracey, near*
> *Newton Abbot. Although secluded, it doesn't take*
> *long to reach either Bovey Tracey or Newton Abbot,*
> *which has a train link. Exeter is only a twenty-five-*
> *minute drive away.*
> *The cottage has vacant possession, so viewing can be*
> *arranged at any time. If you would like to view the*
> *property, please feel free to come into the office or ring*
> *to make arrangements.*
> *With kind regards,*
> *Philip Chandler*
> *Senior agent and partner*

'Well,' Quentin mused aloud, 'they certainly don't hang about.'

Wanda drew back from the computer, her expression thoughtful.

'I don't suppose they would. A property that price is a fair amount. I think I should go to the office to meet Philip Chandler. Eleanor King could just be the type to prefer the personal touch.'

'OK,' Quentin said, 'but don't answer right away. Like you said, we don't want to seem too keen. On the other hand, Eleanor King is a rich widow. What else has she got to do with her time?'

'We'll give it a couple of hours at least,' Wanda decided.

Quentin nodded, looking through the front window for the umpteenth time that day, sweeping his gaze along the pavement as far as he could and wondering if they were being watched. It was definitely a possibility. After all, Lorna was.

'See anyone?' Wanda asked.

'Lots of people, but no one suspicious. I'll have a look from upstairs. You can see more from there.'

From the upstairs front window, he gazed down into the Greenwich street. The terraced houses were identical on both sides – flat-fronted with small, gated forecourts, punctuated with alleyways that gave access to the rear. Those alleyways provided good cover, as Quentin knew from experience. Anyone watching the house could duck in there if they didn't want to be seen.

'Can't see anyone,' he told Wanda. 'If someone is watching, they're being more discreet than our friend from the boat was.'

'Well, he can't be in two places, so if he's watching Lorna, maybe they sent somebody else.' Wanda thought before continuing. 'We'll have to be careful. If I'm going back to Property Perfections in disguise, I'll have to change after I've left here.'

'You didn't last time,' Quentin pointed out.

'True, but we don't know if we were being watched then. Anyway, if Philip Chandler already knows who I really am, why would he bother sending me properties? Or do you think he'd try and lure me into a trap?'

Quentin shrugged. 'It's possible, if he *is* involved. We don't know what information he's got from Boatman.'

'We'll have to risk it,' Wanda said firmly. 'Either that or sit about waiting for something to happen.'

'OK, but it's a good idea to take Colin with you. Safety in numbers and all that.'

Chapter Twelve

The next morning, Quentin watched as Wanda left the house to drive her own car to the busy garden centre where she'd arranged to meet Colin and don her Eleanor King disguise.

Quentin went separately, ostensibly to ensure their safety, but mainly so he wouldn't be left out. When he was sure he wasn't being followed, he found a parking place near Property Perfections and sat waiting, his mobile in his hand. He didn't know what he would do if he suddenly got a distress call from Wanda or Colin – rush to their rescue? Call Philmore?

Why was he worrying? Wanda was perfectly capable of handling the meeting. He pictured her sitting in front of Philip Chandler, talking in that low, seductive voice, charming him as she charmed everyone. Colin, however, was a different story. He'd agreed to play a supporting role only, to go along with everything Wanda said. Somehow, that didn't reassure Quentin.

His mind strayed to the phone call he'd had the last time he'd sat waiting for Wanda. His sister was coming to England. Something to look forward to. Something–

His thoughts were interrupted by the shrill of his phone. He jumped as it vibrated in his hand.

'All done, Quentin,' Colin said cheerfully. 'Meet us at the garden centre café.'

'Well?' Quentin demanded when they were seated, drinking coffee. 'What happened?'

'I've arranged to go and see the cottage in Devon,' Wanda answered.

'Have you?' Quentin asked. 'What about Philip Chandler? Did he swallow your story?'

'I think so. He was very interested when I introduced Colin as my financial advisor–'

Quentin spluttered into his coffee, sending brown droplets over the table. 'Your what?'

'What's wrong with that?' Colin asked. 'Why wouldn't a rich widow have a financial advisor?'

Wanda nodded. 'Yes, Quentin, it adds weight to the pretence that I've got money. It makes people careful when they talk to you about finance. I thought it was a good idea.'

When he'd considered it, Quentin had to admit that it was.

'So,' he said, 'a nice trip to Devon to see something you can't afford. How is that going to help the case? They'll get someone to meet you in Devon–'

'No,' Colin interrupted. 'Chandler said he had business in that part of the world so he'd show us around himself.'

'Oh. Well, that's good, I think,' Quentin answered, beginning to feel like he was being sidelined. 'Though I don't see how it will help. He's not likely to give anything away.'

'If I look like I'm serious about getting a property, I'll have more reason to keep in touch with him,' Wanda pointed out. 'I can string it out, say I need time to make up my mind. The more dealings we have with the company, the more we're likely to find something out.'

'Yes,' Colin said. 'And if they mention anything about Eleanor King's late husband being in antiques, Wanda can draw on what she learned from Gerry.'

Quentin couldn't argue with that. Gerry, Wanda's actual late husband, had been a dealer in antiques, mainly furniture and Victoriana. Colin had been Gerry's friend long before he'd met Wanda.

'I suppose you're right,' Quentin said reluctantly, 'but we need another lead. There must be something else we can do. I wish–'

'You wish what?' Colin asked.

'Oh, nothing.' Quentin had been about to say he wished he knew how far the police investigation had got. He knew that, officially, neither Steve Philmore nor Debbie Francis could part with any information, but unofficially…

'When is this visit?' he asked.

'Tomorrow,' Wanda told him. 'There's no point in you going all the way down there as well. Colin can come with me.'

'OK,' Quentin said, deciding she was right. He watched Colin clean his glasses with the bottom of his shirt for the third time that day. Same old same old, he thought, and went to get himself another drink.

* * *

Feeling excluded and tired of inaction, Quentin went for a run in the park the next day and tried to think. Where would Dave Brown hide vital information? He pictured himself coming upon a covert operation and deciding to blow the whistle on it. What would he do if he found evidence of wrongdoing in the workplace? Steal it, photograph it, copy it to a flash drive? Whatever evidence the dead man had, in whatever form, it seemed unlikely it had been found, either by the criminals or the police. If he'd guessed right, the criminals would have searched Dave's house, as the police must have done when they'd found Dave's address book with his sister's number inside.

Sinking onto an empty bench, he sat with his head in his hands, wishing he knew what they were looking for. Frustrated, he thought of his second mobile and wished he'd brought it with him. He couldn't call Philmore direct so he pulled out his everyday mobile and dialled Philmore's office number.

'Is DCI Philmore there please?' he said when a female voice answered.

There was a lull before the voice came again. This time, Quentin recognized it.

'Is that Quentin Cadbury?' DS Francis asked.

'Yes, Debbie, sorry, DS Francis,' Quentin replied, judging from her tone that it was definitely a DS Francis day, not a Debbie day. 'Is he there?'

'No, he's not.'

Quentin hesitated, then decided just to go for it.

'Look, I know I'm not on the case—'

'No, you're not,' came the sharp retort.

'I don't see why you can't answer a few questions, as I'm the one who found Dave Brown, met his sister via you, and I'm looking after his dog. All I want to know is…' He paused. There were so many things he wanted to know.

'Why wasn't his sister allowed to go into his house?' he blurted.

'I think,' DS Francis said slowly, 'that you know the answer to that as well as I do.'

'You're treating it as a crime scene? Or at least you're searching it for something. Have you found anything?'

'You know I can't answer that.'

'All right, I'll put it another way. When will Anne Roberts be allowed to go and sort out her brother's things?'

'Why? Are you working for her? You said you weren't on the case.'

'I'm just trying to help a bereaved woman, that's all.'

'Right,' said Francis with a sigh. 'We know what that means, don't we?'

Quentin tried a different tack.

'How's giving up smoking going?' he asked, recalling that the detective sergeant had mentioned this the last time they'd worked together.

Another sigh. His ploy seemed to work though. Despite being a stickler for the rules and her determination to rise above the rank of sergeant, Debbie Francis was human.

'I've cut down. Have you heard from Anne Roberts since you met with her?'

'No.'

'Well, let us know if you do. And Quentin – don't do anything stupid. We're talking murder here.'

'As if I would,' Quentin said, responding to her softer tone. 'Don't worry, Debbie, I'll be around to annoy you for a long time yet.'

His flippancy was rewarded by the detective sergeant cutting him off. He grinned, knowing she hadn't forgotten that he'd once deflected a blow that could have caused her serious injury. He sat for a while, watching the squirrels as they darted up and down various trees. Amusement filled him when he witnessed a spat between two of them – a large one with a huge bush of a tail trying to take a nut from a smaller one. The wronged squirrel hung on tenaciously, then snatched it away and fled, leaving the would-be thief to find its own food.

There are bullies even in the animal kingdom, Quentin thought, and by the time he left the park he'd decided on his next course of action.

Chapter Thirteen

Breaking into a property wasn't new to Quentin, but it was the first time he'd disobeyed a direct police order to keep away. He'd chosen daytime for his foray, not wanting to have to rely on torchlight.

With Wanda and Colin in Devon, he was on his own, something he knew they would chastise him for when he told them. Normally he would tell Wanda what he was doing in case something untoward happened, but what could happen in an unoccupied house in broad daylight, and what could they do about it from Devon?

As he often did during investigations, he'd brought a pair of latex gloves and his Swiss army knife, but decided to use the credit card trick to gain entry. It was early afternoon, and the road was relatively quiet. To his relief, the front door wasn't difficult to open, and, wearing the gloves, he slipped unobtrusively into Dave Brown's house. No police tape or notices hindered him, signalling that no violence had taken place there. No violence, except that wreaked on the house itself. It was immediately obvious that someone had been there, apparently looking for something. Cupboards and drawers stood open, cushions had been slashed, clothes were scattered on the floor, everything was in disarray. Stepping over the things in his path as best he could, he made his way through the ground floor, wondering at the irony if someone associated with Property Perfections had made this mess. If it was like this when the police had come, they'd have had a hard job looking for anything, let alone finding anything.

In the kitchen, a dog bowl and some tins of dog food lay amidst the utensils strewn over the worktops, reminding him of Victor. Upstairs, the disarray continued, and Quentin's dismay grew. If there had been anything to find, surely it would have been found during this rampage?

Part of the second bedroom had been partitioned for a bathroom, the cabinet emptied and its contents swept into the sink. The lid of the toilet cistern sat askew, and Quentin guessed it had been removed in case it concealed something.

'Bloody hell,' he muttered, throwing up his hands in a helpless gesture. 'What a waste of time.'

He wondered what he'd expected to find. If the killer had found what they were looking for, they'd have taken it, and the police would have removed anything of interest.

Glancing through the back bedroom window, he took in the small garden, completely paved over. No borders, no shed, just a low, plastic cloche, partially collapsed. Dave evidently hadn't been a gardener, and there was nowhere outside to hide anything. Also, it may explain why Dave had been walking his dog late at night instead of letting him into the concrete garden.

He hadn't seen any sign of forced entry, he realized. The front and back doors were intact, as were the windows. Then he remembered that there had been no keys found on Dave's body, so the killer must have taken them and either used them to gain access or passed them on for someone else to. The police, of course, had their own methods.

Dispirited, Quentin was turning to go back downstairs when he noticed a crossword book on the bedside cabinet. Something drew him to the book and he picked it up, flicking through the pages until he came to the last completed puzzle. The one on the opposite side was untouched except for two words. In the top right-hand corner, four letters were entered: CODE. Quentin read the clue: Disguised communication. At the bottom, one word was placed across: TRAFALGAR. The clue read: Where Nelson was killed.

Just an ordinary crossword with ordinary clues. But why were those clues the only ones to be completed, and why out of order? Most of the others were just as easy to work out. Did it mean something or was he clutching at straws, desperate to find some reward for his illegal entry? After finding nothing else unusual, he replaced the book.

Deciding it was useless trying to search through the various piles and heaps that littered the place, he picked his way over the floor and down the stairs. After a final look round, he made his way carefully to the front door and stepped into the forecourt, not noticing the letter box attached to the wall until he reached the gate and turned to close it. Retracing his steps, he pushed his hand inside the box as far as it would go but felt nothing. It needed a key to unlock it, he saw, and that was probably on Dave's keyring. What did it matter? There couldn't possibly be anything of interest in there. But still…

Surreptitiously, he cast a glance behind him, then to either side. Seeing no one nearby, he took out his Swiss army knife. Seconds later, the front of the box swung open. It was empty, apart from an advert for a pizza parlour and a flyer for an upcoming event at the community centre. Ridiculous, he thought. Whoever had rifled the house would have checked the letter box.

Deflated, he pushed the box's metal door shut, then turned and left, closing the gate behind him.

* * *

On the way home, he diverted to the room above a bakery on the main Greenwich road which he and Wanda used as an office. "Cadbury and Merrydrew, Private Investigators" was written on the door, something that still gave Quentin a thrill. From university dropout to running his own detective agency in the space of a few short years; quite an accomplishment, even if the adventure that had led to him setting up the agency had come about accidentally.

Their everyday work was mostly mundane, and today was no exception. He listened to the messages, deciding there was nothing that couldn't wait until after they'd planned to be back from the Tresco marathon. He felt a pang of regret, knowing he would miss the race, but the pull of finding a murderer was greater.

He thought over what he'd seen among the detritus at the dead man's house. Nothing, except those words in a crossword book that probably didn't mean anything. He never did crosswords himself, but Wanda did. As far as he recalled, she filled in the answers systematically, from top to bottom, if she could.

He went over his covert visit again, picturing each room. Something was bothering him, but he couldn't think what it was. He'd walked through every room, looked at the garden, all to no avail, then come out into the forecourt and checked the letter box. There was nothing there, but an idea was forming, an idea he couldn't shift. If Dave had proof that something was going on in Property Perfections, and he'd decided to blow the whistle, would he only trust it to one source? Wouldn't he have a back-up?

Snatching up his phone, he called Anne Roberts.

'Anne, it's Quentin Cadbury. Listen, I know you said Dave didn't tell you anything when you spoke to him, but did he send you anything? A message, a letter, anything?'

'No,' Anne replied. 'He sent birthday and Christmas cards, but otherwise he never wrote. He always replied to my texts, though. Why?'

'Oh, nothing really. I'm just checking.'

Next, he called Lorna West. If Dave had sent information to someone, Lorna was the obvious choice. After all, he'd already promised her the story. But if he had, Lorna would have received it by now.

'Hi, Lorna,' he said as the voicemail kicked in. 'It's Quentin. Just wondering if you've discovered anything useful. Give me a call when you can.'

Switching on his computer, he typed in "Property Perfections" but there was nothing new. He tried "Philip Chandler" with the same result. Was Philip Chandler the main player in the company? Surely there were other agents, top management, directors, accountants and the like? The website painted a glowing picture of the services provided, but nothing about what made the company tick. Perhaps Companies House could provide some answers. He typed in "Companies House" but the website was down.

His phone rang and Lorna's voice chirped in his ear.

'Hello, Quentin. I've just picked up your message.'

'Hi, Lorna. Just wondered if you'd found out anything. I'm trying Companies House but the website's down.'

'I did that last night,' she told him. 'The company was founded in 1998 by two people, Jeremy Black and Hayley Lamb. They sold out in 2003 to someone called William Chandler.'

'William Chandler! The senior agent there is called Philip Chandler.'

'Yes, a brother from what I can make out. They're both directors of the company, alongside someone called Henry Lawson. They have branches in Paris, Amsterdam and Barcelona. Barcelona's the HQ for the European division, but their registered office is the London branch. Since their takeover, the profits have doubled.'

'Excellent work,' Quentin said. 'Seen anything of our friend from the Scilly Isles lately?'

'No, thank goodness, nor anybody hanging around or looking suspicious. Have you?'

'No, but be careful, Lorna. The police should be keeping an eye on you.'

'They are,' Lorna said. 'I'm in the office most of the day. Don't worry, I'll be all right.'

When he'd rung off, Quentin stayed at his desk, brooding over the case. He was pleased to learn that Lorna had some measure of protection, but still felt that he should be doing something more proactive. Picking up his notebook, he jotted down everything they'd done since he'd found Dave's body and everything they knew now. It only just filled a single page.

'Bloody hell!' he muttered, throwing down his pen.

Deciding there was nothing else he could do at the moment, he locked the office and went downstairs. He was in the bakery paying for two sausage rolls and a cherry Bakewell when he spotted a figure in a doorway on the opposite side of the road. He dashed outside just as a bus trundled by, obscuring his view. By the time it had passed, the doorway was empty. Quentin looked left and right on both sides of the road, but there was no sign of the man he'd seen. No black jacket, but it had looked like Nick Crawford, alias Boatman.

Crossing the road, he ran to the nearest junction and stared into the side road. Nothing. He hovered, turned to double-check the other direction, then turned back just in time to see someone step out of an alleyway. This time, Quentin could see it was definitely Boatman. Whirling round, Boatman sprinted away. Quentin sprinted after him, confident that he'd catch his quarry up with no trouble.

It wouldn't have been any trouble if, a few hundred yards along, a girl with a double pushchair hadn't emerged from a gate immediately in front of Quentin. Too late to swerve, Quentin barged into the pushchair, making it skitter sideways as he fell onto the pavement, jarring his shoulder joints when he put his hands out to save himself.

'Sorry!' he panted after he'd straightened up. 'Everyone all right?'

He nodded towards the two small children strapped into the pushchair. They gazed up at him with surprised eyes.

'Yes, no thanks to you,' the girl snapped. 'There are proper places to run, you know.'

'Sorry again,' Quentin said, and seeing that no harm had been done except to himself, he ran on. He was at the next junction before he saw the man he was chasing – too late. Boatman was wrenching open a car door. Quentin heard the engine burst into life, and seconds later, he watched helplessly as Nick Crawford got away from him for the second time.

Frustrated, and with grazed hands and aching shoulders, he walked home. When he got indoors, he cleaned his grazes, his recent escapade uppermost in his mind. Why was Boatman still following him? Had he seen him go to Dave's house? Quentin hadn't noticed him there, but then Boatman wasn't meant to be noticed. Somehow though, Boatman knew where he lived, or at least where he worked.

He made tea, thinking longingly of the sausage rolls he'd left on the bakery counter, then fed Magpie and Victor. Magpie was still wary of Victor, occasionally biffing him on the nose, an indignity that Victor bore patiently. Victor no longer wore the plastic cone, but the splint wasn't due to be removed for another two weeks.

Pleased that Mozart had gone with Wanda, Quentin sat brooding while Victor settled at his feet. Magpie mewed and looked up at Quentin.

'What's up, boy?' Quentin said, bending to stroke him. 'You don't need to be jealous. Victor won't be here much longer.'

He patted his lap, trying to entice the cat up. Magpie simply flicked his tail and stalked off.

'It's all right for you,' Quentin called after him. 'We can't all afford to get on our high horse and gallop away.'

And for a despairing moment, Quentin wished he could escape as easily as Magpie.

Chapter Fourteen

'How did it go?' Quentin asked when Wanda returned from Devon.

'All right,' Wanda said. Apart from her make-up, Wanda looked as she always did, apparently having discarded her disguise on the way back. 'It's a beautiful cottage. I'd have it like a shot if I could.'

'Where's Colin? Gone on home?'

'Yes. Philip Chandler is quite a charmer. I can see why he's the senior agent. We tried to get some information about the company out of him without being too obvious, but we didn't have much luck beyond finding out that he's been there five years and lives in Chelsea.'

'Chelsea, eh? What car was he driving? The Maserati?'

'No, a Lexus, but maybe he's got more than one. Anyway, I said I'd think about the cottage; you know, it's a big step after losing my husband and all that. What have you been doing all day?'

Her eyebrows shot up when Quentin told her about his visit to Dave Brown's house.

'You broke in? There'll be hell to pay if Philmore finds out.'

'Why would he? Anyway, the place is in such a mess, a herd of elephants could go through and it wouldn't show.'

He went on to tell her what Lorna had learned about the company.

'It looks legit then,' Wanda commented when he'd finished. 'Still, lots of things look legit. That doesn't mean they are. Anything else to report?'

Quentin hesitated, wondering whether to mention his ineffectual pursuit of Boatman.

'There obviously is,' Wanda said discerningly. 'Come on, out with it.'

'I saw Boatman, just across the road from our office,' Quentin admitted.

'Oh? He's still around, even though we caught him at it?'

'He scarpered when I spotted him. I chased him, but he got away.'

'Really? He must be a fast runner if he got away from you.'

'He had a car nearby,' Quentin said. 'A green Corsa.'

'OK. Is there the remotest chance you got the registration number?'

'Not all of it. I was so mad that he got away I only thought to look at the last minute. It ended in 567. Do you think I'm losing my touch or am I being paranoid?'

Wanda shook her head. 'I don't think you're the type to suddenly develop paranoia. Then again, there's a first time for everything.'

'Thanks. The thing is, if Boatman saw me at Dave's house, whoever's behind his murder won't leave us alone.'

'No, of course they won't.' Wanda stood up and went to the window. 'Can't see anyone now. Hold on, I'll go upstairs and look.'

Quentin followed her up and together they surveyed the length of the road as far as they could. There was nothing out of the ordinary to see.

'I'm getting this feeling of déjà vu,' Quentin remarked, recalling previous times when they had been watched.

'Still, they may not know where we live, only where we work.'

'Maybe, Quentin, but whatever's going on at Property Perfections, it's important enough for someone to kill for. They'll have their ways of finding out things. We're private investigators – it's easy to find out where we operate from. They just need to follow us from the office to see where we live. They're obviously well organised. After all, they found out Dave was going to blow the whistle.'

'Yep. That's why I can't understand why they'd use a dunderhead like Boatman for surveillance.'

Wanda chewed at her bottom lip. 'Maybe they didn't know he was a dunderhead when they employed him. Maybe they still don't.'

'What, you mean he hasn't told them we've spotted him? Not just spotted him, confronted him?'

Wanda shrugged. 'You never know. Let's face it, if he's getting paid to tail us and he needs the money, why would he risk getting kicked off the job? They don't know we cornered him on the Scilly Isles any more than they know you chased him today. They'll only know what he tells them.'

'Yeah, I suppose that would explain why they're still using him. Still, it's no good speculating. I don't know about you, but I've got brain ache. Why don't we have a nice supper and an early night?'

Wanda gave him a sultry look. 'Good idea,' she said.

* * *

The following morning, after Wanda had gone back next door, Quentin answered a phone call and Lorna's voice filled the airway.

'Hello, Quentin. Fancy meeting up for a coffee? I've been doing some more digging into Property Perfections and–'

The rumble of traffic in the background increased when what sounded like a car or a truck very close to the phone drowned out Lorna's words.

'What was that, Lorna?'

A strangled gasp, then what sounded like a stifled scream, rang in Quentin's ear, followed by a few words from a male voice that Quentin couldn't discern.

'Lorna?'

The line went dead.

Confused, Quentin lowered the phone as he tried to process what he'd heard. Something had happened, of that he was sure. He quickly called her number. There was no ring tone. The phone had been switched off.

Chapter Fifteen

'How do you know she didn't just run out of battery?' Philmore said after Quentin had hastily located his second phone and rung him direct.

'Journalists don't let themselves run out of battery,' Quentin answered darkly. 'She wanted to meet up. She'd found out something about Property Perfections. And before you say she should have told you, not me, I agree, but let's not split hairs. She could be in real danger.'

'Well, I'm glad you've called me, Quentin, instead of taking matters into your own hands as you usually do.'

'Not when someone's life is under threat I don't,' Quentin snapped. 'Something's happened to her, I can feel it. I thought one of your guys was keeping an eye on her?'

'So did I.'

Philmore didn't sound happy. Quentin guessed that whatever had happened to Lorna, he had expected to hear of it from one of his own.

'All right,' Philmore continued, 'we'll get on it. Leave it with me.'

Quentin had no intention of leaving it with Philmore. He knew the DCI would take immediate action, but he had to do something himself. The feeling that he owed it to Dave to find his killer was supplanted by the need to find Lorna. Dave was dead, but Lorna could still be alive, and the sooner they found her, the more chance there was that she would stay alive. He hoped.

Hurrying next door, he used his key and rushed straight in, calling for Wanda. She appeared from the kitchen, a bundle of washing in her arms.

'Oh, no!' she exclaimed when Quentin told her what had happened. 'Surely, they won't—'

She broke off, unable to voice what they were both thinking. She dropped the washing into a basket and gripped Quentin's arm.

'We have to do something,' she said. 'Or… or do you think they'll be coming for us next?'

'I don't know, but we can't shy away when who knows what could be happening to Lorna. I'm pretty sure about one thing – it wouldn't have been Boatman who abducted her. It's not easy to kidnap someone in broad daylight without being seen, especially if a copper's watching.'

'Was a copper watching?'

'Supposedly. That doesn't matter. What matters is finding out where she is.'

'I know.' Wanda nodded, her face pale. 'You don't have to tell me.'

'No, of course I don't,' Quentin said. 'The question is, where do we start?'

'Well,' Wanda said after fifteen minutes of throwing ideas into the air and coming up with nothing, 'we can't go marching into Property Perfections. Even if we're right and they're involved, they're not likely to hold Lorna on the business premises, and let's face it, they've got plenty of empty places to hide her.'

'Bloody hell,' Quentin moaned. 'She could be anywhere. The only person we know who might be involved is Boatman. All we've got on him is his name, make of car and a partial car reg.'

'I don't think that would be enough for the police to trace his address,' Wanda replied. 'They wouldn't tell us anyway. Philmore will think we'll go rushing off to find the guy. Which is exactly what we need to do. We didn't get much out of him on the Scilly Isles.'

They were interrupted by a knock on the door.

'That's Colin's knock,' Wanda said, and went to let him in.

There was a thunderous look on Colin's face as he entered the lounge.

'Some stupid idiot almost caused an accident,' he rasped. 'Parked on double yellows and pulled out right in front of me. I must have missed him by an inch. I've a good mind to report him for careless driving.'

'Did you get his reg?' Wanda asked.

'No, he sped off in a hurry,' Colin said.

'You'd have a job reporting him then,' Wanda commented.

'Yes. It was green, I know that much.'

Quentin jerked his head up. Could it be?

'Was it a Corsa?' he asked.

'That's what it looked like,' Colin answered, looking surprised. 'How did you know?'

When Quentin had brought him up to speed, Colin gave a low whistle. He looked horrified when he heard what had happened to Lorna.

'You'd better be careful,' he warned, looking at Wanda. 'You don't want to be going through that again. Maybe leave it to the police this time?'

'We have to do something,' Wanda told him. 'We just don't know where to start.'

Colin's mouth tightened but he said nothing, as though he knew protesting would be useless.

'If only we knew where Boatman lived,' Wanda went on.

'Well, he's nothing if not persistent,' Colin said. 'If I spot him again, I'll follow him. The body you found – Dave Brown, wasn't it? What was his role in Property Perfections?'

'IT mainly, according to his sister,' Quentin answered.

'That could be how he discovered what was going on,' Wanda suggested. 'He might have come across something he wasn't meant to see on their computer.'

'They'll need a replacement for him, won't they?' Colin asked. 'They can get away without too many staff, but all businesses rely on IT these days.'

'Why? What are you thinking, Colin?' Wanda asked.

'Only that if I hadn't gone there with you, if they didn't know my face, I could have applied for the job. I can find my way round a computer screen. If I only lasted a few days, I might have found out something.'

'Good thinking, Colin,' Quentin said, meaning it. 'That's a no-no now, though, and we don't want you going the same way as Dave, even if you do get on my nerves.'

'That's what I like about you, Quentin, you're so tactful. Thanks anyway.'

'Never mind about tactful,' Quentin snapped. 'All we're doing at the moment is wasting time while Lorna–' He broke off, unwilling to voice what could be happening to Lorna.

'Have you told Philmore about this Nick Crawford, Boatman, or whatever you call him, following you yesterday?' Colin asked.

'No, not about yesterday,' Quentin admitted. 'What would I say? I saw Boatman then lost him? What's up, Wanda?'

Wanda had opened her laptop and was looking up from it, a surprised expression on her face.

'I've got an email from Philip Chandler,' she said. 'It was sent late yesterday. It's another property. There's a photo, and a few details. Looks a bit Spanish. "Quiet location in Surrey."'

'That's a bit quick after you told him you need time to think,' Quentin said. 'Still, we need to keep him sweet. Go back to him, say you're busy for a few days and will contact him about it soon. I wish…'

'What?' Wanda and Colin asked together.

'Well, I wonder if there's anything to give us a clue to what Dave found out on the premises. At Property Perfections, I mean. It might be worthwhile having a good, uninterrupted look around there.'

'No,' said Colin at once. 'They're hardly likely to leave things around for anyone to find. After all, the police must have been there. When they found out Dave worked there, they would have questioned his work colleagues, wouldn't they?'

'Of course they would,' Wanda said. 'If there's anything to find, it'll be on their computer.'

'It might have been,' Quentin put in. 'But if Dave found something on their system, they'd have wiped it by now, and the police have probably checked it anyway. They could try to retrieve the information, but that will take time. So what can we do?'

'Well,' Colin said, sounding uncharacteristically decisive. 'Why don't you both come and stay at mine? You were meant to be away anyway. You can give your boatman friend the slip and you'll be able to come and go without being watched. It'll take time for them to find out where you are.'

Quentin exchanged a glance with Wanda, knowing the suggestion was a good one.

'Thanks, Colin,' Wanda said, beaming at him. 'That would be a great help, wouldn't it, Quentin?'

'Yes,' Quentin replied, nodding. 'That's good of you, Colin.'

'I know,' Colin said good-humouredly. 'Mr Nice Guy, that's me. Shame it's never got me anywhere.'

Quentin noticed Colin's deliberate look at Wanda as he said this. Colin still wanted her, he could see.

'You and Mozart go on with Colin, Wanda,' he suggested. 'I'll bring Victor with me when I've sorted out a few things. I'll use your car, if that's all right, save me going to the lock-up.'

He went home, filled the automatic cat feeder and fixed a water bottle by the cat flap while Magpie eyed him with suspicion.

'Sorry, boy,' Quentin said fondly. 'I'll try not to be too long. At least you'll have the place to yourself for a bit.'

He collected Victor's food bowl and lead, and packed a small holdall for himself, yet he couldn't bring himself to simply leave. He donned his anorak and made sure he had both his phones and chargers, along with a torch, a compass and his Swiss army knife. Leaving his holdall in the hall, he sauntered out of the house with Victor. If Boatman was watching, maybe he could draw him out, trigger a reaction that could lead him to Lorna.

He took his normal route to Greenwich Park, walked the circuitous path he usually ran around, then went back down the hill, diverting onto the main road near the office. There was no sign of Boatman or anyone following him, so he let himself into the office and watched the road from the upstairs window. That's when he spotted a green Corsa disappearing into the same road where he'd seen it before. Hurrying from the office, he ran home as fast as Victor and his still healing leg would allow. Once he'd ushered the dog safely into the house, he grabbed Wanda's keys and sprinted to her Toyota. As far as he knew, Boatman had never seen Wanda's car. He got in, slumped down, and waited.

Five minutes later, the green Corsa passed him at a snail's pace, as if looking for a space to park. Definitely Boatman, Quentin decided as he caught sight of the driver. A little further on, the Corsa stopped on a single yellow line and the driver stared towards Quentin's house. Nick

Crawford, Quentin decided, may have discovered where he lived, but he wasn't prepared to be chased again. Or perhaps he was tired of standing about in the hope of seeing either of the people he was meant to be watching. Perhaps, Quentin thought, he was trying to watch from the comparative safety of his car. Stupid, really. He knew Quentin had seen him in the car, so why drive round the same area in the same car? Whatever else Boatman was, he wasn't the brightest star in the sky.

As if realizing he couldn't stay on the yellow line for long, Boatman indicated and the Corsa pulled out. Quentin did the same, managing to round the corner with only one vehicle between him and the Corsa. He followed it into the adjacent street, keeping enough distance to avoid arousing Boatman's suspicion. They were driving round in a square, Quentin realized. The space left when Quentin had driven off had already been filled, but after the second lap, Quentin saw a space as a van exited. He drove into it, worried that continuing in the Corsa's wake would give him away.

When the Corsa didn't reappear, Quentin cursed his caution. He restarted the engine and drove around again. Nothing.

Stopping in a street a little further afield, he slapped his hand down on the steering wheel, catching the horn and making it toot. At the same time, a green car came towards him from the other end of the road. Panicked in case Boatman recognized him and accelerated away, Quentin snatched up Wanda's sunglasses from the well by the gearstick and shoved them on. The oncoming vehicle was almost on him when it stopped and its lights flashed. A truck was parked awkwardly and there wasn't room for both cars to get through. Quentin edged the Toyota through the gap, keeping his head down as much as possible. The day was dull, and with the dark glasses impairing his vision, Quentin misjudged the width of the space and knocked the other car's wing mirror.

'Bloody hell!' he muttered, seeing the driver's door opening. The last thing he wanted was an altercation with Boatman in the middle of this busy road, where it could draw unwanted attention. He was about to drive away when a woman climbed out of the other car. She gave a cursory glance at the wing mirror then turned towards him.

'Sorry,' he said, winding the window down as she approached.

'I should think so too,' she said. 'I pulled over enough for you to get through.'

'I know, and I'm sorry. I'll pay for the damage.'

'It looks all right,' the woman said, seemingly placated. 'Just look where you're going in future.'

'I will.'

Quentin watched as she returned to her car, a Nissan Micra he could see now. Deflated, he decided to call it a day. He might as well have gone to Colin's with Wanda for all the good he'd done.

Grasping the sunglasses, he dropped them back into the central well. 'Waste of time,' he murmured as he rounded the corner onto the main road. Suddenly, he jerked himself upright. Coming from a side road and stopping at the traffic lights was the green Corsa.

For an instant he had a clear view of the number plate, not time to take in the whole thing but part of it registered in his memory. Then his view was obscured, and by the time he'd reached the traffic lights, there were two vehicles between him and the Corsa. He kept following and managed to keep track of it until he found himself on the outskirts of Brixton. And that's where he lost it.

Cursing, he pulled over and sat with his head in his hands. Frustration filled him. It had been hours since he'd heard Lorna's strangled gasp over the phone, and what had he done? Alerted the police, yes. But anything to help find Lorna? No.

For no reason other than he needed to hear a reassuring voice, he rang Wanda.

'Where are you?' she asked.

Feeling foolish, he explained what had happened.

'Never mind,' she said. 'At least you tried. I've brought my laptop and all our notes so I'll work on them till you get here.'

Immediately afterwards, Quentin rang Philmore.

'Steve,' he gabbled when the call was answered. 'Is there any news on Lorna?'

'Not yet, Quentin. I told you we'll let you know.'

'Why can't you bring Philip Chandler in?'

'On what grounds? We've no proof he's involved with the kidnapping. There's no proof there even was a kidnapping. There could be a perfectly reasonable explanation why Lorna ended her call as suddenly as she did–'

'That's rubbish, and you know it! Just bring Chandler in on suspicion or something, make something up, anything.'

A sigh sounded in Quentin's ear. 'A few years ago, we might have got away with that. It's not just Chandler we have to worry about. Property Perfections is an international company.'

'Never mind that. It's Lorna you should be worrying about. Surely there's something you can do?'

Quentin stopped, knowing he was being unfair. Steve Philmore was a good policeman with several high-profile cases under his belt. But he was tied to the rule book and the police code of practice.

'Sorry, Steve,' he added. 'I know you're doing what you can but I feel so helpless. I feel… I feel like it's my fault somehow.'

'How could it possibly be your fault? It's not your fault a man was murdered. Dave Brown was in touch with Lorna before you found him. They would have got to her without your involvement. Now get off my back and don't call again unless you've got some vital information. OK?'

'OK, Steve, but let me know if there are any developments.'

'I will. Goodbye, Quentin.'

Quentin ended the call feeling slightly better. Philmore hadn't told him to stop investigating. Contact him with any vital information, he'd said. How could he gain vital information without investigating? With a new determination settling on him, Quentin started the engine and drove.

He'd only gone a few yards when he realized he'd have to turn round and go back the way he'd come. If he'd brought his holdall and Victor, he could have gone straight to Colin's in Wanstead. Instead, he'd have to return to Greenwich.

Passing a side road, he pulled over, waited until the way was clear and backed into it, checking his rear-view mirror as he did so. He was about to ease forward again when he spotted the bumper of a green car sticking out behind other parked vehicles. Anticipation and apprehension filling him, he reversed further, gasping when he got a full view of the car. It was a green Corsa.

Chapter Sixteen

After a moment's hesitation, Quentin kept reversing until he reached the junction of an intersecting road and began backing around the corner, causing an oncoming vehicle to brake suddenly and its driver to glower impatiently as he waited for Quentin to complete his manoeuvre. When the way was clear, Quentin drove back to where the green Corsa was parked, slow enough to see some of the front number plate. The part he remembered jumped out at him. Yes, it was definitely the car he'd seen Boatman in.

After several circuits around the block, he finally found a parking space. Donning the sunglasses again, he jumped out and made his way to where he'd seen the Corsa, wondering if Boatman lived in one of the adjacent houses or whether he'd parked wherever he could and walked to where he lived.

'Excuse me,' said a female voice.

Roused from his thoughts, Quentin turned to see an elderly lady pushing an equally elderly man in a wheelchair.

'Sorry,' he said, stepping aside to let them pass. For a wild moment, he thought of stopping them, giving Boatman's description and asking if it was anyone who lived near them, then dismissed the idea. The chances of that in a road this long were negligible. After fifty minutes, when he'd walked the length of the road on both sides as well as two parallel roads, he decided he was wasting his time. He went back to the Corsa and photographed the front number plate. It was difficult, squished in between two other vehicles as the Corsa was, but after removing the sunglasses and checking the image, he saw that the whole of the registration plate was there.

An idea forming, he hurried back to the Toyota and got in, his phone still clutched in one hand. He hesitated, knowing that if he made the call, he might lose the only link he had to Property Perfections. But Lorna's life might be at stake, so how could he even think of not telling Philmore?

He sighed. Automatic number plate recognition. He knew the public couldn't access personal information, but Philmore could use it to find Boatman's address. Then the police would be all over Nick Crawford.

Quentin stopped his reasoning, his attention caught by the couple with the wheelchair coming towards him on the opposite side of the road. They stopped at a gate to a house sporting a tall hedge on one side. As the woman turned the wheelchair to pull it backwards up the concrete step, a bag slid from the man's lap and hit the ground, its contents spilling onto the pavement.

Quentin climbed out from the car, darted across and began gathering up the fallen items.

'Thank you so much,' the woman said.

The man in the chair mumbled his thanks too, though his words were indistinct.

'He hasn't got the grip in his hands since his stroke,' the woman explained. 'I really shouldn't get so much all at once. That store is expensive, but it's convenient, being so close.'

'No problem,' Quentin said, looping the handles of the bag over his arm and stepping through the gate. 'I'll take this to the door for you.'

'That's kind of you,' the woman said, trying to manoeuvre the chair through the gate.

'Here, let me do that.' Quentin put the bag down and grasped the wheelchair's handles, lifting it up the step. It was surprisingly heavy, and he wondered how the woman managed.

The house was terraced, the ground floor separated from the one on either side by an arched alleyway leading to the back garden. There were two steps up to the front door.

'We're still waiting for a ramp from the council,' the woman explained. 'Our son fitted a temporary one at the back, so we're using that at the moment.'

Looping the shopping bag back over his arm and taking hold of the wheelchair again, Quentin turned and made for the alley.

'It's all right, I can manage now,' the woman assured him.

'No trouble,' Quentin said, carrying on. When he emerged from the alley, he turned into the back garden. Quite long, he noticed, and the tall hedge continued a few feet from the house to the end of the garden.

Quentin waited while the woman walked up a wooden ramp, rummaged in her pocket for her key and opened the door. Quentin pushed the chair up the ramp to the threshold, then handed her the shopping bag.

'There we go,' he said, flashing her a smile.

'Thank you again,' she said. 'It can be difficult sometimes, getting in and out of places. They're not all wheelchair-friendly. I've nearly tipped poor Tom out a few times, haven't I, Tom?'

The man in the wheelchair nodded and mumbled something Quentin couldn't catch.

Quentin leaned down. 'Sorry?' he said.

The slurred words came again, and this time Quentin made sense of them.

'It's hard for Maureen. Too much for her.'

'I heard that, Tom Berkley,' the woman called Maureen said. 'It's not too much for me. I'd say if it was.'

A memory stirred in Quentin's brain – his Aunt Josie, in her older years, crippled with arthritis and losing her mobility.

'Anyway,' Maureen was saying, 'there are always kind people like this young man to help us – we'll be all right.'

'Pleased to help,' Quentin said, stepping back. 'Well, I'll be off now. Bye.'

'Goodbye,' Maureen called, and pulled the wheelchair inside.

Quentin turned to descend the ramp. As he did so, he caught a movement on the other side of the hedge. Seconds later, someone appeared in the gap between the hedge and the house. Quentin gasped, then froze. It was Boatman.

Nick Crawford didn't look Quentin's way. He walked purposefully to his back door and disappeared inside the house. Recovering, Quentin carried on, walking fast until he was across the road and safely seated in Wanda's car. Swivelling round, he stared at the house he'd seen Boatman go into.

'Must be dark in there,' he muttered to himself, noticing a high fence on the opposite side from the hedge. 'Pretty private, if that fence goes all the way back.'

He sat for a moment, wondering what to do. He was sure Boatman hadn't taken Lorna. Not capable enough. He wondered again why whoever had killed Dave would employ someone so slapdash.

It didn't matter. What mattered was, he now knew where Boatman lived; he was here, outside his house. So what was he going to do about it?

After scanning the road and waiting until there was no one nearby, Quentin walked quickly and quietly through Boatman's front gate onto a weed-strewn path. Relieved that he didn't need to pass the front window, he went through the alley to the back garden, glancing sideways through to the garden he'd been in a few minutes ago. All he could see before the hedge began was a four-foot-wide patch of concrete and the ramp. He guessed that Maureen would be too busy with Tom to be either coming outside or looking through the back window. From that angle, she wouldn't see much anyway, he decided, turning to face into Boatman's garden.

With the hedge on one side and a high fence on the other, this was a totally private garden, Quentin realized, if you could call it a garden. What may once have been a lawn resembled an African savannah, and a variety of weeds tumbled out of the borders. The only relief from this was an elongated cabin-like shed that ran along the bottom, from the hedge on one side to the fence on the other. A trail of trodden-down grass wound its way to the door of the shed.

Flattening himself against the wall of the house, Quentin sidled along until he reached a window. The kitchen, he guessed. On the far side of the window was the back door. Quentin hovered, trying to decide on a course of action. Go back to the front, knock on the door, confront Boatman? Risk a peek through the kitchen window? He guessed the back door wasn't locked. Did the man live alone? Should he barge in, take the man by surprise?

His thoughts stopped abruptly as the back door swung open. Quentin ducked back into the alley just as Boatman came out with something in his hand and hurried to the shed. Moving forward, Quentin peered around the hedge. Boatman had reached the shed and was opening the door. Bright light spilled from inside, lightening the gloom of the garden. Just a flash, while Boatman went in and the door was shut again. Was Lorna in there? Unlikely. Too close to neighbours.

Desperate to see what Boatman was up to, Quentin crept along the hedge towards the shed. No windows, he noticed as he drew nearer, not on this side anyway, but a padlock swung free on the door. Squeezing into the narrow gap between the shed and the hedge, he shuffled his way along to the back of the wooden structure.

Bugger it, he thought grimly. No windows. Clearly there had been windows, but they'd been boarded over. He thought of his Swiss army knife nestling in his pocket. He could prise the boards away, but Boatman would hear. Inching his way back towards the front, he wondered whether to make a dash to the alley. He was still dithering when he heard the door open and saw a flash of bright light before the door was closed again, just seconds later.

Seconds. But long enough for the brightness to enlighten not only the garden, but Quentin's brain as well. Because, from this distance, light was not the only thing that seeped into the dull April air; it brought with it a smell, an unmistakable odour that Quentin recognized instantly. He'd been to university. He'd dropped out before gaining his degree. But he didn't need a degree to tell him what was inside that shed.

Chapter Seventeen

The shrill of a phone penetrated Quentin's thoughts – not his phone, but Boatman's, he realized. Instead of coming out of the shed, Boatman had retreated inside to answer the call. Quentin crept round to the front and put his ear to the wooden wall.

'I am following him,' he heard Boatman say. 'I can't be watching him every minute. I've got to eat … No, I don't need anyone else, I can do it … I told you where the woman was, didn't I? When am I going to get my money? … All right, all right … Look, you know where he lives, and where he works, so why do you need to know what he's doing all the time? … OK, I get the picture … No, of course he hasn't spotted me … Yes, yes, all right, I will.'

Quentin assumed the caller had rung off when Boatman uttered a string of profanities.

'Let him try waiting about for hours then following someone around when you don't know why you're doing it,' Quentin heard him complain. 'I've a good mind to tell him to stuff it. Must be an easier way to make money.'

So they'd been right. Boatman was a very small cog in a much bigger wheel. He didn't know what was going on at Property Perfections. And the less he knew, the less he could give away; a good strategy in the criminal world, Quentin had to admit.

The shed door opened and Quentin sprang away. Too late. Boatman saw him before he had time to either hide or make a run for it.

Shock showed on Boatman's face, but he soon recovered and leapt at Quentin, delivering a hefty blow to his midriff. Winded, Quentin gasped, then rammed him, head down. In the tussle that followed, Quentin was pushed against the door, the padlock digging into his back. Using all his strength, he managed to get the upper hand, gripping the other man by both arms. The man squirmed and tried to kick out.

'Stop!' Quentin shouted, then lowered his voice. 'Listen to me. You're being played for a fool. These people you work for have already killed someone, and they'll kill you too if you cross them.'

Boatman looked sullen but stopped wriggling. 'I won't cross them.'

'No?'

Pulling Boatman away from the wall and yanking the shed door open, Quentin pushed Boatman in front of him, stepped inside and closed the door.

'What about this lot? You'll be crossing them if you're arrested for growing this.'

Boatman's face set into a stubborn mask, but fear showed in his eyes. His gaze flickered over the illicit crop, then around the cabin as though seeking escape.

'Where's Lorna?' Quentin blurted. 'The woman you led them to – where have they taken her?'

'How do I know? They wanted to know when she was in a public place with lots of people and I told them. That's all I know.'

'Yeah, right,' Quentin said with scorn, although after what he'd overheard, he was inclined to think this was true. 'What did you think they wanted her for? Don't you care what's happened to her?'

'S'none of my business.'

'None of your business? They could be murdering her right now, and it'll be your fault,' Quentin hissed, disbelief and rage filling him. Did this man have no morals? No feelings?

When Boatman didn't answer, he tried a different tack. 'You could be done for being an accessory to murder,' he said, although he suspected this wouldn't hold up in court.

For the first time, Boatman seemed uncertain. 'They won't really kill her, will they? Why, what's she done?'

Quentin gave a heavy sigh. He wasn't going to get anything useful from Nick Crawford.

'Look,' he said, nodding toward the rows of plants. 'I won't let on about your little sideline if you cooperate with me.'

Quentin jumped as his mobile vibrated against his hip and sang out its tune. His grip on Boatman slackened a little. Mistake. His captive wrenched himself free, and in a whirl, had both hands round Quentin's throat.

'Give me your phone,' Boatman rasped, his eyes fixed on Quentin's face. Not relishing the thought of being strangled, Quentin slid his hand into his pocket.

'Slowly,' Boatman commanded, digging his fingers deeper into Quentin's neck. Clutching the phone, Quentin raised his arm, banking on the fact that Boatman would have to remove one of his hands in order to take the phone. But Boatman, it seemed, was having a less than dull-witted day.

'Throw it over there,' he said, jerking his head towards the door.

Not likely, Quentin thought, and brought his knee up hard into Boatman's groin. Boatman yelled in pain, and Quentin grabbed at his arms, trying to break the stranglehold on his neck. In the process, his phone flew from his grasp, landing on the floor by the door.

'Bloody hell!' he spluttered, then let out a loud moan as Boatman gave an almighty shove and sent him sprawling backwards into the bed of vegetation. By the time he'd struggled onto his elbows, Boatman was through the door.

Quentin groaned as the door was slammed shut and he heard a metallic clank. He groaned again when he looked at the floor. Not only was he locked in, Boatman had taken his phone.

* * *

It was a few panicky minutes before he gathered his wits. Blinking against the bright light, he got to his feet and tried the door, although he knew it would be useless. The windows were boarded over on the outside, yet he supposed the boarding might give if he broke the glass and punched at it for long enough. The walls seemed pretty solid, as did the door. This definitely wasn't a run of the mill garden shed.

He thought of shouting, alerting the neighbours, but doubted they would hear. He'd had to put his ear to the wall to hear Boatman on the phone. How long would he be stuck here? No one knew where he was. He'd have to dig his way out with his Swiss army knife…

'You stupid idiot, Quentin,' he chided himself aloud. Shaking his head, he delved into his left-hand pocket, sighing with relief when he felt his other phone. Grimacing, he realized he'd have to call Philmore, the only contact on this mobile, unless he could recall either Wanda's or Colin's number. Except, he noticed suddenly, this wasn't his second phone, it was his usual one. Which meant Boatman had the one with Philmore's number on it.

A shiver ran down Quentin's back. If Boatman turned the phone over to whoever was employing him and they rang that number… A phone with only a detective chief inspector's number on it? He could end up dead in an alley like Dave Brown. He had to get out of there.

'Wanda,' he barked as soon as she answered his call.

'Quentin! I was wondering where you'd got to.'

'Listen, Wanda, I'm locked in a shed at Boatman's house. I need you to get me out. Bring Colin with you and something to break a padlock. I don't know the house number but it's Coronation Street, Brixton, the far end from the main road, left-hand side going down. There's a big hedge on one side and a fence on the other. I don't know if Boatman will be here, but be prepared, and don't ring me if you can avoid it. I don't want him to know I've got a phone.'

'We'll be there, Quentin,' was all she said. No questions, no fuss, just reassurance that she understood and would come straight away.

There was a bench-like counter at one end of the rows of plants, with a rusty garden chair leaning against it. Quentin pulled it out and sat down. A couple of trowels, several watering cans and some plastic plant ties sat on the counter, along with plastic cartons, like old ice-cream cartons, full of dried or drying flowers. Quentin wondered how long they took to dry, and how big their yield. He knew cannabis was considered by some as medicinal and by some as recreational; he also knew that when it got out of hand, it led to much more serious drug abuse.

Shaking his head, he pushed away the bitter memories that drugs evoked – the death of his best friend at university, the smuggling ring he'd help to catch – and the man with the cultured voice still making money from illicit drug trading, despite Quentin's best efforts to stop him.

He wondered how long it would be before Wanda and Colin reached him. He calculated Brixton to be about an hour's drive from Wanstead. He couldn't just sit here – he should be doing something to help himself. Suppose Boatman came back with reinforcements?

He stood up and glanced around, hoping to find a hammer or at least a metal fork or shovel, but there was only the two trowels and a wooden mallet. He looked again at the boarded-up windows. Afraid that Boatman might hear and see what he was doing, he ruled out the front and turned to the back. Boatman might still hear something, but he decided to risk it.

He found some empty compost bags and laid them on the floor under the window. With the boarding on the outside, he expected the shattered glass to fall inwards. He could drag the glass-covered bags aside before pounding at the boards and going through the window.

To protect his eyes, he fished in his pocket for Wanda's sunglasses, miraculously still intact, and put them on. He reached for the mallet, knocking one of the plastic containers and cursing as it clattered to the floor, its contents spilling out in all directions. Stepping over the mess, he grabbed the mallet with both hands, raised his arms and swung it as hard as he could. The mallet struck the glass and bounced off, rebounding so forcefully that Quentin staggered back, teetered when his feet hit the wooden edge of the cannabis bed, and toppled back into the plants, his arms recoiling and the mallet striking his forehead as he landed.

Dazed, he struggled to get up, then froze as he heard a noise from outside. Boatman? Or someone he'd called to deal with Quentin?

He picked up the mallet and walked unsteadily to stand by the door. He heard the clang of the padlock being moved and he tensed, ready to spring at whoever came through the door. Hushed voices came to him, and he slumped against the wall as he recognized the familiar tones of a female one.

'Quentin?' it called. 'Are you in there?'

Still feeling woozy, Quentin allowed himself to slide down the wall onto the floor while banging and clanking told him the padlock was being forced from the door. After several minutes, the wood on the door splintered and a metal point showed through.

When the door swung open, it was Mozart that Quentin saw first. He bounded up to Quentin and licked his face, tail wagging furiously.

'Mozart,' Quentin murmured, amazed that his rescuers had brought him along. The casualness of it felt wrong.

'Boatman?' he croaked when Wanda and Colin appeared.

'He's not in the house,' Wanda told him. 'Probably done a runner. There's no green Corsa anywhere outside. The neighbour said she saw him go out about half an hour ago.'

Half an hour, Quentin thought, wondering how long he'd been there. It was hard to gauge time in this artificial light. He glanced at his watch, dismayed when he saw a spider's web of cracks on the glass front.

'What's this then,' Colin said, indicating the plants. 'Is it what I think it is?'

'I'm guessing cannabis.' Wanda eyed the vegetation in amazement. 'I've never seen it, but I know it's got a funny smell, and who grows tomatoes in a shed with artificial light and a padlock?'

'Yeah,' Quentin agreed. 'I couldn't believe it either. Still, it might explain why Boatman's not very good at his job. Probably high as a kite half the time. How come you got here so quickly?'

'We weren't quick,' Wanda said. 'We got stuck at roadworks.'

'Maybe I passed out for a bit, then, or maybe these plants are affecting me. Can that happen? Anyway, I tried to smash a window, force the boarding off, but it didn't work. Must be toughened glass or something.'

'What's that mark on your head?' Colin asked. 'Did he clonk you one?

'Something like that,' Quentin said ruefully, unwilling to admit he'd likely caused the bruise himself.

'So,' Colin said, 'you saw this guy and decided to creep round his garden on your own, without telling anyone where you were or what you were doing? Bit reckless, isn't it?'

'Well, once I'd seen him, I couldn't just walk away.' Deciding to keep his good deed for Boatman's neighbours to himself, Quentin carried on. 'I was there, right outside his house. I had to do something.'

'Well, you'll have to tell Philmore,' Colin said. 'This bloke might know where Lorna is.'

'I don't think so,' Quentin said, and relayed Boatman's telephone conversation.

'So he doesn't know much, and tending his precious cannabis plants is more important to him than watching us. Do you think he's selling the stuff?' Wanda asked, screwing up her nose in distaste.

Quentin shrugged. 'Don't know. Still, I don't think this case is about drugs, not the hard stuff like last time. I'm guessing it's Boatman's sideline.'

'Some sideline,' Colin said. 'Must be a nightmare trying to keep it from the neighbours.'

'Whatever,' Quentin said, standing up. 'I'm more worried that he's called whoever he was speaking to earlier and told them where to find me. We need to leave.'

'We'd better hurry,' Wanda said. 'Here, Mozart.'

'Come on then,' Quentin said. 'I've had enough of this place.' He started towards the door, stopped, and turned back. 'I don't care if Boatman's done a runner or not, I'm not leaving this lot for him or anyone else to profit from.'

Locating the mallet, he picked it up and swung it up at the florescent tubes that lit the cabin. He swung again and again until all the tubes were smashed and they were in darkness.

'Better?' Colin asked, switching on the torch on his phone and pushing open the door.

'Much,' Quentin replied. After several swipes at the plants themselves, he stepped gratefully outside.

Chapter Eighteen

With the possibility hanging over them that Boatman had passed on Quentin's location, Wanda drove Quentin straight back to Greenwich in her Toyota to pick up his holdall and collect Victor. Colin returned to Wanstead in his own car.

'If they come looking for me and I'm not in the shed, then they'll be watching my house like hawks,' Quentin said. 'They won't have had time to do anything yet, but they won't take long once they see I've scarpered. I'd better put a few more things in my bag. Perhaps you should too. We'll fly in and out as quickly as we can.'

It wasn't until they were on the way back to Wanstead with Victor that Mozart began barking excitedly and springing up, putting his front paws on the back of Wanda's seat.

'Down, Mote,' Quentin said, knowing how distracting this can be for a driver.

Mozart, usually so obedient, kept up what was more of a yap than a bark, jumping down and nudging at Victor with his nose. Victor, apparently not in a playful mood, drew away, while Mozart twisted round and round on the seat, still yapping.

'Mozart!' cried Wanda in her best schoolmistress voice. 'Sit!'

By the time they got to Colin's, streetlamps were keeping the encroaching night at bay. Victor lumbered out of the car and walked sedately beside Quentin onto the driveway. Mozart shot past them and ran onto the front lawn, continuing his frantic yapping and frenzied darting about. Heedless of Wanda's calls for him to stop, he skipped around the garden, somersaulting over an ornamental water feature. His back legs caught the rim of the basin and tipped it over. The basin crashed onto the terracotta edging of a flower bed and split in half, felling several tall fritillaries in the process. Light shone from the hallway when Colin came out to see what was going on. Surprise registered on his face as he watched the dog cavorting on the manicured lawn, looking for all the world like a mechanical toy that had been overwound.

'What the devil's wrong with him?' Colin demanded, frowning at the sight of water spewing from his broken water feature.

'I don't know,' Wanda said, looking upset. 'He never acts like this. I can't understand it.'

'I can,' Quentin said, unable to stop a smile at Mozart's comical antics. Stepping onto the lawn, he knelt down, waited until Mozart came zigzagging past, reached out and scooped him up.

'Come on, Mote,' he said. 'Let's get you inside.'

Mozart wriggled in his arms, and Wanda caught hold of his collar while Quentin got to his feet.

Indoors, in the light of the kitchen, Quentin held the dog's head and examined his face.

'There's the answer,' he said, picking a dried petal from Mozart's fur. 'He must have eaten some of those plants. Bloody hell! I never thought I'd see a dog stoned on cannabis.'

*　*　*

After Mozart had thrown up and finally settled down on a blanket in Colin's conservatory, Wanda called the out-of-hours vet for advice.

'I've got to keep his fluids up,' she said afterwards. 'If he's still ill in the morning, I should take him in, but because he's getting it out of his system and he's in good general health, he should be all right.'

No one felt like cooking, so they rang for a takeaway delivery.

'It's been quite a day,' Quentin said over their Chinese meal. 'And we're still no closer to finding Lorna.'

'No,' Wanda agreed. 'All the time we're dithering, anything could be happening to her. We need to be more proactive.'

There was a short silence. Victor limped up to Quentin and laid his head on his lap. He was rewarded with a gentle pat on the nose.

'Shame you can't talk,' Quentin said. 'You're the only eye witness to your master's death.'

After another short silence, Quentin reached for his mobile.

'What are you doing?' Wanda asked.

'Being more proactive. I'm calling Philmore.'

When Philmore answered, Quentin gave him Nick Crawford's car registration, address and an abbreviated account of how he'd come by it. As he finished, he hesitated, wondering if he should keep the final piece of information to himself. No, he decided, it could have serious consequences for Philmore, and not telling him would break the trust between them.

'What?' Philmore rasped when Quentin blurted it out. 'So now there's a criminal walking around with a mobile phone with my number in it?'

'Well, he won't know it's yours unless he rings it, so don't answer any calls from it. I'm sorry, Steve. Look, I spotted the guy and followed him, that's all. He may not know where Lorna is, but he may know something about Property Perfections. If you need a reason to arrest him, look in his shed. There's enough cannabis growing in there to supply the whole street. No news on Lorna, I take it?'

'No. We've been checking up on the company, questioned Philip Chandler again, but he says he's never heard of Lorna.'

'What about the other partners? Chandler's brother and the other one?'

'William Chandler's in Barcelona – that's been confirmed – but no one seems to know where Henry Lawson is. He's a sleeping partner, apparently. We'll keep digging.'

'What about Lorna's editor, or anyone at her paper? Have you spoken to them?'

Philmore sighed. 'Of course we have, but it's a newspaper. People come and go all day so nobody took much notice. Our guy had eyes on her from across the road. He could see her on her phone, then a van went in front of her and after it passed, she was gone.'

'Bloody hell! She was on the phone to me. Did your guy get the reg of this van?'

'No. By the time he'd scanned the area looking for her, it had gone. It was white, that's all he could say. Might have been false plates anyway, and there's no proof she was in there. She could have gone anywhere, or been dragged into a car or an alleyway. He only noticed the van because that's what obscured his view. It's central London. The street was heaving.'

'Someone must have seen something, surely?' Quentin persisted.

'He asked people in the vicinity but got nowhere. The busier a place is, the less people see. We'll check CCTV but it doesn't cover every inch of the street. Our guy went back to her office, but found nothing on her desk to suggest she was acting on new information. We're arranging for someone to get into her computer but that will take a while.'

'Great.' Quentin groaned. 'Well, let me know if you come up with anything.'

'You seem to forget I'm the officer in charge here, Quentin,' Philmore snapped. '*You* let *me* know if you come up with anything.'

'Point taken,' Quentin said as the call ended. He relayed what he'd learned from Philmore to Wanda and Colin.

'What do you reckon to Lorna's chances?' Colin asked Quentin when Wanda went to check on Mozart.

Quentin pulled a face. 'If she can convince them that Dave didn't tell her anything, she might be all right. I mean, they've got no other reason to kill her. She hadn't found out anything, although in that last call to me she said she'd discovered something about Property Perfections. If only she'd had time to tell me before she was taken.'

'Hmm, that's a bummer,' Colin said. 'What I can't understand is why they didn't move Dave's body instead of leaving it there. If they'd have hidden it, you know, dumped it in a lake or something, he may not have been discovered for ages.'

Quentin shrugged. 'Wanda thinks maybe they had meant to but didn't for some reason. Perhaps the attackers were interrupted. They could have been planning to come back and move him, but couldn't. I mean, it was really early when I found him – only just getting light, then the police were there.'

'Or maybe because they swiped all his ID, they thought it would take a while for him to be identified,' Colin suggested. 'Long enough for Property Perfections to clean up their act, remove any trace of incriminating evidence from their premises and computer system.'

'Yeah. Still, seems slapdash to me. How's Mozart?' Quentin added as Wanda came back into the room.

'Sleeping. I think he'll be OK.'

'Maybe we should get an early night, too,' Colin said. 'Get some rest and be bright-eyed and bushy-tailed tomorrow.'

'We can't just go to bed,' Quentin snapped. 'We need to make a plan, now, tonight.'

'All right, Superman,' Colin conceded. 'What do you suggest?'

Stumped, Quentin shook his head.

'How many empty UK properties do you think Philip Chandler's got on his books?' Wanda asked.

'A few, maybe,' Quentin said. 'I should think most places will still be occupied, though.'

'What does it matter how many are empty?' Colin demanded. 'We can't go to them all.'

'No, but there's three of us,' Wanda pointed out. 'Between us we could at least check out the nearest ones. If we knew where they were, that is.'

'I daresay Philmore's thought of that,' Colin countered. 'He could get a list of the properties they're dealing with if he hasn't already.'

The glance that passed between Quentin and Wanda made Colin look from one to the other with suspicion.

'What?' he said. 'You can't ask him. He's not going to print off a list and let you go running off looking at empty houses, is he?'

'Why not?' Quentin said. 'They're empty houses, not dens of iniquity. We can't do any harm checking them out, and we might find something useful.'

'Except,' Wanda cut in, 'if they're keeping Lorna in one, they'll have taken it off the list, probably off their records altogether.'

Quentin's face fell. 'Of course they would. Oh well, it was a good idea at the time.'

After a pause, Quentin continued. 'I vote we go back to Property Perfections. There might be more staff there this time. There's the colleague who reported Dave missing, a woman, wasn't it? Maybe it was the person you saw initially, Wanda.'

'Yes,' Wanda said. 'And she can't be in on whatever's going on there or she wouldn't have reported Dave missing.'

'I thought you were steering clear of Property Perfections, Quentin, in case someone recognizes you,' Colin said.

'Only if Boatman took photos when he was watching us and sent them to Chandler, and we don't know for sure that he did. We don't even know for sure that Boatman's working for him. Anyway, Chandler's never seen me in the flesh.'

Colin looked sceptical. 'Hmm. Perhaps me and Wanda should go. After all, Chandler knows us, and you look too young to be able to afford the sort of properties they deal with.'

'That's a bit ageist, Colin. Anyway, I could disguise myself, and I don't have to be looking for a property. I could be, I don't know... a salesman or something.'

'A salesman!' Colin snorted. 'What would an upmarket company like Property Perfections want with a salesman?'

'A student then. I could be writing a thesis on the property market.'

'Yeah, right. You don't look *that* young.'

'He could be a mature student,' Wanda said. 'You can go to university at any age if you've got the qualifications and the credits. I think it's a good idea, Quentin.'

Quentin's self-esteem grew, as it always did when Wanda took his side in front of Colin.

'It would be good to go when it's a bit busier,' Wanda went on. 'They'd need more staff on then. Tomorrow's Saturday. It should be busier.'

'You'll need to make an appointment,' Colin said, as if realizing any further objections would be overruled. 'You can't expect them to drop everything and speak to a student, any of them.'

'I'll play it by ear,' Quentin told him. 'And if nothing comes of it, then you and Wanda can go and talk to Chandler about that new property he sent her, see if you can suss anything out.'

'OK,' Colin said, somewhat appeased.

'And we'll forget Boatman for now,' Quentin added.

'I'm not forgetting him,' Wanda declared. 'I hope he's in a ditch somewhere being as sick as Mozart.'

'Hear, hear!' Colin quipped.

'Well,' Quentin said, feeling more relaxed now they had something positive to do the next day, 'I don't think Boatman can tell us anything useful. We'd be better to concentrate on finding Lorna. I don't know about you two, but I could do with a drink.'

And without waiting for a response, he helped himself to a generous measure of Colin's single malt whisky.

Chapter Nineteen

'You look like a hippy,' Colin said to Quentin as he parked his Honda a few roads away from Property Perfections.

Quentin wasn't sure what a hippy was, although he vaguely recalled his mother mentioning hippies. Before his time. He knew he looked totally ridiculous, but he didn't care. He wore what Colin assured him were John Lennon glasses, a flowered shirt and, in the absence of flared jeans, corduroy trousers, salvaged from a box in Colin's spare room. A felt hat covered his hair.

Wanda had stayed behind with Mozart to ensure he wasn't suffering any lasting effects of the cannabis, although he seemed much better today.

'Right,' Quentin said, opening the passenger door. 'I'll call if I need to, otherwise keep out of sight. We don't want them making a connection between Eleanor King's financial advisor and a random student.'

Colin grunted and Quentin left him. Minutes later, Quentin approached Property Perfections. It was eleven-thirty and the place was, if not bustling, at least busier than before. From the description Wanda had given him, he recognized Philip Chandler in a navy-blue jacket with a matching tie over a pale-blue shirt. He sat talking to a silver-haired man on one side of the room, a stylish, modern desk between them. A young woman sat at a second desk, a phone held to her ear. A second man – another estate agent, Quentin assumed – sat on the far side, pointing to a brochure opened in front of a middle-aged couple. They didn't look particularly affluent, but, as Quentin had learned, appearances could be deceptive.

The young woman put down the phone and looked at Quentin as he approached her.

'Can I help you?' she said, eyeing his mismatched attire with uncertainty. A scarf obscured most of her name badge.

'I hope so,' he said, giving her a winning smile. 'I'm writing a thesis on the impact of the property market on society, and I was wondering if I could ask you a few questions?'

Glancing across at Philip Chandler, the woman hesitated, then looked towards the door as another couple entered. 'Not today,' she replied. 'Perhaps if you could come back in the week when we're not so busy?'

Still smiling, Quentin said, 'Well, I've got plenty of time. All right if I wait till you're quieter?'

Without waiting for an answer, he moved back and sat on one of the chairs just inside the door, while the new couple approached the young woman's desk. He swept his gaze over the office, taking in the hessian wallpaper, the discreetly placed plants and the expensive-looking carpet. Telephone handsets matched the colour of the walls. Everything was understated. It screamed money to Quentin, especially when he studied the few well-displayed photos and descriptions of properties for sale.

'Can I help you?'

Quentin was jolted out of his reverie when Philip Chandler called to him as the silver-haired man he'd been engaged with left. Jumping up, Quentin hurried over and sat opposite him. The couple who had come in last were leaving with a bundle of brochures and expressions that told Quentin they'd made the wrong choice of estate agent. The young woman who'd served them leaned towards Philip Chandler, her scarf falling away to reveal her name badge. "Tina Patterson", Quentin read. The colleague who'd reported Dave missing.

'This gentleman is a student and would like to ask some questions about the business,' she said apologetically, as though she feared a reprimand for not deflecting such a trivial intrusion.

A look of irritation flashed across Chandler's face. He glanced at his watch. 'I've got a few minutes before my next appointment. What do you want to know?'

Quentin quickly repeated what he'd told Tina, adding the university he'd attended for good measure. He asked what he thought were relevant questions, jotting down the other man's measured answers and wishing he could ask what he really wanted to know, but the polished and practised Philip Chandler wasn't going to give anything away. Quentin wished he could ask Tina, but what could he say? Do you know what Dave Brown found out?

He was just wondering how he could bring the conversation round to IT when Chandler's mobile phone rang. He pulled it from his pocket, checked the display and immediately stood up, his efficient composure slipping a little.

'You'll have to excuse me,' he said, already turning towards a door behind him. 'I've got to take this.'

A call important enough to take in private? A client? His wife? Some inner sense told Quentin otherwise.

He rose and flashed a smile at Tina, who was once again on the phone.

Deciding it would be difficult to question Tina at that moment, he left, walked a while until he was out of sight, then picked up pace and headed to the rear of Property Perfections where he'd seen the red Maserati. When he got there, he looked towards the back of the premises and felt a stab of disappointment. No door left ajar, no open window. He wouldn't be able to hear anything.

He was about to turn away when the back door opened and Chandler came out, his head down and his mobile clamped to his ear. Quentin ducked behind the Maserati and held his breath as Chandler moved closer and leaned against the other side of the car.

'It's all right, Henry, really,' Quentin heard him say. 'Yes, the police have been here but they didn't find anything–'

As if in agitation, Chandler took a few paces, coming to rest by the bonnet. Praying he wouldn't turn round, Quentin shrunk back.

'You keep fading, Henry. What did you say? Hold on a minute.' Chandler punched a key, the loudspeaker key, Quentin realized when the caller's voice sounded intermittently loud then hardly audible.

'There's nothing to worry about,' Chandler said. 'Everything's in hand.'

There was a pause. Quentin racked his memory. Henry. Lorna had spoken of a Henry Lawson, a sleeping partner in Property Perfections. Was that who Chandler was talking to? Whoever it was, they were making the suave and smooth Philip Chandler very nervous.

'Don't worry, Henry, your money's quite safe – hello? Can you hear me?'

Chandler held the phone away from his head and looked at the screen as though checking the call was still connected. Quentin knew it was when the caller's voice came through, sudden and very clear.

'I certainly hope so, Philip. I wouldn't want you to–'

What the caller wanted or didn't want Chandler to do, Quentin didn't hear. He didn't hear and he didn't need to hear. Chandler moved away, but the few words Quentin had heard were enough – enough for him to freeze in his ungainly, uncomfortable crouching position, enough to paralyse his mind and his body.

Because the voice that had emanated from Chandler's phone was one he recognized. One that belonged to a master criminal; one that had taunted and threatened Quentin many times; one that carried the refined, well-modulated tones of the man Quentin knew as Cultured Voice.

Chapter Twenty

'Are you sure?' Colin asked when Quentin was back at the car. 'I mean, if you only heard a few words–'

'Of course I'm sure,' Quentin said. 'I'd know that voice anywhere. It's him, Cultured Voice – Whitelaw, as he used to call himself in the UK. He used the name Hoeker in the Netherlands, now apparently it's Henry Lawson. Well, I'm assuming it's Lawson.'

'So, this just got even more dangerous for you then, Quentin. Isn't there anything this bloke hasn't got a hand in?'

'Not much. And if he is Henry Lawson, then he's a sleeping partner, which means–'

'He's got money in the business,' Colin finished.

'Yep. Well, he makes enough from his illegal dealings. He's got to put it somewhere.'

Quentin caught Colin's eye, knowing that, for once, they were completely in tune.

'Money laundering?' Colin asked softly.

Quentin raised his eyebrows. 'Could well be.'

'OK,' Colin ventured after a pause. 'You know what you've got to do now, don't you?'

Quentin didn't answer. He simply sighed, took out his phone and called Philmore.

* * *

'Not Cultured Voice again,' Wanda said over the table outside the café where they'd arranged to meet for lunch. 'That man's like a jack-in-the box – he keeps jumping up when you least expect him.'

She leaned over to pat Mozart, who seemed sluggish but otherwise unharmed after his escapade yesterday. Victor, as though resenting being left out, put his head on Quentin's knee.

'Yeah,' Quentin said glumly, absently stroking Victor. 'And I thought he'd let his threat to kill me lapse. If he finds out I'm involved with this… Well, now the stakes are doubled.'

'Why would he find out?' Wanda asked. 'The papers just called you a member of the public and Philip Chandler doesn't know who you are. From what you heard, it sounds like Chandler's just been told to sort things out. Cultured Voice must know about Dave's death, but he may know nothing about you or Lorna. Chandler's not going to risk his sleeping partner getting spooked and pulling his money out of the company. If this Henry Lawson is Cultured Voice, then I'm sure Chandler and his brother have been made very aware that if anything goes wrong then they're on their own.'

Quentin nodded. He knew his nemesis had an army of people to call on to do things for him, but he also knew that none of them knew his true identity. As Cultured Voice had said to him during their one and only meeting, being dependent or getting emotionally involved with anyone raised the risk of being caught.

'So we're pretty sure Property Perfections is just a front for laundering money?' Colin asked.

'Sounds highly likely,' Quentin replied. 'Cultured Voice has been in since the takeover, according to Companies House. You can't believe it, can you? I mean the guy was banged up in the Netherlands before he escaped. The Dutch police couldn't have known about his connection to Property Perfections, or the company would have been in trouble.'

'He used an alias there,' Wanda reminded him. 'He must have ID for each name he uses. What did Philmore say?'

'Only that it's all the more reason for us to keep out of it. They're still trying to track down Boatman, but they think he's small fry. He didn't say as much, but I'm guessing they'll be looking into Philip Chandler even more closely now.'

'What time does Property Perfections close?' Wanda asked.

'Four, I think, on a Saturday,' Quentin said. 'Why?'

'The woman you saw – was she the person I saw the first time? Youngish, red hair, glasses?'

'Sounds like it. She's Tina Patterson, the person who reported Dave missing. Why?'

'Well, I was thinking…'

'That we should wait till she finishes and approach her? I thought of that while I was there, but it went out of my head after I heard Cultured Voice. What reason can I give for asking her about Dave? I suppose I could say I'm a relative or friend of Dave's, but she might mention it to Chandler and it might spook him if he thinks someone's sniffing around. Anyway, I'm sure Philmore's already questioned her, and Chandler can't think she knows anything or she wouldn't still be working there.'

'It might be worth the risk,' Wanda said. 'She thought enough of Dave to try to contact him when he didn't show for work, then report him missing.'

'You're right,' Quentin said. 'I'll catch her when she leaves and see if I can learn anything.'

'I'll come with you.' Wanda looked from Quentin to Colin. 'No arguments. You don't know if she'll leave by the front way or the back. She might drive to work. Did you see another car apart from the Maserati?'

Quentin frowned. 'There was one,' he said, trying to remember. 'I think that was all. To be honest, after I heard Cultured Voice I couldn't focus on anything else. I just needed to get away from there.'

'Well,' Wanda resumed, 'you watch the car park and I'll watch the front. She might respond more to another woman.'

A sigh came from Colin. 'I suppose I'm on dog-sitting duties again.'

* * *

Quentin shed his disguise, and he and Wanda left her Toyota and walked to their agreed lookouts.

As he waited at the rear of Property Perfections, Quentin wondered if they were doing the right thing. He knew they were taking a risk – Tina Patterson might not talk to them, and even if she did… A variety of scenarios opened up in his mind. He pushed them away, refusing to talk himself out of their plan. He'd been right, there were only two cars in the car park, the Maserati and a Jaguar. Would Tina really be driving a Jag? He thought it more likely that the Jag belong to the other estate agent he'd seen that morning, so it seemed safe to assume that she wouldn't be leaving this way. Perhaps he should abandon his post and join Wanda at the front.

He stopped speculating when his mobile rang.

'She's just come out,' Wanda told him. 'Looks like she's heading for the bus stop. I'm going after her.'

'OK.' Quentin was already sprinting round the corner and soon caught her up. 'Come on,' he urged as they left the parade of shops behind and a row of bus stops came into view.

'Let me do the talking at first,' Wanda puffed as they neared Tina Patterson.

'Excuse me,' she called when they were almost level with her. When there was no reaction, she called, 'Tina!'

Tina stopped walking and turned.

'Hello, Tina,' Wanda said, smiling. 'Sorry to hold you up but we were wondering if we could have a word with you.'

Tina looked from her to Quentin with suspicion. 'What about?'

For a moment Wanda hesitated. Then, as if making up her mind, she stepped closer to Tina.

'About your colleague, Dave Brown.'

Tina looked taken aback. 'Dave?' she said. 'Why?'

'Is there somewhere we could talk?' Wanda asked. 'Could we buy you a coffee or something?'

'Why? What's Dave got to do with you?'

'I'm his sister.'

Tina's face softened. 'You're Anne?'

Wanda nodded. 'The police told me you're the one who reported him missing, and I just wanted to know if you could tell me… well I don't know really. It's just I hadn't seen him for a while and I'd like to talk to someone who'd been with him recently.'

Quentin looked at Wanda in admiration. How had she come up with that on the spur of the moment?

Tina cast an uncertain glance at Quentin.

'This is my friend,' Wanda said smoothly. 'He's been looking after me while I've been in London. So, can you spare us a few minutes?'

'Of course. There's a pub a bit further up. We could go there.'

Ten minutes later, the three of them were seated in a faux Tudor public house, drinks duly purchased and on the table in front of them. Tina sat with one hand in her lap while the other played with the edges of a beer mat. She showed no sign of recognizing Wanda as Eleanor King, or Quentin as the hippy student who'd come to Property Perfections that morning, although she glanced at Quentin frequently.

'I don't know what I can tell you,' she said, 'except I liked Dave. He was kind.'

'Did you see him outside of work?' Wanda asked.

A flush stained Tina's face. 'Only lunchtimes. We didn't have a date or anything.'

From the way she said this, Quentin thought Tina would have liked a date with Dave.

'Did he seem all right to you? Wanda asked. 'He wasn't worried about anything?'

'Em… Not really. Why?'

Remembering what Anne Roberts, Dave's actual sister, had told him, Quentin intervened.

'Didn't he tell you there was something at work that he had to sort out, Anne?' he said, looking at Wanda. 'You know, the last time he rang you?'

He felt Tina's gaze on him as he spoke.

'Yes,' Wanda answered, 'that's right. He didn't sound right so I asked him what was wrong. He said he'd be OK when he'd sorted something out at work. Did he say anything to you?'

Tina shook her head. 'No. He didn't.'

'Well, did he say anything to make you think he was worried about something?'

'I've been through this with the police. Poor Dave. He can't even rest in peace.' Tears trembled on Tina's eyelashes.

'Tina,' Wanda said, catching hold of her hand. 'That's exactly how I feel. Dave was killed and I want to know why. Don't you?'

'Of course I do, but why are you asking me? I don't know why he was killed.'

'When Dave didn't turn up, you tried to contact him, and when you couldn't, you reported him missing. Did you tell the people you work with that you were going to do that?'

Tina hesitated. 'I told Phil we ought to do something, but he said I was worrying over nothing. He said Dave probably had to go off on a family matter, or some simple explanation, and to leave it, but I wasn't happy. It wasn't like Dave not to come to work. Even when his dog was sick, he rang in to say he'd be late, and when he went to the dentist, he asked for the time off. I looked up his address on our records and went to see him, but he wasn't there and the neighbour hadn't seen him or the dog for days. So I reported him missing.'

'What did they say at work when they found out you'd reported him missing?' Quentin asked, leaning forward.

'Philip thought I was jumping the gun.'

Tina looked at Quentin, frowning. Then her face cleared. 'You're the guy who was asking questions this morning,' she said accusingly.

Knowing it was useless to deny it, Quentin nodded. He'd thought it possible that Chandler had agreed to Tina going to the police. After all, he would have realized that Dave's body would be identified and his workplace discovered sooner or later, despite the removal of Dave's ID. Chandler might have thought it would look less suspicious if he'd appeared willing to find out why Dave had disappeared. From what Tina was saying, though, it seemed he wanted the dead man's identification to be delayed for as long as possible.

'Yes,' he admitted, sure now that Tina genuinely didn't know why Dave had been killed or that Chandler was involved. He glanced at Wanda and she nodded.

'The truth is—' Quentin paused, wondering how much he should reveal. 'The truth is, Anne's asked me to help find her brother's killer.' That was the truth, at least. 'She... we think, and the police think, that Dave was killed because of something he knew, something he'd found out about Property Perfections.'

Tina's pale face grew paler. Her eyes were wide behind her red-framed glasses. 'Wh-What?' she stammered. 'What did he find out?'

'We don't know,' Wanda said gently. 'That's what we're trying to get to the bottom of.'

'What do you think of Philip Chandler?' Quentin asked.

'Phil? He knows his job. He can be a bit short sometimes, but he's very good with clients.'

A charmer, when he needs to be, Quentin thought, recalling what Wanda had told him on her return from Devon.

'Why?' Tina was sounding agitated now. 'You don't think he had anything to do with Dave's death, do you?'

'We don't know,' Quentin said. 'But if he did, we don't want him to get away with it.'

Ignoring Tina's gasp, Wanda resumed the questioning.

'Who took over the IT when Dave didn't come in? What I mean is, have there been any computer problems since the last time Dave was there?'

Tina thought for a moment. 'The day after he didn't show, Phil said there was a problem with the system. He said it couldn't wait till Dave came back and he was getting someone in to fix it. The next morning, he rang and said not to bother coming in until after lunch because the computers would be offline till then. I don't know why – there was stuff I could do without the computer.'

'So you didn't see who came in to fix the system?'

'No. Look, Anne, I understand you want to know what happened to your brother, but surely the police will be looking into it all? They've been into the office twice, and Phil's answered loads of questions. The police checked the computer and the accounts but they said it was routine, and everything was in order.'

'Well, it would be,' Quentin said grimly. 'Dave had been dead days before they found out where he worked. Plenty of time to wipe computer records and put their house in order.'

'You really think...' Tina's voice quavered. 'You think Phil knew Dave was dead all that time? All the time I was wondering where he was?'

'We don't know for sure, but it's possible. The police seem to think there's more to Property Perfections than selling houses. What about the other guy who was there this morning?'

'Adam? He's only part time, works Fridays and Saturdays unless Phil's showing clients around a property, which isn't all that often. Phil usually vets places to see if he wants to take them on, but he doesn't always attend viewings. He's got an arrangement with various agents round the country to show people round if he can't go himself. We only take on upmarket properties.'

Quentin grimaced. 'Adam is on call all the time? What if he's not available?'

'I field enquiries and arrange for Phil to call them back. Phil's even shut the office before.'

'What's Adam's surname?'

'Holden. He's all right. Just had twin boys.'

Quentin exchanged glances with Wanda and guessed she was thinking the same as him. Could a family man who'd just had twins be involved in any illegal dealings at Property Perfections?

'How does he get on with Philip Chandler?' Quentin went on. 'Do they have private conversations?'

'Not especially. Adam's on the phone to his wife a lot, and he always wants to get home on time. He brought the babies in. They're lovely.'

'Right,' said Quentin, deciding it was unlikely that Adam knew anything untoward.

There was a lull. Tina sipped her drink, then resumed fiddling with the beer mat. 'Is that all you want to know?' she asked, breaking the silence.

'What about Chandler?' Wanda asked. 'Has he got a family?'

'He's divorced, got a son at university. He doesn't talk about himself much. Do you really think he knows something about Dave's death? I can't believe it. I'll leave. I'm not going back. I can't work for someone who can lie like that, pretending to know nothing when he might have known about it all along.'

'We don't know if Chandler was personally involved with his death,' Quentin said. 'But he knows something. We just want justice for Dave.'

'So do I.' Tina sat staring straight ahead, as though letting what had been said sink in. After another silent moment, she shook her head, a strand of red hair falling over her forehead. Then she seemed to come to a decision.

'Dave didn't tell me anything, but thinking about it, after he went missing Phil asked a few times if he talked about work when we went to lunch together. Maybe Phil was trying to make sure I didn't know something. Anyhow… I don't think there's anything I can tell you that might help find who killed Dave. But that doesn't mean there won't be.'

She look directly at Quentin. 'I won't leave,' she said emphatically. 'I'll stay. If you're right and Phil is involved, I might find out something.'

Quentin and Wanda exchanged glances again.

As if noticing this, Tina said, 'Look, if there's anything I can do, I want to do it. Dave's dead and he was the only one in that place I really liked. It's boring without him to talk to.'

'Tina.' Wanda leaned forward. 'Listen, it might be helpful if you stayed, see if you notice anything suspicious or unusual, anything different from the norm in Chandler's behaviour or in his telephone calls, but it could be dangerous.'

'How will it? All I have to do is watch and listen.'

'Yes, but…' At Quentin's nod, Wanda continued. 'There's something else. Before Dave was killed, he contacted a journalist. He was going to blow the whistle on Property Perfections.'

Tina looked surprised. 'He didn't say anything to me about that. He seemed like he was going to say something a few times, though, then changed his mind. I thought he was trying to get the courage to ask me out,' she said, blushing.

'Maybe he was,' Quentin said. 'And maybe he thought telling you what he'd found out would be dangerous for you. The thing is, it *is* dangerous. Dave's dead and the journalist… well, she's been kidnapped.'

Tina gasped. 'Kidnapped!'

'Yes,' Quentin continued. 'And we think she could be held in one of the company's empty houses. So while we'd love your help to find her, and to find Dave's killer, it could be dangerous.'

'You mean I could end up like Dave or this journalist.' Tina let go of the beer mat and sat back in her chair.

'I'm sure you won't–' Wanda began, then changed tack. 'I mean, you mustn't do anything to put yourself in danger.'

'I'll do it.' Tina's voice was firm, and her face set in a determined mask. She finished her orange juice. 'Well,' she said grimly, 'I think I need something stronger than this.'

Over a gin and tonic, they exchanged mobile numbers.

'Let us know if you see or hear anything,' Quentin said as they finished their drinks. 'We've always got our phones but if for any reason you can't contact us, ring the police, especially if you get an inkling as to where Lorna – that's the journalist – is.'

'OK.'

'Are you sure about this?' Wanda sounded anxious.

'Yes.' Scraping back her chair and standing up, Tina carried on. 'I can't stand by and do nothing. Dave didn't deserve to die.'

'No,' Quentin said, an image of Dave slumped between the bins flashing into his mind. 'No. Of course he didn't.'

Chapter Twenty-one

'I hope we've done the right thing,' Quentin said when they were back at the car. 'I didn't intend for her to spy on Chandler.'

'She seemed pretty determined once she'd decided to stay,' Wanda pointed out. 'I'm sure she'll have sense enough to get out if she feels the need. She volunteered. We didn't ask her.'

'I know, but we didn't even tell her you're not Dave's sister. Lucky she didn't recognize you as Eleanor King.'

'I didn't want to admit to tricking her into talking to us,' Wanda said. 'She had enough to take in as it was. Anyway what matters most is that Lorna's been missing over twenty-four hours now.'

'Yes,' Quentin said dejectedly, 'and we still have no idea where she is.'

* * *

It was after they were back at Colin's and filling him in that Quentin had a call from Philmore.

'I thought you'd like to know we've tracked down Nick Crawford,' he said, sounding a little happier than he had previously. 'We're bringing him in for growing illicit plants so we'll see what he can tell us, if anything.'

'That's good. How did you find him?' The question Quentin really wanted to ask remained unspoken.

'We searched his house,' Philmore told him. 'We didn't find anything useful but there was an address book. Guess the bloke forgot about it when he cleared off. There wasn't much in it, but there was an address in Brentwood under Mum, so we sent someone there. The mother said she hadn't seen him but the green Corsa was parked outside. He tried to get out the back but he wasn't quick enough. We'll speak to the mother in due course, but we'll wait till he's here and we've interviewed him; done all the usual checks.'

'OK, Steve, what about… the phone?'

'Yes, we've got it. Looks like he didn't have time to pass it on. Let's hope he didn't give my number to anyone.'

Relief swept over Quentin. Somehow he felt he'd let Philmore down by the phone being taken.

'I'll hang on to it,' Philmore said. 'I don't think it's safe to use it at the moment.'

'I'll get a new one,' Quentin offered. 'I won't put your number in as a contact – I'll learn it by heart.'

'Good idea,' Philmore said curtly. 'Let me know when you've got it.'

'They've got Boatman,' Quentin told Wanda and Colin when he'd rung off. 'And he still had my emergency phone, so that's a weight off my mind.'

'What happened wasn't your fault,' Wanda assured him. 'It's not as if you lost it or anything, it was forcibly taken from you. It was Philmore's idea to get it in the first place, and you've always been really careful with it, so don't blame yourself.'

'Thanks, Wanda,' Quentin said, appreciating that she was trying to lift his spirits.

'Anyhow, they've got Boatman, so that's something,' Wanda said. 'But I bet he doesn't know where Lorna is.'

'Probably not,' Quentin agreed. 'But he told whoever hired him where to find her.'

'He sounds a bit of an idiot,' Colin said. 'He doesn't sound the type that your friend with the cultured voice would trust with important information, but if he's left it to Chandler to sort things out, then he probably doesn't know anything about Boatman.'

'Maybe,' Quentin said doubtfully, 'but Cultured Voice normally has his finger on the pulse.'

'This is different though, Quentin,' Wanda put in. 'He's surely not in the property business himself – he's just using it to hide his dirty money.'

Quentin nodded, but he was agitated. Although the arrest of Boatman was a positive, he still felt they weren't doing enough to find Lorna. Now that he knew Cultured Voice was involved, he felt even more anxious, and not just for Lorna. If his nemesis found out he was sniffing around Property Perfections…

He glanced towards Wanda. She was worried too, he knew, but she was doing a good job of covering it up.

'Cheer up, you two,' Colin said, meaningfully. 'I might have something for you to do tomorrow.'

'Really? What's that then?' Quentin asked, hoping Colin wasn't going to suggest something mundane.

'Well, it might not lead to anything, but I had to alleviate the boredom somehow. There's only so much dog-sitting you can do while your friends are out doing the important stuff.'

'Just tell us, Colin,' Wanda said.

'All right,' Colin said, as if realizing he'd laid it on thick enough. 'You know that Spanish-looking property they sent you, Wanda, the vacant one? Well, I phoned Property Perfections just before they closed, you know, as Eleanor King's financial advisor, and asked if they could give me the exact location.'

Colin paused.

'And did they?' Quentin said impatiently.

'No. Because it's been withdrawn.'

'Withdrawn!' Wanda and Quentin repeated in unison.

'Did they give you any idea where it was?' Quentin asked.

'Only that it's in Farnham. I asked why it was withdrawn, but the person I spoke to didn't know. That's as good as it gets, I'm afraid.'

'Well done for trying, Colin,' Wanda said warmly. 'It's a shame we don't know any more details.'

'*We* don't,' Quentin said, 'but I know someone who might.' He reached into his pocket and pulled out his notebook. 'You never know, Tina might remember.'

He punched in the number Tina had given them and waited. It seemed a long time before he heard a breathless 'Hello?'

'Tina, it's Quentin. Sorry to have to call so soon.'

'It's OK.'

'Tina, is there a property advertised in Property Perfections that's been withdrawn recently?' He didn't want to admit to already knowing this. Best not to complicate things by involving Colin, alias Eleanor King's financial advisor.

'Yes,' Tina replied. 'It hadn't been sold and I wasn't given a reason. Phil only told me it had been withdrawn.'

'Can you remember the address?'

'Why? You think the journalist's being held there?'

'It's worth a try,' Quentin said. 'Can you remember where it was?'

'It's near Farnham, quite isolated from what I could gather. It's a Guildford postcode…em, GU10, I think, can't remember the rest. I think… Yes, it's called The Hacienda.'

'All right, Tina, thanks. We'll do what we can with that.'

'The Hacienda, somewhere near Farnham, GU10,' he repeated when he'd rung off.

'That's a big area to cover,' Colin observed. 'You could drive around for days looking for it.'

'Not necessarily,' Wanda told him, firing up her laptop. 'As long as there's not lots of places with the same name in the same area, the Royal Mail postcode site is very comprehensive.'

After a few minutes, a triumphant smile showed on her face. 'Bingo! The Hacienda, Woodcote Lane, Farnham.'

She copied down the address and postcode, then looked questioningly at Quentin.

'You're not thinking of going now?' Colin asked. 'It'll be dark by the time you get there.'

'All the better,' Quentin said.

'And if Lorna's there, we shouldn't leave her there a moment longer than necessary,' Wanda added.

'Call Philmore,' Colin said in a tone that threatened he would if Quentin and Wanda refused to.

'We will, as soon as we know if Lorna's there or not,' Quentin said. 'It pointless sending the police to an empty house on a Saturday night.'

Colin's normally amenable features hardened. 'What if she is there? It could get messy if someone's guarding her.'

'Maybe. That's something else we need to find out,' Quentin said. 'We can't ignore the possibility of her being there and do nothing.'

'Come with us, Colin,' Wanda suggested. 'It would be useful if you stood by in a separate car ready to call the police if need be.'

'Yes,' Quentin urged. 'You're always saying we don't include you.'

'I'll go on one condition,' Colin said. 'I do the poking around with you and Wanda stays in the car.'

He looked at Wanda. Quentin looked at her too, knowing she hated to be left out.

'All right,' she said. 'It's a deal.'

Chapter Twenty-two

As Tina had said, the property called The Hacienda was isolated. Quentin and Wanda navigated the winding lane in Wanda's Toyota, with Colin following in his Honda Civic, passing woods on one side and a smattering of well spaced-out houses on the other. The houses gave way to an elongated patch of scrubland opposite a fenced-off area set into the woods. A sign attached to the fence showed that the site was used for clay pigeon shooting.

The lane wound to the right of the clay pigeon area, out of sight of the houses. It petered out at a large property practically hidden by fir trees. As Colin had predicted, it was almost dark now, and the streetlamps had stopped at the last of the houses. The property showing in their headlights through a gap in the conifers sported its own miniature lamp post, its yellow glow illuminating high wrought-iron gates with a nameplate declaring the premises to be The Hacienda.

'Ring Colin, tell him to kill his lights and back up,' Quentin ordered sharply.

Seconds later, they had reversed round the bend and were parked out of sight of The Hacienda. Getting out of his car, Colin came up to the Toyota.

'We'll walk from here,' Quentin said, winding his window down. 'It's a dead end and anyone inside will hear our engines and see our lights. If we need you to ring Philmore, Wanda, one of us will call or text. If you have to make yourself scarce for any reason, just go. We'll still have Colin's car. Better for you to go and get help than risk danger here. Come to think of it, we should turn round and face the other way in case we have to beat a hasty retreat.'

'We're probably wasting our time,' Colin answered. 'I didn't see any lights on in the front of the house. Still, those trees are pretty thick.'

'Better safe than sorry,' Wanda said. 'Come on then, let's turn round.'

When both cars were facing the other way, Colin joined Quentin by the Toyota. At Quentin's suggestion, they'd both dressed in soft shoes and dark clothes. Quentin could just make out Colin's form in the moonlight.

'I feel like a burglar,' Colin said as he pocketed the torch he'd brought.

'You look like one,' Quentin told him. 'Put your phone on silent.'

'Nobody rings me except you two and Emma,' Colin said, but silenced the phone anyway.

Quentin did the same with his phone and slid it into his pocket next to his Swiss army knife.

'Go careful, you two,' Wanda said as they moved away.

'I don't think we should approach from the front,' Quentin said when they neared the house. 'The gate might be bolted from the inside or it might clang or something. Might even be electric. Let's go round the side, see if we can get over the wall.'

'That's all right for you,' Colin grumbled. 'I haven't climbed a wall since I got caught scrumping apples.'

'You were caught? That doesn't bode well. Do you want to change places with Wanda?'

'Certainly not. I'm quite capable, I just don't make a habit of it, that's all.'

They swerved left onto the scrubland, picking their way over the bumpy ground, their torches angled down.

'Let's keep going,' Quentin said when they neared the side wall of The Hacienda. 'Maybe there's a back entrance.'

They carried on, the moonlight above and the torch beam below easing their way. There was a slim side gate set into the wall, also wrought iron, and a garage at the rear of the premises with up-and-over doors that looked as though they were operated electrically. On the far side of the garage was a track for access.

'We could risk opening the gates,' Colin said, 'but they could be alarmed. It's the type of place that might be.'

'You're right,' Quentin said. 'Looks like it's a wall climb then.'

They were whispering now, although anyone listening would have to be in the garden to hear them.

'Wait,' Colin said. 'The garage would be the easiest bet.'

Quentin looked to where Colin was pointing. The wide garage had been extended outwards, the access doors jutting out from the perimeter wall while its rear was firmly inside the grounds. At the side, on the front end, a foot or so from the perimeter garden wall, was a small window.

'If we can get onto that window ledge and onto the roof, we could jump down into the garden,' Colin suggested.

'Spoken like a true burglar,' Quentin jibed. 'Good idea, Colin.'

They walked the few feet back to the garage and shone a torch through the window. It looked empty.

'Right,' Quentin said. 'How about you give me a leg up and wait here for me? I mean, it won't take long to go round the building to see if there are any lights on or anything to indicate that someone's there. Keep your phone on silent but keep checking it – if I need you, I'll text, and if anyone apart from Lorna is in there, they're less likely to spot one of us rather than two.'

Colin seemed uncertain, so Quentin added, 'I'll probably find nothing and be back in ten minutes. If you haven't heard from me and I'm not back in half an hour–'

'I'll call the police,' Colin finished. 'OK then, get going.'

Colin cupped his hands together under Quentin's raised foot. Seconds later, he staggered back, almost toppling under Quentin's weight. Quentin lurched forward, jarring his wrist as his hands hit the garage wall.

'Bloody hell! I'm not that heavy,' he complained, though he was four inches taller than Colin.

'Sorry!' Colin said. 'We haven't all got your athletic build.'

Athletic build or not, Quentin couldn't get onto the window ledge without help. Colin insisted on trying again and, after a few precariously balanced moments, Quentin gripped each end of the ledge and managed to get both knees onto it. Then, wobbling unsteadily, he placed his right hand on the perimeter wall and grasped the drainpipe running from the garage guttering with the left. Manoeuvring himself into a standing position, he placed his right foot on the perimeter wall and heaved himself up onto the flat roof, the drainpipe creaking under the pressure.

'OK,' he called softly, then edged forward. In the moonlight, he could see the extensive grounds, with shrubs and bushes lining the wall. He looked for a grassy area to drop onto, but there wasn't one immediately below, neither was there a convenient drainpipe to shin down. The lawn was on the other side of the gravel path, but he knew he couldn't jump that far. It was the path or the bushes. Gritting his teeth, he leapt, hands outstretched in an effort to break his fall. 'Ouch!' he muttered as sharp gravel pierced his palms and penetrated his jeans at the knees.

Getting to his feet, he rubbed his hands to dislodge the gravel and brushed at his knees. Then, afraid that the gravelly crunch might betray his approach, he moved onto the lawn and crept up to the back of the house. He could see why it was called The Hacienda. The building was painted white, with a flight of steps either side of double doors. The doors looked to be glass, but had some sort of blind or shutters making it impossible to see inside. Through a shuttered window, he could see a shaft of light from somewhere inside; perhaps the hall, Quentin thought. Even if the owners had left and the property was empty, there could still be lights timed to come on automatically to deter burglars.

Without using his torch, he continued cautiously on to the front, where another sweep of steps led to the main entrance. Wow, was Quentin's first thought as he took in the vista in the light from the miniature lamp post. He wondered how much it would set you back. From the double wrought-iron gates, a gravel drive skirted manicured lawns edged with shrubs, leading up to a widened space, presumably for visitors' cars.

Quentin's gaze travelled over the building. Was Lorna here? If only he knew. He thought of breaking in, but hesitated. It wouldn't be like breaking into Dave Brown's house. This place would almost certainly have alarms. Did it matter? If it was empty, no one would hear. The nearest houses were at least a quarter of a mile away. Unless the alarm went straight to the security company, as he knew some of them did. He spotted the outline of what looked like an alarm under the eaves. A long way to climb for any burglar to disable. He stood for an uncertain moment, wondering what to do.

Suddenly, light showed beyond the front wall and the purr of an engine disturbed the evening air. Quentin darted back round the corner of the building and waited. He peeked out just as the gates swung open and a car drove in, its tyres crunching on the gravel. It came to rest in the widened space near the entrance. Quentin shrank back until the headlights were switched off, then leaned forward again. The car's front doors opened and two men got out. Quentin couldn't see clearly, but when one of them spoke, he was sure it was Philip Chandler.

'Don't worry, no one can see or hear us here. That's why I chose it, and because it's not too far. Come on.'

Quentin watched Chandler climb the steps. The man who followed him was of similar height but looked chunkier.

'It's certainly private enough,' the chunkier man said.

'Yes, that's the point,' Chandler said, producing a set of keys and opening the door. 'Hold on a moment while I unset the alarm.'

The chunky man hovered on the threshold before stepping inside and closing the door.

'Bugger it,' Quentin muttered. He could learn nothing more now. Or could he? The alarm was off, so breaking in now should be a simple credit card job. Chandler and his companion would be in one of the rooms, and there were plenty to choose from. Quentin shook his head. Why did Chandler think a massive place like this would appeal to a widow living alone?

It didn't matter, he told himself. What did was getting inside and listening to what was being said.

Realizing that Colin would have seen Chandler's headlamps and not wanting him to panic, Quentin sent a short text.

Chandler and another gone into house. Didn't see me
– stay put.

Stealthily, he moved from his hiding place. He stopped at the car – a Lexus, he saw. Didn't Wanda say Chandler had driven a Lexus in Devon? Moving on to the steps, he climbed up. He listened at the door, but heard nothing. Satisfied that the men were out of the hallway, he slid his credit card between the door frame and the lock with a practised hand, pushing the door gently when he heard a faint click. Once inside, he pushed the door back into place, leaving it slightly ajar so he could leave quickly and quietly. The hall was dimly lit, and there was a room either side with doors open but dark inside. Further down, brighter light and voices spilled from another room.

The owners may have left, but there were still some pieces of furniture in evidence, perhaps no longer wanted or to be collected later. An ugly-looking cabinet stood against the wall just before the room where the light and voices emanated from. Quentin crouched beside it so he wouldn't be seen if Chandler or his companion came out. Which Chandler did at that very moment. Quentin held his breath. Surely they weren't leaving already.

'I'll get some glasses,' he heard Chandler say, and breathed again when he realized Chandler had turned the other way. Towards the kitchen, he guessed.

Seconds later, the chink of glasses heralded Chandler's return as he went back to the other man. A pop like a cork being removed, and the glug of liquid, told Quentin they weren't drinking tea.

'Single malt, ten years old.' Chandler sounded pleased with himself.

Quentin's mouth watered at the thought of his favourite tipple.

'Right, so let's get down to business.' The second voice was similar to Chandler's but deeper. 'I haven't come all the way from Spain to drink whisky, though I wish I had that luxury. I'll need to get back soon.'

'You can stay a few days, surely, Will.'

Cogs turned in Quentin's brain. Will. Spain. William? Barcelona? Was this William Chandler, Philip's brother, in charge of the Barcelona branch of Property Perfections?

He pulled out his phone and switched on the recording facility. He didn't know if it would pick anything up, but he had to try. If William had jetted in from Spain and was now here at this remote location, whatever he had to discuss with his brother must be important.

'You've got cover over there,' Philip was saying.

'Not for long,' the man called Will said. 'I don't like leaving anyone else in charge, and my return flight's already booked. Anyway, what's going on with this woman? Henry's not happy – some random staff member finding something out about our operation and then his body being left to be found. He'll blow if he finds out about this journalist.'

'We've got to deal with it. I didn't expect them to kill Dave. They were told to get what evidence he had and make him swear not to tell anyone, bribe him, blackmail him, anything to shut him up. It got out of hand. We're not murderers, Will.'

There was a pause. 'We weren't, Phil, but it looks like we are now. Why the devil didn't they get rid of him once they realized he was dead?'

'They didn't have time. They took everything on him so he couldn't be identified immediately in case he was found while they went to find a van, but they left it too long. Then that runner turned up. Who the hell runs at that time of day?'

'Bloody messy business. Well, as I see it, Phil, we've got two choices. Pull out and give up our income and lifestyle, or go along with Henry. I don't know about you, but I like my lifestyle. I don't feel inclined to give it up.'

'Nor do I, but I don't like the thought of prison either. Look, Will, we've had a good run. We could cut Henry loose and still make money from the business.'

A snort sounded through the air. 'You really think we'd survive without Henry's money? Dream on. Look, I've always watched out for you, and I will now, but you don't make the kind of money we do with a legit business. We need to keep Henry sweet.'

There was a spluttering sound, as though Philip Chandler was choking on his drink.

'Keep him sweet?' he said when he'd recovered. 'Then we've got to do something about this reporter, and the bloke who found Dave.'

Quentin swallowed, wondering what was coming.

'What's he got to do with it?' Will Chandler demanded.

'He's a private investigator and he was seen talking to the reporter. He may know what she knows.'

'How do you know they know anything?'

'I don't. The journalist admits that Dave arranged to meet her but says he didn't tell her anything, and she admits to talking to the PI but says he doesn't know anything either.'

'So what's the problem?'

'A journalist and a private dick sniffing around isn't good news, is it? They sussed Crawford, the bloke I asked to keep an eye on them, so now my bloke's out of action. Not that that's any loss – he's bloody useless. Just as well, really. He doesn't know anything beyond he was told to watch those two, and he hasn't got the brains to work anything out, so he can't give anything away.'

'He must have rung you with information. Won't they find your number on his phone?'

'You don't think I gave him my number?' Philip sounded indignant. 'I'm not that stupid. I got a burner. I've got rid of it now. Anyhow, now you've seen this place, are you happy with bringing the journalist here? There's a cellar. She'll be all right down there. We can hold her until either she tells us what she knows, if anything, or until we decide what to do with her. I can't keep her where she is.'

'What about the owners?'

'They're in South America for at least a month, then they're going straight to their new property.'

'OK. When do you want to move her?'

'Soon. Tomorrow night would be good.'

Quentin's legs were beginning to ache, but his heart soared. Lorna was alive and they were bringing her here tomorrow night.

Chapter Twenty-three

'Tonight?' Philmore sounded doubtful.

Having already endured a lecture about taking things into his own hands, Quentin sat in the DCI's office the next morning with Wanda. After a call from Quentin telling him they had important information on Lorna's kidnapping, Philmore had called Debbie Francis and here they were, at work on a Sunday morning.

'Yes,' Quentin answered. 'That's what they said.'

'And Henry Lawson, probably our old friend Whitelaw, doesn't know about Lorna or you, Quentin?'

'From what I heard, no. If he knew about me, he'd be on to me by now.'

Quentin shivered at the thought of those cultured tones taking him to task. He could almost hear that measured voice threatening to take his revenge.

'Anyway,' he continued, producing his phone, 'you can listen for yourself.'

He played the recording of the Chandler's conversation. The voices sounded indistinct but audible.

'The tech boys should be able to enhance it, so that's good,' Philmore murmured, as though reassuring himself. 'Whitelaw, I mean Henry Lawson, he's likely not in the country if the Chandlers think they can keep Lorna's kidnapping a secret. Your man, Nick Crawford, doesn't seem to know who's in charge. He's more worried about his ruined cannabis crop. We've traced a number with no caller ID shown on his recent calls but it got us nowhere. Still, getting to Lorna is our first priority. Her father's been ringing in every few hours.'

'Wouldn't you, if she was your daughter?' Wanda asked. 'Did he report her missing or did you tell him about the kidnap?'

'We had to wait twenty-four hours,' Philmore admitted. 'Her editor contacted us as well. We had to tell them both. It wasn't easy. Her editor agreed not to print anything until we've had a chance to locate her. And now we have.'

Quentin waited for an acknowledgement that the chance they had was thanks to him, but it didn't come. Quentin was disappointed. In the last case they'd tackled together, Steve Philmore had treated him almost as a colleague.

'So,' Quentin said, 'you'll have people in place to nab the Chandler brothers when they arrive at The Hacienda?'

'Yes. I'll get things moving as soon as you've gone.'

Quentin and Wanda exchanged glances.

'What about us?' Wanda said. 'We'd like to be there to see Lorna. After all, Steve, you wouldn't know where she was if it wasn't for us.'

Francis looked at Philmore as if waiting to see his response. Philmore caught her eye, then looked away.

'You wouldn't listen if I told you to keep out of it,' he said. 'Stay in the car and keep quiet. If you get in the way—'

'What, Steve?' Wanda asked, her voice sultry and her blue eyes wide. 'You'll have us arrested?'

Philmore had threatened this before; usually, as Quentin knew, for their own safety.

'We'll have someone there as soon as I can arrange it, in case it kicks off early,' Philmore said, not rising to the bait.

'OK, Steve,' Quentin said, deciding not to push the point any further.

He stood up and Wanda did the same. As a parting shot, Wanda smiled and looked directly at Philmore.

'Don't worry, Detective Chief Inspector,' she said tantalisingly. 'We won't cramp your style.'

Hurriedly, Quentin ushered her out.

* * *

'That was uncalled for,' Quentin said when they were driving away.

Wanda tossed her head. 'Well, honestly, you'd think he'd give us some credit. We're all on the same side.'

Quentin sighed. 'Yeah. I think he's under pressure.'

An uneasy silence fell between them. Quentin knew that, despite her parting words, Wanda had gained as much respect for Philmore as he had.

'You know what I think?' Wanda said suddenly. 'I think it's definitely him. Cultured Voice, Henry Lawson – or Whitelaw, as Philmore knows him. Philmore always tries to steer us away from getting involved with police business, but he's worse now he knows Cultured Voice has reared his ugly head again.'

'Why? It means he got another chance to nail him.'

'Yes, but how many chances does he need? Another failed attempt won't look good on his record, especially if one of us gets hurt in the process.'

'I suppose not, but then he's not the only one who's failed to catch him. We have, and the Dutch police managed to let him escape. We've been within inches of him, but when he doesn't want to be seen, he might as well be invisible.'

Wanda nodded. 'True. I suppose I shouldn't be too hard on Philmore. I mean, how did you feel when you found out Cultured Voice was behind this Property Perfections business?'

'Bloody terrified,' Quentin admitted.

'And with good cause,' Wanda answered. 'Philmore probably feels the same. Anyway, now that Boatman's out of the running, do you think someone else will be watching us?'

'Philip Chandler didn't say anything about anyone taking Boatman's place. I should have stayed a bit longer, but I was so pleased that Lorna was alive and that there was a chance to rescue her that I left as soon as I heard that.'

'I probably would have as well,' Wanda said. 'Let's get back to Colin's. We'll have to take him with us tonight or we'll never hear the end of it.'

* * *

'Why are we waiting till tonight?' Colin demanded. 'If Philmore's sending someone straight away, shouldn't we be there too? If the Chandlers change their minds about the time and Lorna's moved this afternoon, we'll miss the whole shebang. The Hacienda isn't overlooked, so who would see them taking her in there?'

'It may be a case of where they're taking her from,' Quentin suggested. 'They didn't mention where that is.'

'Whatever,' Colin said, sounding impatient. 'They took her where she is now in daylight, so why can't they take her out in daylight?'

'That's right,' Wanda put in. 'It's not the first time someone's been kidnapped in broad daylight. OK, why don't we go down to Farnham now so we're in place whenever they get there?'

'We could be gone ages,' Colin pointed out. 'We can't leave the dogs that long, and I'm not staying here with them.'

'We'll take them with us,' Wanda said. 'There's bound to be a Travelodge somewhere. They take dogs and we can get in after four. Then we could come and go as we like and stay the night.'

'Good idea,' Quentin said. 'We'll take our things. After all, when the Chandlers are nicked, we can go back to Greenwich and sleep in our own beds tomorrow.'

Chapter Twenty-four

It was nearly one o'clock in the morning before Quentin's mobile rang. Stretching his long limbs out as far as he could, he snatched the phone from the well by the gearstick.

'Steve?'

'Looks like a no-show, Quentin. I'm leaving two people on surveillance but I'm telling the others to stand down. Some of them have been here since midday.'

'What if they brought her earlier? She could already be in there. Can't you break in?'

'Not without a warrant. It's a private residence, the homeowners aren't suspects and all the signs point to the place being empty. There are no vehicles so if she's in there, she's on her own, but I think it's unlikely she was moved between when you saw the Chandlers last night and when we arrived at midday today. I'm guessing they intended to do it tonight as they said but something stopped them. I'll request an urgent warrant first thing in the morning.'

'Can't you apply for a warrant retrospectively?'

'Yes,' Philmore said patiently, 'but only to help someone in imminent danger of dying or being killed, or to stop a wanted criminal from escaping, and none of those things apply. Anyway, we're going, and so should you.'

'OK, we will,' Quentin said, knowing that Philmore was probably right and wondering what had stopped the Chandlers moving their captive.

'Maybe they weren't going to do it themselves,' Wanda said when Philmore had rung off. 'They're not really the strong-arm types. They could be using whoever kidnapped her to move her as well.'

Quentin grunted. He wished he'd stayed in the house until the Chandlers had left last night. They might have revised their plan to move Lorna or scrapped it altogether for all he knew. He thought longingly of the room in the hotel from where Wanda and Colin had already collected the keys, imagining its warmth and comfort.

'You go back to the hotel with Colin, Wanda,' he said. 'I'm going to stay here just in case.'

'But if they show, you'll be on your own,' Wanda warned.

'No I won't. The surveillance guys are here and Philmore and Debbie are staying locally like us. I'll call them if I need to.'

'All right,' Wanda said. 'The dogs are getting restless anyway, even though I've taken them out a few times.'

Minutes later, Philmore's Audi and a black van emerged from where they were hidden behind some tall shrubs on the far side of The Hacienda. Colin's white Honda was also hidden, while gorse bushes camouflaged Wanda's blue Toyota on the scrubland.

Soon Quentin was on his own. The surveillance vehicle was still secreted from view, and he guessed its occupants were as bored as he was. His eyes grew heavy as tiredness overcame him. Why was he staring into the darkness as if the Chandlers would suddenly materialise with Lorna? If anybody arrived, their headlights would show. Grabbing Mozart's travel rug from the back, he took a few mouthfuls of the water Wanda had left him, reclined the seat as far as he could, pulled the rug over him and closed his eyes.

* * *

It was five forty-five when he awoke, stiff with being cramped in the car. Groaning at the crick in his neck, he tried to ignore the message his bladder was sending him. After a few minutes of trying to get comfortable, he located his torch and made use of the bushes that were camouflaging the car. It was then that he saw the headlights of a vehicle approaching. He ducked down and listened for the sound of the engine as it drew nearer. It's quiet, he thought. If I'd been asleep it wouldn't have woken me.

As the car reached The Hacienda's gates, Quentin risked standing in a stooped position, watching as the gate swung noiselessly open and the car drove through. From its shape in the light of the miniature lamp post, it didn't look like the same car Quentin had seen previously. Not Philip Chandler then, or if it was, he was in a different car.

The gates didn't close. Fleetingly, Quentin wondered if the surveillance officers had seen the vehicle; then, making an instant decision, he collected his mobile and Swiss army knife from the Toyota, pushed the door to and picked his way carefully over the uneven ground, keeping the phone torch beam angled down. He would be too easily seen from the front, so when he was in the lee of the wall, he crept towards the wrought-iron gate at the side. From there, in the breaking dawn, he had a clear view of the car now parked in the widened space in front of the premises.

The driver's door stood open and the burly shape of a man stood beside it, smoking. Quentin could see the red glow of a cigarette as his hand went to his mouth. Another man was leaning into the rear door. When he straightened, he was holding on to something, and Quentin stifled a gasp as someone was dragged out. Lorna! Her hands tied in front of her, Lorna was placed in front of the man who'd pulled her out and pushed roughly towards the steps. The driver threw his cigarette to the ground and followed them up the steps to the door.

'Thugs,' Quentin muttered under his breath. 'And not the Chandler brothers.'

He fought back the urge to call out, to rattle the gate, anything to distract the men and to let Lorna know he was there. Instead, he went swiftly and silently to the front. By the time he got there, Lorna and her two captors were inside the house with the door shut. He slipped through the gates, keeping to the lawn as he approached. When he came to the Vauxhall they'd driven, he risked turning on the flash on his phone and photographing the number plate, guessing that the two men were occupied with getting Lorna into the cellar. Whoever they were, they'd either been given the code for the alarm or Philip Chandler hadn't set it when he'd left on Saturday night.

Quentin was wondering how long the two thugs would be inside when another set of headlights lightened the darkness. Quentin just had time to dash round the corner of the building before a second car swept through the gates. As it pulled up alongside the Vauxhall, the headlights were switched off. In the light from the front lamp post, Quentin could see it was a Lexus. Philip Chandler, Quentin thought. Time to call Philmore.

He pulled out his phone as the door of The Hacienda opened and the thug who'd manhandled Lorna appeared. Not wanting to miss anything and afraid his voice would be heard, he sent a text to Wanda, hoping she would hear the alert as the message was delivered.

> *Lorna at Hacienda, two heavies plus Chandler. Call*
> *Philmore.*

The Vauxhall's driver now appeared in the doorway of the house, puffing at another cigarette.

'All done?' the new arrival called. The depth of his tone told Quentin that although the Lexus may belong to Philip Chandler, the voice didn't, neither did the chunky build. This was Will Chandler.

The man who had pushed Lorna was descending the steps.

'Come on, Joe,' he urged the driver, who remained in the doorway.

'I ain't going nowhere till I've got me money,' the man called Joe said.

Will looked up at him. 'I've got your money.'

'That's what the other bloke said,' Joe growled. 'We ain't seen it yet.'

Will reached into the Lexus and took out a bag. 'Here's your money.'

Throwing down his cigarette, Joe stepped heavily out of the house, pulling the door shut behind him. He lumbered down the steps and walked up to Will, staring at the bag. He waited until Will had pulled the bag open, then moved forward and shone a torch inside.

'Better be all there,' he snarled.

'Looks all right to me,' said the other thug, coming up beside his partner in crime and peering inside. 'Come on, Joe, let's get out of here.'

Joe snatched the bag and made to walk away.

'How did it go?' Will asked. 'Any trouble?'

'The bitch bit my hand,' answered the second thug.

'But everything's all right inside? You found the cellar?'

'Yeah. She's safe enough.'

'Good. Where are the keys?'

The thug handed over a set of keys while Joe got into the Vauxhall's driver's seat. Seconds later, they were speeding through the gates and away. Clutching the keys, Will Chandler stepped towards the house, hesitated, glanced at his watch, swung round and returned to the Lexus. Then he too was driving away.

Breathing a sigh of relief, Quentin emerged from the side of the house. 'Where the bloody hell are the surveillance boys?' he muttered. He could understand how they missed the first car arriving, but missing the second one as well?

He stood debating whether to wait for Philmore or seize the opportunity to go in and rescue Lorna now. She must be terrified. It had been bad enough when he'd been locked in Boatman's shed, but at least there had been light. He imagined Lorna in a cold, damp cellar, alone in the dark. With that thought, he made his decision.

He pulled out his mobile and rang Wanda. 'Did you get my message and have you rung Philmore?' he said as soon as she answered.

'Yes and yes,' she told him. 'Is Chandler still there?'

'No, everyone's gone, and it wasn't Philip, it was Will. I don't know what's happened to the surveillance boys but they're not here either. I'm going in–'

'OK, but maybe wait for Philmore or at least ring him first, save yourself another earbashing? He'll be there in ten minutes.'

Quentin stopped walking towards the steps. He heard Philmore's voice as he'd heard it yesterday. *If you get in the way...*

'OK,' he said, 'but if he's not here in ten minutes – bloody hell!'

Quentin began running.

'I'm going in now!' he gasped into his mobile. 'The place is on fire!'

Chapter Twenty-five

In a few strides Quentin had reached the steps and was racing up them.

Smoke was curling its way through the cracks around the front door. Quentin shoved the phone into his pocket, pulled out his wallet and yanked out his credit card. When the door swung open, smoke billowed out. Waving his hand in front of him, Quentin could see that the mat on the inside of the door was smouldering, causing a cloud of acrid smoke and threatening to erupt into flames any moment. Belatedly remembering that oxygen fuelled fire, he slammed the door and rushed along the corridor to the kitchen, his hand over his nose and mouth trying not to breathe in. Coughing, he grabbed a plastic washing-up bowl and filled it with water. Then he walked back as quickly as he could and emptied the whole lot onto the mat. Gingerly touching the edge of the mat and feeling that it was cool enough to handle, he opened the door and hurled it down the steps.

'Bloody thugs!' he muttered, between coughs, realizing that when the driver had thrown down his cigarette butt, it must have fallen inside rather than outside the door.

He made his way along the corridor, shining his torch into each room as he went; the two smallish rooms he'd seen before, both empty, then the room on the other side of the ugly cabinet where the Chandlers had sat drinking whisky. Opposite was a cloakroom, then the kitchen. Where was the entrance to the cellar?

Grey smoke hung in the air and Quentin coughed again. He darted into the kitchen and closed the door. This room was relatively smoke-free. Looking around, he saw a door on either side of the units. He opened the first to find a larder, shelves bare. The second was locked. He searched for keys, but then recalled that Will Chandler had them. He tried his credit card, but it didn't work. The mechanism looked old, different from any he'd seen before. Perhaps this was an original door, installed before the house was extended and modernised.

He banged on it and shouted. 'Lorna! Can you hear me?'

It was a few seconds before a muffled reply came. 'Yes!'

'Alleluia,' muttered Quentin. When her answer hadn't come immediately, he'd thought for a tortuous moment that the ruffian she'd bitten had rendered her unconscious – or worse. The image of Dave's body flashed before him, and he shook it away.

'Are you OK?' he called.

This time the reply came at once. 'Yes.'

'All right. I'm going to find something to open the door with. Hold on.'

Quentin gazed around the kitchen. There was nothing he could use to open the door.

'Looks like it's old faithful,' he murmured, taking out his Swiss army knife and chastising himself for not using it in the first place. He selected a tool, inserted it into the lock, patiently twisting it this way and that until at last the mechanism clicked. He pulled the door open and a dim shaft of light showed from the bottom of some concrete steps. He descended slowly, the dank odour of a little-used space assailing him. As he reached the bottom, Lorna came towards him, her relief evident.

'Quentin!' she said, her voice tremulous. 'Thank goodness. I thought– I thought they'd brought me here to kill me.'

She collapsed into his outstretched arms and sobbed. Quentin gave her a moment, looking over her shoulder at the mattress and blanket on the floor, the bucket, the bottles of water and packets of crisps. If they did intend to kill her, they weren't planning on doing it yet. At least they had untied her hands.

'Come on,' he urged. 'Let's get you out of here.'

'What's burning?' Lorna asked as they climbed the steps and emerged into the corridor. The smoke was beginning to dissipate, but there was still enough to make them both cough.

'I'll explain later,' Quentin said. 'Mind you don't slip – it's wet by the door.'

When they got outside, the first thing Quentin saw was Philmore's Audi. Philmore was talking to two men in crumpled clothes, one of whom Quentin recognized as a surveillance officer he'd caught a glimpse of yesterday. He and his colleague looked sheepish, and as Quentin appeared, Philmore looked up at him. His expression was thunderous, a scowl marring his pleasant features.

'I'm surrounded by idiots!' Quentin heard him growl. 'I'll deal with you two later.'

DS Francis got out of the Audi. She ran forward when she spotted Lorna. At the same time, a Honda Civic drove through the gates. It pulled up and Wanda and Colin tumbled out. Wanda hurried over to Lorna as Francis led her down the steps. In the growing daylight, Quentin could see that one side of Lorna's face was swollen and there was a bruise around her eye.

'Bloody thugs,' he muttered for the second time that morning.

He went ahead to join Philmore and Colin.

'Is Lorna all right?' Colin asked Quentin.

'She's shaken up, but I think she'll be OK,' Quentin answered.

'I thought Wanda said the place was on fire,' Philmore said.

Quentin nodded. 'It was, or it would have been if I hadn't got in there. I'll show you.'

As they approached the front door, Philmore wrinkled his nose.

'There were two of them,' Quentin told him. 'When they came out, one was smoking. He threw his cigarette down – it must have fallen inside because after they'd gone, I saw smoke coming through the door. I got to it just before the fire caught hold.'

Philmore stared down at the mat at the bottom of the steps, brown singe marks making a mottled pattern on the plain fibres, then at the water still evident inside the threshold. He called to Francis to cancel the fire engine they'd requested, then turned back to Quentin.

'All right,' he said, grim-faced. 'Show me where you found her.'

* * *

After Lorna had used Wanda's phone to call her father and her editor, Philmore agreed to her going back to the hotel for a shower and a meal before giving a statement.

'She can use our room,' Wanda said. 'I'll look after her.'

'You go on,' Quentin said. 'I'll come back with Colin.'

'Go with them, Debbie,' Philmore instructed. 'I can drive myself.'

When they'd left, Quentin took Philmore through everything that had happened since Lorna and the kidnappers had arrived.

'What happens now then, Steve?' he asked when he'd finished. 'I mean, presumably someone's going to be coming back here to check on Lorna and bring her some food, so...'

Quentin stopped at the impatient click of Philmore's tongue. 'Give me a chance, for goodness sake, Quentin. Obviously they'll be back at some point, so that's when we need to nab them. Did Chandler say anything about anyone coming back?'

'No. The kidnappers were paid off, so that might be it for them.'

'Right.' Philmore ran his hand over his chin. 'Well, based on what you've seen and heard, we could arrest the Chandlers straight away, but I wouldn't mind waiting until they get here. All the relevant parties think Lorna's still in the cellar. We could have someone on surveillance here. Not those two' – he jerked his head towards the surveillance officers – 'and someone on Property Perfections. Will Chandler might be staying with his brother so we'll cover Philip's home address too. They're bound to try to scarper as soon as they know Lorna's gone. If we can get all four of them, it'll be good, but the Chandlers are worth more than the muscle men.'

'Will said he wouldn't be staying in the country long,' Quentin told him.

Philmore nodded. 'I'll get an APB out on him, and arrange a watch on all ports and airports in case he tries to slip through the net. Ah, here's the back-up I asked for.'

Two cars, one plain grey and one with blue and yellow police markings, drew up, and Philmore went to talk to them.

'What do you reckon then, Quentin,' Colin asked. 'Another day of waiting around here or back to London?'

Quentin shrugged. 'We could take turns,' he suggested. 'They've only just brought her here so they're not likely to come back just yet. To be honest, I could do with something to eat and a shower.'

'OK,' Colin said good-humouredly. 'You go to the hotel for a bit. I'll stay, park out of sight where I did yesterday and call you if anything happens. Come back and relieve me as and when. I've got some water and biscuits to keep me going. Just a minute.'

Colin opened the Honda door and took a key from the central well. 'Take this. You can use my shower if Lorna's in yours, or she can use mine, whatever.'

'Cheers,' Quentin said, grateful for the offer. 'Hopefully Philmore will get someone to give me a lift.'

To his surprise, Philmore instructed the surveillance officers who were due to go off duty to take Quentin to the hotel.

'I'm waiting for forensics,' Philmore explained. 'I want that cellar gone over and the room where you saw the Chandlers dusted for prints and DNA. It needs to be done quickly in case anyone else turns up. We'll do a more thorough sweep of the whole place later if we need to. We need to catch the Chandlers inside if we can, but we don't want them wiping it clean.'

'I took a photo of the thug's car, but I think my battery's dead now,' Quentin said. 'I'll let you have it later.'

Philmore nodded. 'Good thinking.' Then, as if recognizing that he'd hadn't acknowledged Quentin's role in saving Lorna, he added, 'Lucky you were here or the whole house could have gone up. Right place, right time. That's the key to everything, eh Quentin?'

Quentin's ego swelled. It was strange, he thought, that over the last few years his relationship with Philmore had alternated between camaraderie and resentment.

'It is, Steve. And...' Moving out of earshot of the two surveillance officers, he went on, 'I know your boys messed up, but to be honest, I might have missed the first car if I hadn't been out of my car at the time.'

'That's big-hearted of you, Quentin, but you wouldn't say that if Lorna had suffocated or burnt to death in there. I think they'll be back on the beat or traffic for a while. Either way, they can start by giving you a lift.'

It was a silent journey back to the hotel.

'Thanks guys,' Quentin said when they got there. 'Don't feel too bad. I nodded off myself, just woke up before you, that's all.'

The grunts he got in reply told him that these particular members of the police force hoped they would never set eyes on him again.

Chapter Twenty-six

It was lunchtime before Lorna insisted she was well enough to go back to London. After a shower, two hours' rest and a meal, she'd given Debbie Francis a full statement.

'I want you to catch those two brutes,' she said. 'I bet they're the ones who killed Dave.'

Francis looked up at that. 'Did they say anything to make you think that?'

'Not exactly. They didn't talk much, but the smaller one said… what was it? Yes, he said, "It's a pity that bloke wasn't down here where he wouldn't have been found." Then the one who was always smoking told him to keep his mouth shut.'

'"That bloke"? You think he meant Dave Brown?'

'That's what I assumed. I hope you catch them, but they're only the brawn. It's the brains I'd like to see behind bars.'

Me and you both, Quentin thought. But if his old enemy, Cultured Voice, was behind Property Perfections' clandestine business, then he didn't hold out much hope.

After Lorna and Francis had left and they were alone, Quentin took his much-needed shower.

'Hail the conquering hero!' Wanda greeted when he emerged wrapped in a towel.

Quentin gave her a weak grin and sat on the bed. 'Oh yeah, a right James Bond, that's me!'

'Really? I was thinking more Austin Powers.'

'Thanks. I love you too.'

'I know. And I love you.'

Wanda stood in front of him, her face bare of make-up and her fair hair still tousled from her dash straight from bed to The Hacienda. Her eyes locked on his.

'Do you?' Quentin's heart pounded. He wound his arms round her waist and drew her to him. 'Do you, seriously? Enough to marry me?'

He held his breath, waiting for the usual rebuttal. It didn't come. Instead, Wanda held his face between her hands, kissed him, and pushed him down onto the pillow.

* * *

Quentin's blissful sleep was interrupted by the persistent ringing of his phone. He scrabbled groggily on the bedside table, but his phone wasn't there. The ringing stopped as Wanda, her hair swaddled in a towel, stepped out from the en suite and swept his mobile up from the dressing table.

Quentin sat up, thinking it could be Philmore, or Colin demanding to know why he hadn't been back to relieve him. He looked sleepily at Wanda as, moving towards him, she said, 'Hello?'

Wanda stopped in her tracks and she lowered the phone to look at the display.

'Who is it?' Quentin asked.

'I don't know,' she whispered, her face contorted into a frown. 'The number's withheld.'

Bloody hell, Quentin thought, taking the proffered mobile. Could it be?

'Hello,' he said tentatively.

'Well, Mr interfering Cadbury, you've really done it this time.'

Quentin flinched, not only at the cultured tones but at his old adversary's words. It seemed the threats that had been absent in recent months were about to resume.

'What have I done?' Quentin countered, every vestige of sleep falling away.

'Don't play the innocent with me, you jumped-up little nobody. You know exactly what I mean.'

'Look,' Quentin said, deciding it was useless delaying the inevitable and holding the phone so that Wanda could hear. 'It's not my fault your thugs left a body for anybody to find, and it's not my fault I'm the one who found it.'

'I totally agree, Mr Cadbury, but you could have left the matter there. But no, you couldn't, could you? You're a detective, or you think you are. How is your little agency doing?'

'Well enough to suss out some of the people in your precious Property Perfections,' Quentin snapped, irritated by the man's sarcasm.

'Watch your tone, Mr Cadbury, or you'll be sorry you ever crossed paths with me. I thought, after I was so lenient with you last time, you'd be a bit more considerate.'

'Why's that? Because you didn't kill me when you had the chance? You seem to forget we're on opposite sides.'

'Oh, I haven't forgotten, I assure you. My memory is just as long as it's always been.'

'Is that right? Thanks for the champagne, by the way. Still, I suppose you can afford it with your dirty money.'

'My money's not dirty, Mr Cadbury. It's perfectly clean.'

'After it's been laundered, you mean?'

Silence. Quentin could almost hear the caller's anger.

'Quite,' said Cultured Voice at length. 'Anything that stops the cash flow through one of my enterprises is very inconvenient. Still, in this case I'm partly to blame. I broke my own rule and relied too heavily on other people. I believe I warned you against that when we met, Mr Cadbury.'

The anger in the cultured voice had ebbed a little.

'You did.' Quentin recalled that meeting when Cultured Voice had stated categorically that the only way to success was to depend on no one but oneself.

'I thought I could trust my Property Perfections partners to run things properly, and they have – until now. That's the problem, you see, Mr Cadbury. Complacency. Never assume that because things are in order they'll stay that way. If I'd known the threat to my income would be handled so ineptly, I'd have dealt with it differently. And if I'd known you were involved, I'd have put a stop to it much more quickly.'

'What do you want?' Quentin asked, trying not to sound intimidated.

'What do you think I want?'

'You want me to leave you alone so you can carry on with your sordid dealings?'

'It's a bit late for that now, don't you think? And, sordid… that's a little unfair.'

'Unfair?' Quentin almost choked on the word. 'Killing someone in cold blood, kidnapping a defenceless woman – where's the fairness in that?'

'Come now, Mr Cadbury, as I understand it, Miss West is perfectly comfortable, and you've known me long enough to know I'd never soil my hands with such despicable crimes.'

'No, you make sure someone else takes the rap for you.'

'Of course I do. It's called looking after number one. After all, if you don't look after yourself, no one else will. Although you *have* got the delectable Mrs Merrydrew. I take it she's with you? Or has she seen the light and traded you in for someone more suited to her intellect and maturity?'

Quentin's face burned and his mind seethed. How dare this– this criminal make assumptions about him and Wanda? How dare he?

'I see that's offended you, Mr Cadbury. Wading in where you're not welcome is offensive, isn't it? Your meddling has offended me greatly. I'll be in touch.'

Quentin sat staring at the phone long after the line went dead.

'Don't let him get to you,' Wanda said softly. 'You knew he'd contact you at some point. After all, we found out about his involvement in Property Perfections so why wouldn't he find out about you?'

'I know. It's just… he's so…' He knows how to make me feel inferior, Quentin wanted to say, but didn't. It wasn't the first time his nemesis had taunted him about Wanda, but each time it made him afraid that he would be proved right: that Wanda would leave him, if only for someone nearer her age.

'Snap out of it, Quentin,' Wanda urged. 'He only does it to wind you up.'

'Well, he's succeeded.' Quentin pictured the man as he'd seen him several months before. Neatly dressed, brown well-cut hair, regular features set in a stony expression, nothing that stood out except the eyes, steely grey and icy cold behind gold-rimmed glasses.

'Stop worrying about what he said and think about how we're going to catch him,' Wanda persisted.

'Right,' Quentin said despondently. 'Like we've caught him all the other times? Anyway, sounds like he knows about Lorna being kidnapped. He said he thought she was comfortable, so he obviously doesn't know she's free now.'

'Ring Philmore,' Wanda said. 'Tell him he's been in contact. Then we'd better decide what to do next.'

Chapter Twenty-seven

Thirty minutes later, they were parked by the houses in the lane leading to The Hacienda, Victor and Mozart sharing the back seat. Colin had left his car in its hidden spot and joined them in Wanda's Toyota.

'Crikey,' he said when he heard about the call. 'You've got to give it to the guy, he's got some balls. Shame someone doesn't castrate him.'

'Yeah,' agreed Quentin. 'Like that's ever going to happen. You'd have to get close enough first, and he doesn't get close to anyone.' Nevertheless, Quentin couldn't suppress the image of himself brandishing a very sharp knife at the relevant part of Cultured Voice's anatomy.

'You were close to him that time, Quentin,' Colin reminded him.

'Yep,' said Quentin. 'But he had his minders with him and he made damn sure I couldn't do anything to harm him.'

'At least Lorna's free now,' Wanda said. 'Thanks to Quentin.'

'Yes,' said Colin, sounding reluctant to give Quentin credit. 'If you hadn't been there, Quentin, and that fire had taken hold, Lorna might have died.'

'*And* he was the one who found out where she was,' Wanda said, and Quentin blessed her for it.

'Granted,' said Colin grudgingly, 'but don't forget I'm the one who pointed you to the right house. So what's the plan now?'

This met with a stony silence.

'We haven't got one,' Wanda admitted. 'All ideas gratefully received, Colin.'

Colin grinned. 'OK. I'll rack my highly intelligent brain and see what I can come up with. What did Philmore say when you rang him?'

'More or less the same as me,' Quentin said, recalling Philmore's frustrated reaction. 'He's planning on covering The Hacienda as well as Property Perfections and Philip Chandler's home address.'

'Well,' Wanda said, 'as I see it, we need to choose where we want to be – here at the house, at Property

Perfections or Philip Chandler's home address. Perhaps we should split up.'

'Do we know his home address?' Colin asked.

Quentin shook his head. 'No, but I know someone who will.' Taking out his mobile, he rang Tina Patterson.

'Hi, Tina, it's Quentin. Are you at work and can you talk?'

'I've got a client with me at the moment. I'll call you when I'm free.'

It was ten minutes before Tina rang back.

'Sorry,' she said. 'I'm on my own now.'

'Tina, is Philip in today and do you know his home address?'

'He's been in but he's gone again.'

'Do you know where he's gone?'

'No. He had a phone call and he didn't look happy. He went out the back to talk, then came in and said he might be out for the rest of the day and rushed off.'

'Right,' replied Quentin, wondering who the call had been from. Philip Chandler couldn't know that Lorna had been rescued – nobody could. The new surveillance officers and Colin had been watching all morning and no one had been to The Hacienda since the forensic team had left at nine-thirty.

'What about his home address?'

'Just a minute while I check our records.' There was a pause before Tina gave an address in Chelsea. 'Have you found out anything?' she asked.

Quentin hesitated, wondering how much to reveal. The less she knew, the less she could give away if Philip Chandler suspected her for any reason, and the longer he thought Lorna was still a prisoner, the more chance there was of him returning to Property Perfections.

'We're getting there,' he said. 'Ring if there's anything you think I should know. Don't put yourself in danger.'

'Philip's not there,' he told the others as he lowered the phone. 'Still, if Philmore's done his bit, someone will be following him. If he's gone home, someone will be there too, and if he comes here, we'll see him.'

'Why would he come here?' Wanda said, passing Colin the last of the quiche and coffee they'd bought for him. 'Surely he wouldn't drive all the way from London just to bring food for Lorna in the middle of the day?'

'I don't know,' Quentin said, 'but it's pointless going back to Property Perfections if he's not there. Then again, by the time we get back he could be too.'

'We're getting nowhere like this,' Wanda said. 'Why don't we—'

She stopped at the sound of an engine and, seconds later, a sleek red car swept by them, the driver's focus directly ahead.

'It's him,' Quentin gasped. 'That's his Maserati.'

'Is it?' Colin queried. 'A Maserati *and* a Lexus?'

'Why is he in such a hurry?' Wanda asked.

'Something's up,' Quentin said. 'Come on.' He started the engine and drove to the spot on the patch of scrubland where he'd been before.

'I'm going after him,' he said. 'Wanda—'

'I'm coming,' Colin interrupted. 'I'm the one who's been cooped up here all morning.'

'Go the round the back, then, in case he tries to leg it,' Quentin barked, deciding there wasn't time to argue.

'I'll ring Philmore,' Wanda called as he got out of the car.

Quentin didn't answer. He made his way to the outside wall of The Hacienda, then turned to see Colin disappearing around the far side of the property, where the track to the garage ran alongside the wire fence separating it from woods.

The front gates were open and Quentin slipped through them. Assuming Philip was already inside the house, he positioned himself around the corner as he had before and from where he could both see and hear any movement. He'd resisted the temptation to use his credit card trick, as much as he wanted to witness Philip's reaction when he realized Lorna was gone. He knew he could make a citizen's arrest, but he also knew Wanda would have called Philmore, and Philmore would organise something even if he couldn't get there himself.

Before he had time to make a decision, a sound carried through the air; a sharp report, like a gunshot. A gunshot? Surely not. The sound came again, and this time Quentin knew it was definitely a gunshot. Bloody hell, he thought, panicked. Philip's gone out the back way and he's shooting at Colin!

Breaking into a run, he followed the track that led to the garage at the rear of the house. As he neared the garage wall, a figure came charging round the corner. It was too late to avoid a collision and Quentin's head recoiled as a forehead hit his chin. A man's forehead, but not Colin's, he realized, his stomach churning – and not Philip Chandler's.

Sweat beaded his upper lip as fear gripped him. Whoever this person was, they had a gun. He braced himself, every nerve in his body tingling as he prepared to barge at the man and throw him off balance.

'You!' said a gravelly voice. 'What the devil are you doing here?'

The man stepped back and Quentin's fear fled as he recognized him from when he'd arrived earlier that day. He'd totally forgotten about the new surveillance officers.

'I heard shots,' he gabbled. 'My friend–'

Another shot rang out, and another. If someone was shooting at Colin, they were making a proper job of it. At that moment, Colin came round the corner, followed by the second surveillance officer. A volley of shots sounded, and Quentin gasped as between shots, a voice was carried on the wind, faint but clear. 'Pull!'

'Bloody hell!' he groaned. 'Clay pigeon shooting!'

* * *

The noise of a powerful car engine stopped the earbashing Quentin and Colin were getting from the officers. All four men rushed to the front in time to see the Maserati speeding away.

The first surveillance officer – George, his colleague had called him – swore loudly.

'We should have called that guy's arrival in as soon as he got here. Now we're for it, and it's your fault!' he concluded, glaring at Quentin.

Quentin retaliated. 'No it isn't. You rushed round here when you heard the shots the same as we did.'

Before anyone else could speak, the purr of an engine and a car bonnet protruding into the driveway heralded the arrival of another vehicle. The four men darted back out of sight as the crunch of tyres on gravel came to a standstill. From his vantage point, Quentin saw a grey Volvo in the parking space. He was yanked back by George, who glared at him again and stood in front of him.

'It could be Will Chandler,' Quentin whispered to the back of George's head. 'He's the brother of the bloke who drove away. He's in on the kidnapping.'

'You know more than we do,' grumbled the second surveillance officer.

Quentin thought that quite possible. These guys, as were the ones yesterday, would be from the local force, appointed at Philmore's request. It would be up to the Surrey Constabulary to process Philmore's threat to "deal with them later".

Risking a second reprimand, Quentin edged up beside George and peeked round the corner. Instead of heading for the steps up to the front door, the driver of the Volvo sat in his car staring at the gates as though he was expecting someone. With just a side view, and with his head tilted towards the gates, Quentin couldn't see his face clearly, but it could have been Will Chandler.

Explanations ran round Quentin's head. Philip, in his speedy Maserati, must have been out of the lane before

Will turned into it. Will was probably waiting for his brother to arrive with the key.

'Aren't we going to do something?' Colin asked from behind.

'Our orders are to call any activity in,' George told him. 'John's done that now.'

'Does any activity include letting the suspect get away?' Quentin said, unable to keep the sarcasm out of his voice.

'We weren't supposed to do anything until back-up arrived. And we can't arrest someone for sitting in a car,' George snapped. 'He needs to be doing something illegal.'

Just then, the Volvo door opened and the driver climbed out. His hand went to his jacket pocket. Before he could do anything else, a figure jumped out from the shrubbery bordering the lawn and flung itself at the driver, yanking his hand away from his pocket.

'Oh no, you don't, you kidnapping crook,' cried the attacker.

Quentin flew round the corner, gasping as he saw Wanda's blonde head next to that of a bewildered-looking elderly man – who was definitely not Will Chandler.

Chapter Twenty-eight

'What's going on? Who are you?' the elderly man demanded, looking from Wanda to Quentin when he appeared at her side, followed by Colin, and John and George, the two surveillance officers.

George stepped forward. 'May I ask what you're doing here, sir?' he said.

The man he was addressing straightened his back and looked indignant. 'More to the point, what are *you* doing here?'

George flashed his ID.

'Police? Why? What's the trouble, officer?'

'Just tell us who you are,' George insisted.

'I'm Adrian Pritchard. This is my house.'

'Oh!' exclaimed Wanda, reddening. 'I'm so sorry. I thought you were somebody else.'

'We understood you were abroad,' Quentin told him.

'I was, but my wife was ill so we came back early.'

Quentin saw George exchange glances with John, who shrugged.

'Er, are you planning on staying here?' Quentin asked, thinking of the cellar with its obvious signs of recent occupation.

'No, we're at our new property. I just came to get a few things we left here and make sure everything was all right. Our agent's got the keys. I'm waiting for him.'

'Well, I'm sorry, Mr Pritchard,' George said, 'but we can't give you access at the moment.'

'What do you mean? It may be up for sale, but it's still my property.'

Adrian Pritchard turned at the sound of a car coming through the gates. A dark-blue Audi drew up and Philmore got out. Obviously he'd opted to stay around, or something had delayed him going back to London.

George drew him aside and Quentin guessed he was updating him. Philmore shook his head as though in disbelief before striding over to the group of people on the driveway.

'Mr Pritchard,' he said with authority. 'I'm Detective Chief Inspector Philmore. I'm sorry you've had to come home to this.'

'I should think so too,' said Pritchard. 'Perhaps you'd be kind enough to tell me why I'm not allowed into my own house.'

'I'm afraid I can't divulge that at present, but I can assure you we'll let you know immediately once our investigations are complete.'

'Investigations? Into what?'

'As I've said, I can't divulge that. If there's anything in the house that you need urgently, please tell me and I'll arrange for one of my officers to get it for you.'

Pritchard looked uncertain. 'Well, it's not urgent, it's just that I've come especially, but I suppose it can wait.'

'What a shame you've had a wasted journey,' Wanda said, giving him her most alluring smile. 'It's such a nuisance after you had to cut your trip short because your wife isn't well. Is she feeling better now she's home?'

'Yes, a bit better,' Pritchard replied, somewhat mollified.

'That's good then. There's nothing like your own bed when you're under the weather, is there? And I'm sure the chief inspector will have everything here wrapped up soon and you'll be able to collect your things. I'm so sorry about jumping out at you like that. I hope I didn't hurt you.'

Pritchard looked at Wanda as if seeing her for the first time.

'I expect I'll get over it. Did you think I was a burglar?' he said, apparently not having picked up on the word "kidnapping" in Wanda's accusation.

'Something like that,' Wanda admitted. 'Why don't you give the inspector your contact details and he'll ring you as soon you're able to get back in.'

For the umpteenth time, Quentin was awed by Wanda's ability to calm difficult moments. The three policemen looked impressed too. Wanda's husky, Lauren Bacall voice had tempered Pritchard's anger and diffused the situation.

'All right,' Pritchard agreed, turning to Philmore.

John, the second of the surveillance officers, stepped forward, produced a notebook and pen and wrote down the information as Pritchard relayed it.

'Thank you,' Philmore said. 'Before you go, would you mind telling me why you chose Property Perfections as your estate agents?'

A flicker of suspicion crossed Pritchard's face. 'I saw their advert,' he said. 'We spent a lot on revamping the place, and I wanted to recoup the money. Mr Chandler was confident he could get the top price for it so I went with them.'

'Did you instruct them to withdraw it from the market?' Quentin asked.

Pritchard looked surprised. 'No. Why would I? I don't need both houses, and our new one suits our needs more.'

'Did you know Mr Chandler, or anyone connected to Property Perfections, before you put the house up for sale?' Philmore asked, glaring at Quentin as if daring him to interrupt his questioning.

'No. I'd never seen or heard of him or anyone else there before I contacted Property Perfections. Why? Is it him you're investigating? You can't divulge that, I suppose.'

'I'm afraid not. When did you tell them you were back in the UK?'

'This morning, when I rang and said I wanted the keys. I've mislaid mine. Come to think of it, he tried to put me off, but I said I wanted to come today. I even offered to pick the keys up, but he insisted on being here with me.'

Well, of course he did, Quentin thought. He'd want to make sure Pritchard went nowhere near the cellar. Maybe he planned to move Lorna out before the owner arrived.

'That was after I'd said I still had the electric control for the garage and was going in there to find something I thought I'd left there,' Pritchard added.

'All right, Mr Pritchard, thank you,' Philmore said. 'We'll be in touch as soon as we can.'

Pritchard looked at each of them in turn, his gaze settling on Wanda, who gave him another beguiling smile. Still looking perplexed, the owner of The Hacienda nodded at Wanda, got into his car and drove away.

'Well, there's a turn-up for the books,' said John. He may have been referring to Pritchard, but his eyes were firmly fixed on Wanda.

Quentin was used to men eyeing Wanda with a certain gleam in their eyes, and usually he ignored it. Today though, he moved towards Wanda and put his arm around her possessively. Perhaps it was the call from Cultured Voice; he didn't know. He only knew he needed to show, if only to himself, that Wanda was his.

'So,' he said, 'it looks like Mr Pritchard caught Philip on the hop and Philip rushed to get here before him. Lord knows why he went off in such a hurry. When he realized Lorna wasn't here, he could have just locked the cellar and said he'd mislaid the key. Pritchard wouldn't have been any the wiser.'

'He probably panicked when he saw Lorna was gone,' Philmore speculated. 'Thought the game was up. After all, he knew we'd be involved once Lorna told her kidnap story, and we'd make the connection to Property Perfections. He could be rushing back to warn his brother, maybe do a runner, so we need to get moving.'

Dropping into the Audi, Philmore barked instructions into the police radio, then rang Debbie Francis. When he'd finished, he got out and spoke to the surveillance officers.

'Wait for uniform to get some crime scene tape round this place, then you can stand down,' he said. 'I can't see either of the Chandlers coming back here. We've got prints from the cellar and the room the Chandlers were in, hopefully some DNA as well, but forensics will come and finish off properly. Thanks, boys.'

George shrugged. 'It's OK, sir. We didn't really do anything.'

'At least you were awake,' Quentin couldn't resist saying.

A glare from Philmore.

'Sorry,' Quentin said, realizing it wasn't his place to pass comment.

'What now then?' Colin ventured.

Philmore looked at him as if he'd just noticed he was there. Then he looked at Quentin and Wanda.

'I think you should all go home and leave it to us now,' he said. 'You've done your bit, so thanks for that. We'll put out APBs on the Chandlers and watch all the ports and airports. We've got Lorna's description of the two guys who brought her here, and we know what car they drove, so we'll be after them as well.'

'What do think the odds are that the kidnappers are the ones who killed Dave Brown?' Quentin asked.

Philmore shrugged. 'Quite possible, especially after what Lorna said in her statement, but why the Chandlers would use the same people for the kidnapping after things went wrong with Dave Brown is anyone's guess.'

'Maybe they couldn't find anyone else, or didn't have time to,' Quentin suggested. 'As far as we know, the Chandlers have never been involved in violence before. They're businessmen, used to pushing money from pillar to post, putting on a legitimate front, and they're good at it. What about Cult– Henry Lawson?'

Philmore pursed his lips and said nothing. Quentin guessed at his thoughts. If the Chandlers were found, they would be arrested and Property Perfections would be out of business. If the two kidnappers, possibly murderers, were caught, they would stand trial. But the chances of the man behind it all, the international criminal that Quentin knew as Cultured Voice, being caught were slim – so slim that Philmore refused to discuss it.

'OK,' Quentin said resignedly. 'Come on, Wanda. Let's get back to London and see how Lorna is.'

Chapter Twenty-nine

'I heard gunshots,' Wanda explained when they stopped at a café on the way back to Greenwich. 'I left the dogs in the car and ran to the house. I just got inside the gates when Chandler came out. I managed to hide before he rushed down the steps and sped off like a bat out of hell. Then the owner turned up and I thought it might be another member of the gang. I thought he had a gun in his pocket. I had visions of him going for you so that's when I jumped him.'

'You made a good job of it,' Colin said, grinning. 'Remind me not to get on the wrong side of you.'

'It's all very well for Philmore to say to leave things to them…' Quentin said, after taking a sip of his coffee. 'OK, so Lorna's safe, thank goodness, and we know how and why Property Perfections is involved and why Dave was killed, but none of the crooks have been caught, and the brains behind it will likely stay free even if they're all caught.'

'And we still don't know where the proof that Dave found is,' Wanda added.

'It's frustrating,' Colin agreed. 'But let's face it, the police have got far more resources than we have. *We* can't cover all the ports and airports.'

'They might not go abroad,' Wanda pointed out. 'They could hide out in Britain somewhere, though I don't suppose they'll use one of their own properties. They'll know every empty house on their books will be checked. Oh my God!'

Wanda stopped and colour drained from her face.

'What is it?' Colin asked.

'Tina!' Quentin blurted, picking up on Wanda's thought at the mention of empty properties. 'The Chandlers will know someone got the information about The Hacienda from somewhere. If they suspect Tina, who knows what will happen?'

'You're overreacting,' Colin said. 'She could have given out that address to anyone who enquired about the place before they told her it was withdrawn from the market. You've been ringing her on her personal mobile, and even if the call I made to Property Perfections was recorded, as far as she knew, I was a genuine customer. She was just doing her job. All she has to do is carry on as she is, act the innocent.'

'We still need to warn her,' Quentin said.

Wanda was already punching Tina's number into her mobile. 'You're both right,' she said. 'And they might be too busy trying to sort themselves out to think about her, but better safe than sorry.'

Five minutes later, Wanda lowered her phone. 'She's fine. She says Philip's got no reason to suspect her, and she's going to email a list of empty properties like she did for Philmore.'

'Still, maybe we should get her some police protection,' Quentin suggested.

'Yeah,' Colin scoffed. 'Like they protected Lorna, you mean?'

Quentin grimaced. 'That was bad luck. Anyway, the Chandlers will probably go to ground until they think it's safe to try to escape.'

'Well,' Colin went on, 'we've already said they're unlikely to use one of their empty properties now they've been rumbled.'

'You never know,' Quentin countered. 'If they're desperate, they could move from one to another as they need to.'

'What we need is a plan,' Wanda said. 'Something to draw them out, lure them into a trap.'

'I can't see Philmore being happy with that, not if we do it without his say-so,' Colin pointed out.

'Maybe,' Wanda replied darkly. 'But if we'd waited for him at The Hacienda, where would Lorna be now? We need to do something.'

Even as she spoke, Wanda was punching a number into her mobile. Quentin and Colin exchanged glances as they listened to one side of the following conversation.

'Lorna? Are you home yet? ... Oh good ... And are you OK? ... Are you up to answering some quick questions? Say if you're not ... OK. I just wondered if there's anything you've remembered since this morning ... I mean, when they first abducted you, do you have any idea where they took you?'

There was a pause while she listened to Lorna's answer. Quentin gestured for Wanda to turn on the loudspeaker facility, which she did.

Lorna's voice filled the air.

'...some sort of lock-up unit or garage. 'It was about an hour's drive from where they snatched me. I was so traumatised I couldn't even tell you which direction we drove in. It's still a bit hazy if I'm honest.'

'Never mind, Lorna. At least we know what car they used, and the registration number. Quentin's sent the photo he took at The Hacienda to DCI Philmore, so the police will be on the lookout for it. Give us a ring if you think of anything else. Bye for now.'

Wanda had no sooner put down the phone when it rang. She turned on the loudspeaker when she realized it was Lorna again.

'I've remembered something,' Lorna said. 'It's just come to me. When they came to transfer me it was dark, nobody around, so they tied my hands but didn't bother with the blindfold straight away. When we got to the main road, I saw a sign for Putney High Street. Then they made me lie down and not move, so I didn't notice anything else till we got to the house in Farnham. Don't know how much help that will be, but I can't think of anything else, sorry.'

'It's all right, Lorna. You take it easy.'

'Well, she was right, it wasn't much help,' Colin commented as Wanda put down the phone.

'It might be.' Quentin frowned, trying to think how knowing where Lorna was initially held could help them. He recalled part of the conversation between Philip and Will Chandler at The Hacienda: *I can't keep her where she is.*

'It's somewhere Philip knew about but he couldn't keep her there for some reason,' he mused aloud. 'Putney. South west London. Not exactly a small area.'

'Why are we wasting our time trying to figure out where they took Lorna initially?' Colin demanded. 'What good will it do if we do find out? She's free now, and the police will be on the lookout for the Lexus and the Maserati, and the Vauxhall the kidnappers used. That's much more likely to bear fruit. Let's face it, Maseratis aren't two a penny. If they've got any sense, the Chandlers will ditch it.'

'Yeah,' said Quentin thoughtfully. 'That's a lot of money to ditch.'

'Whatever,' Colin said, shaking his head impatiently. 'I think we've done all we can do. Lorna's safe and Property Perfections won't be running their little game again now they've been sussed. Hopefully the police will get them at some point. I'm going home.'

Wanda nodded. 'All right, Colin. We'll let you know if we hear anything from Philmore.'

Colin dropped a kiss on her head, nodded to Quentin, then turned and walked away.

Quentin stared after him, wishing he could let things go as easily as Colin. But somehow, even though they had achieved most of what they'd set out to do, Quentin still had a feeling of incompleteness. The perpetrators of two crimes, killing and kidnap, were still at large, and that didn't sit well with Quentin at all. Over and above that was the certain knowledge that the call he'd had, from the man he knew as Cultured Voice, wouldn't be the last.

He felt Wanda's hand on his arm.

'I know what you're thinking,' she said softly. 'Don't worry, we'll think of something. Come on, let's get home. We'll both feel better after a good night's sleep in our own beds.'

* * *

Sleep in his own bed was denied Quentin when his mobile woke him at two o'clock in the morning. Scrabbling to pick it up, he saw the number was withheld. Instantly awake, he sat up.

'Yes,' he said, switching on the bedside lamp.

'So, Mr Cadbury, it seems you've foiled my colleague's plan to keep Miss West detained.'

Quentin didn't know how to answer. Cultured Voice had somehow learned, probably from the Chandlers, that Lorna had been rescued. But how did they know it was him who'd rescued her? Neither of the Chandlers had any idea that he knew where Lorna was.

'It had to be you, Mr Cadbury. My partners, if you can call them that, are insisting that only you and Miss West know what's been going on, so by simple process of elimination, it had to be you. I really do think you should have taken up my offer of employment.'

Quentin's hackles rose. That this criminal, dealer in all things contraband, mastermind of numerous crimes and continual evader of justice, could think that he'd entertain the idea of working for him for even a nanosecond, made Quentin's blood boil.

'Lost for words, Mr Cadbury?'

'Why would you want to employ someone who's thwarted your plans more than once?' he choked out. 'How could you ever trust someone like that?'

'Ah, you've hit the nail on the head. Trust. Is there such a thing?'

'Not according to you. Trust no one. That's your mantra, isn't it?'

'You know me too well, Mr Cadbury. Which is why you might have served me well. Sadly, not anymore. I think you've pushed me a little too far this time. I've managed to pull a good portion of my money out of Property Perfections but a lot of it is tied up in the business, so overall I'm making quite a loss. Which, I'm afraid, is unforgivable.'

A chill ran down Quentin's spine as he waited. Waited for the cultured tones to rise, to betray the anger behind the measured cadence. But the voice remained even, confusing Quentin with its next words.

'Nevertheless, I'm prepared to overlook your interference and help you.'

Quentin gasped, unable to believe what he was hearing. 'Help me?'

'Well, you'd be helping me in return. You'd prefer to catch my so-called partners yourself instead of waiting around for the police to do it, wouldn't you? After all, it was you who found Miss West, not them.'

Quentin gulped, unable to answer. The man knew he'd been at The Hacienda before the police. How? Quentin shook his head. He should know by now that Cultured Voice had ways of knowing everything.

'You see, Mr Cadbury, these partners of mine are useless to me now. They're clever in their own way, but they lack my vision and intuition. Even when I was a guest of the Dutch authorities, the Chandler brothers had no idea. They thought I'd left the business in their hands while I was busy investigating a new venture. They may have read about a Henri Hoeker being arrested in the Netherlands, but I've always been Henry Lawson to them.'

A snigger sounded in Quentin's ear, as though Cultured Voice was laughing at the Chandlers' gullibility.

'So what's your point?' Quentin asked.

'The point, Mr Cadbury, is that they are no longer reliable. They have been useful, but they've become ineffective. I don't want to have to worry about where they're going or what they might do next. I need to be rid of them. So if they're nicely tucked up in prison for several years, it would be a great relief.'

Incredulous, Quentin gasped again.

'A good solution all round, wouldn't you say?' Cultured Voice continued.

'You– you want me to get them put in prison while you get away with it?'

'That's the general idea, yes.'

'I won't do it.'

'I think you will.'

'I won't. You're the one who should be in prison.'

A loud sigh told Quentin that his adversary was nearing the end of his patience.

'Come now, Quentin, I know you want to see the people who kidnapped Miss West, and the ones who were running an illegal business, behind bars, not to mention the person responsible for the unfortunate Dave Brown's death.'

Quentin seethed silently. You're responsible, he wanted to say, shout, yell, as loudly as he could. But what good would it do?

'I assure you,' the cultured voice continued, 'that none of the people we've mentioned will lead you to me, so it's pointless letting their crimes go unpunished in the vain hope that they will. Your moral principles are commendable, Mr Cadbury, but letting sprats as immoral as the Chandlers go free just to catch a very elusive mackerel is futile. I'm sure Mrs Merrydrew would agree with me.'

Quentin baulked at this. Once again his enemy was using Wanda as a kind of emotional blackmail. He understood the veiled threat behind the words. He hated this man, yet he knew his enemy was right. He couldn't stand by and ignore something that might lead to the capture of the kidnappers, Dave's killer and the Chandlers.

'So,' he said through tight lips. 'How do I find these people?'

'There, now, I knew you weren't stupid enough to pass up the opportunity I'm offering. I won't bother with the muscle men – I'm sure even the British police force can find cannon fodder like them. Of course, you may well find out where the Chandlers are under your own steam, but a little help won't go amiss.'

'Are you going to tell me or not?'

'Patience, Mr Cadbury. I'm not going to lay it on a plate for you. I'll give you a clue, or rather I'll ask you a question. Where would you hide a very conspicuous car? Not in your own garage, surely. You're a detective. I'll leave it with you.'

The ensuing silence weighed heavily on Quentin. It closed around him, like the oppressive air before a storm. Feeling the need to do something, he resisted the urge to ring Wanda and went downstairs to make tea. Victor opened an eye, then closed it again. Magpie looked on when Quentin began pacing the lounge, the phone call at the forefront of his mind.

Cultured Voice had given him a clue, in the form of a riddle, as to how to find the Chandlers. *Where would you hide a very expensive car? Not in your own garage.* The Maserati belonged to Philip Chandler, and Philip Chandler had access to the empty properties on his books. Quentin needed the addresses of those properties. If Tina Patterson hadn't sent the list she'd promised by tomorrow morning, he'd have to contact her.

Sighing, he went back to bed.

Chapter Thirty

A bark from Victor woke Quentin at seven-thirty the next morning. When he went downstairs, Victor was standing guard over his food bowl, which Magpie was trying to push out of his reach.

'All right, you two,' he said, wondering how much longer he'd have to keep the dog. He'd grown fond of Victor, but these terraced houses with tiny gardens weren't really suitable for big dogs.

His landline rang, and he reached for the handset.

'Quentin? It's Anne Roberts. Sorry to ring so early, but I'm not sleeping well and I wondered if you're any closer to finding out who killed Dave?'

'Oh, hello, Anne. Yes, I now know who was involved, but they haven't been caught yet. It's not straightforward but we'll get there.'

'You're still looking into it then?'

Quentin heard the catch in her voice. It reinforced his determination to bring Dave's killer to justice. Despite his conviction that Cultured Voice was ultimately responsible, it hadn't been his hand that had wielded the knife that had stabbed Dave.

'Yes,' he replied, an image of Dave slumped by the bins coming to him. 'It must be hard, losing your brother like that. Don't worry, Anne, I'm not giving up. The police are still investigating too.'

'OK, thanks. I don't think I'll sleep properly until this is sorted out. Please keep me posted.'

Later, Quentin checked his emails. 'Yes!' he murmured, opening the one promised by Tina. There were only four vacant houses on Property Perfections' books, not including The Hacienda. As Tina's email pointed out, other properties up for sale were still occupied by hopeful vendors.

So, Quentin thought, four places where the Chandlers could be hiding out, or at least hiding the Maserati.

'What's the point of him telling you where to look for Philip's car?' Wanda asked when she learned about the latest call from Cultured Voice. 'Surely he'll realize the Chandlers won't risk staying in one of their own properties now, and even if the car's there, *they* might not be. The Maserati won't tell us where they are, will it?'

'Maybe not, but he's not in the habit of giving pointless information, unless he's giving me the runaround, which I don't think he is. He is furious that I'm involved, but he's more peed off with the Chandlers. They're no longer useful to him, so he wants them out of the way. He's not big on second chances.'

Wanda raised an immaculate eyebrow. 'You've had a few,' she reminded him. 'After all, you're still here despite his threats.'

'Yeah, there is that.' Quentin shook his head. 'I can't work it out, really, except I don't work for him like all the others he's got rid of.'

'True. You've never taken money from him, but you've cost him shedloads. You're a thorn in his side, but you're not a disloyal or inefficient underling. He's known from the beginning that you're out to get him, and since then he's learned that you stick to your guns, so perhaps he respects that.'

'Respects it!' Quentin exploded. 'Funny way to show respect, getting me to catch the Chandlers just to make his wretched life easier.'

'All right, perhaps he just enjoys a challenge. One day he might get fed up with being challenged; who knows? Whatever, we can't afford to ignore him.'

'Well,' Quentin said, 'if he's given me a clue then it's for a reason, so we'll have to follow it. The trouble is, he wants me to find the Chandlers before the police do, so...'

'We can't tell Philmore,' Wanda finished for him. 'So we won't, not yet anyway. It's not as though anyone's in danger like Lorna was. We'll try to track down the Maserati and see if it leads us anywhere. We can call Philmore if it does. I mean, the police get tip-offs and use snouts all the time, so why can't we? We're after the same result.'

'I suppose you're right, Wanda.'

Despite the fact that he had ignored police advice and taken things into his own hands many times, and irrespective of recent bad press, Quentin still had a great respect for the British police. He thought Philmore and officers like him were doing the best they could in the face of budgets cuts, staff shortages and increasing crime rates.

'Right,' he said briskly. 'Which property shall we start with?'

* * *

The empty properties on Tina's list were a converted barn in Wales and an Edwardian house in Essex, along with the Suffolk premises originally sent to Wanda, and the Devon cottage she and Colin had visited. Essex being the nearest, they decided to start there, then go on to Suffolk.

Realizing they might not make it back that day, Wanda packed them a few things while Quentin filled Magpie's automatic feeder, earning him another haughty look from his pet.

'Sorry, boy,' he said fondly, feeling a little guilty to be leaving Magpie again. Then, having agreed they would use his car, Quentin sprinted to the lock-up garage a few streets away.

Twenty minutes later, he'd collected Wanda, Mozart and Victor and they were on their way in Quentin's BMW. Wanda typed the postcode into the satnav, which told them their time of arrival at their destination would be 1.45 p.m.

'That's if we don't get held up,' Quentin commented. 'Or stop for lunch.'

'I brought water, a flask of coffee and some food,' Wanda told him. 'We won't starve.'

It was two-fifteen before they found the property. A few miles off the A12, the landscape turned more rural.

'It's not far from Harwich,' Wanda said when she checked the map. 'Handy for anyone who wants to nip across to Holland.'

Quentin grunted, concentrating on the road ahead.

'Well,' he said eventually, 'it's certainly away from the rat race around here.'

When they found the house they were looking for, it was far plainer than either The Hacienda or the cottage in Devon. The facade was of red brick, with nothing eye-catching to draw attention to itself. Unlike The Hacienda, with shutters still in place, the house looked forlorn, its blank windows reflecting the light like blind eyes. They drove past, waiting until they came to a small copse of trees before parking on the far side of it.

'I didn't see a car anywhere near it,' Quentin said as he switched off the engine.

'Could be at the back or in the garage,' Wanda suggested. 'If the Maserati's here, it won't be on show. Let's take the binoculars, walk through the trees and check it from there first.'

The warmth of the April day dipped in the shade of the wooded area, and a chill settled over them. Quentin cursed as he tripped on a protruding tree root and fell against a tree trunk, scraping his hand on the rough bark.

'Bloody hell!' he grumbled as blood seeped from the fresh graze as well as the reopened cut from The Hacienda's gravel drive. 'I'll need a blood transfusion if things go on like this!'

Wanda handed him a tissue. 'Stop complaining and look where you're going.'

When they emerged on the other side, he raised the binoculars and studied the house. From this angle, he could see there was a double garage at the side and that the back garden, hidden from view by a stout-looking wooden fence, stretched a long way back. The front garden looked smaller, enclosed by a low wall and a driveway to the garage.

'Can't see a window in the garage,' he said, lowering the binoculars and handing them to Wanda. 'Looks like it'll be an army knife job.'

'We can approach it from here, though,' Wanda said. 'There's only one window on this side of the house and that looks like it might be opaque glass. If anyone's in there, they won't see us.'

Quentin took back the binoculars and swung the strap round his neck.

'Right. OK then, let's go.'

They made their way over the uneven ground; primroses, cow parsley and chickweed showed colourful blooms amid the coarse grass. When they reached the side wall of the garage, they stopped, trying to work out if there was any way they could see inside without breaking in. After a scout around the rear fence, Quentin came back to join Wanda.

'Can't see a back gate,' he reported. 'There might be an alarm on the house, but maybe not on the garage. I'll check the front.'

He slid stealthily along the wall to the front corner of the garage, then wondered why he was acting like a secret agent trying not to be seen. There was nobody to see him on this side, no one could have seen him over the high fence when he'd walked round it, and if the house was empty, he wouldn't be seen at the front either. *If* the house was empty… Were the Chandlers here?

Walking normally but careful not to go out far enough to be seen from the front windows, he rounded the corner.

There were ruts in the shingle driveway, tyre marks where vehicles had driven to and from the garage. He looked at the garage doors, two old-fashioned wooden types that met in the middle and would need to swing outwards for a vehicle to enter or exit. There were bolts top and bottom on each door, as well as a more modern-looking lock on each. A gap in the centre gave him a very narrow view of the inside. He put an eye to the gap and peered in. Through the darkness, he could make out a slice of colour, something bright. Red? He took out his phone and switched on the torch, held it to the gap and peeked in again. Yes, red, low-slung, like a sports car. Like a red Maserati.

His pulse quickened. 'Bingo!' he murmured to himself.

'Looks like we've hit the jackpot first time,' he said when he went back to Wanda. 'Can't see properly so can't be sure. We'll have to get the doors open.'

'OK,' Wanda said. 'But if the Chandlers are in the house, they might hear.'

'We'll have to risk it, Wanda, unless you've got any idea how to find out if they're here?'

Wanda chewed at her lip, a sign that she was worried or thinking deeply.

'I might have,' she said at last.

'Really? What are you going to do, knock on the door and see what happens?'

'More or less,' she said. 'Why not? I'll say my car broke down up the road, my phone's out of battery and could they call the AA for me? Will Chandler's never seen me, and Philip's only seen me in disguise as Eleanor King.'

Quentin gave a half-laugh. Wanda may have been in disguise when she'd met Philip Chandler, but there were very few men who would forget Wanda's face after such a short time. He was bound to make the connection sooner or later.

'I think I'll just open the doors and have done with it,' he said. 'I'll close them after me so I can have a look at the car, see if it gives us any clues about the Chandlers' whereabouts.'

He was about to round the corner again to tackle the garage door locks, when they heard the roar of a motorbike. As the bike came into sight, it slowed down. Quentin shrank back as it swung off the road and came to rest outside the front gate.

'What's going on?' Wanda whispered to Quentin's back.

'It's a young bloke,' Quentin told her as the rider dismounted, secured the bike and removed his helmet. 'He's coming in.'

Quentin retreated further from the corner and flattened himself against the wall. Wanda did the same, and they stood motionless, hearing but not registering the tune the rider whistled. The whistling stopped, and the sound of the garage bolts being drawn back reached them. Then they heard the jangle of keys and a clunk as if they'd been dropped on the ground.

'Sod it!' The male voice was full of impatience. 'Bloody stupid doors.'

The young man obviously succeeded in opening the doors because the nearside one suddenly loomed in front of them, the fingers of a hand gripping its edge as it was pushed back as far as it would go. Wanda grasped Quentin's arm, and they froze, praying that they wouldn't be discovered.

The whistling recommenced after the man had stepped away and entered the garage. Seconds later, an engine sounded, growing louder as a vehicle was driven out of the garage. Immediately Quentin was certain of one thing. Whatever the young man was driving, it wasn't a Maserati. And it wasn't being driven away. A premonition coming to him, he moved forward and peered round the open garage door.

'A lawnmower!' Wanda murmured, coming up behind him. 'Not quite a Maserati then.'

They watched the red, sit-on mower going backwards and forwards on the front lawn, making straight lines in the grass. The rider, having discarded his jacket, was dressed in an old-looking jumper and tatty jeans.

'Why cut the grass on an empty property?' Quentin asked.

Wanda gave him a sideways look. 'Because it looks nicer when people come to view it. Come on, we're not going to find out anything hiding here.'

'What are you doing?' Quentin asked when Wanda pulled at his arm and led him round the corner.

As they reached the low garden wall, she waved at the rider on the lawn mower. The man drove the machine up to the edge of the lawn and cut the engine.

'Hello,' Wanda said, giving him her sweetest smile. 'Sorry to trouble you, but we've lost our dog. We were walking him in the woods there and he ran off. I don't suppose you've seen a little white dog anywhere?'

'No,' the young man answered, eyeing Wanda for a long moment before looking at Quentin.

'Oh,' Wanda said. 'Well, I expect he's gone back to the car. He's not usually one to go far, but I should hate him to run into the road, or get into your garden and dig up your lovely flowers.'

'They're not my flowers,' came the answer with a shrug. 'No one lives here. I just come in to cut the grass and keep it tidy till the place is sold.'

Quentin stepped forward. 'Oh, it's up for sale? We're looking to move to this area. How much is it, do you know? Have many people been to see it?'

'No idea,' was the indifferent reply. 'I've never been inside but it looks posh, so I guess it's quite pricey. Don't know about anything else.'

'OK, thanks,' Quentin said, seeing they weren't going to learn any more.

'Hope you find your dog,' the young man said. He started the engine and continued with his work.

'That was a waste of time,' Quentin grumbled as they made their way back to the car.

'No it wasn't,' Wanda said. 'At least we know the Chandlers aren't there, or the Maserati. Talking of dogs, we'd better let them out for a bit before we go any further.'

Back at the car, Mozart jumped out excitedly while Victor climbed down cautiously after him. Quentin's phone rang and he stiffened when he saw the number was withheld.

'Yes?' he said, leaning on the bonnet.

'Mr Cadbury.'

'Yes,' he said again when the caller didn't continue.

'Have you had any luck with the clue I gave you?'

'Not yet,' Quentin said through gritted teeth.

'How disappointing,' the cultured voice mocked.

For God's sake, Quentin thought. How on earth does he expect me to solve his stupid riddle when he only gave it to me at two o'clock this morning?

'I'm working on it,' he said.

'I hope so,' Cultured Voice went on. 'Where are you and what are you doing?'

For a moment, Quentin searched for something to say that would give his enemy the impression that he was further afield with his task than he was, but he gave it up. Nothing came to mind, and Cultured Voice had a way of finding out about everything that concerned him.

'I'm in Essex checking on one of Property Perfections' empty houses,' he said at last.

'Very enterprising, I'm sure. I see your logic, but perhaps you should try closer to home, and soon. I'm looking forward to hearing that my former partners are safely out of harm's way.'

'Out of *your* way, you mean,' Quentin said before he could stop himself.

'Precisely. You know I'm a patient man when I need to be, Mr Cadbury, but there are times when being patient isn't conducive to my well-being. Now is one of them. I want those two found quickly, or I may have cause to dispose of them in a more unpleasant manner.'

Quentin shuddered. The Chandlers deserved to be punished for breaking the law and their role in Dave's death, but Quentin wanted justice to be meted out legally, not for them to be victims of Cultured Voice's kind of punishment.

'I'll ring you tomorrow,' Cultured Voice was saying. 'I hope you'll have better news for me by then.'

Silence told Quentin the call was over. He gave Wanda the gist of the conversation then watched as she walked with both dogs towards the wooded area. From the periphery of his vision, he saw something suddenly dart across the open ground into the trees. A rabbit, he realized after it had disappeared. Mozart barked and bounded after it. Victor, still hampered by his injured leg, gave up the chase after a few yards.

A few minutes later, Wanda reappeared at the edge of the woods and spread her hands in a helpless gesture.

'Bloody hell!' Quentin groaned. 'Now we really have lost our dog!'

Chapter Thirty-one

It was Victor who found Mozart. Tugging at his lead and giving several loud barks, the dog pulled them away from where they'd spent fifteen minutes looking and led them back to the BMW, where Mozart sat looking as though he was waiting for them to return from a leisurely stroll. Wanda's relief was apparent, and when Mozart had been duly fussed over, they got into the car.

'I don't know what's wrong with him lately,' Wanda complained. 'He never runs off.'

'Maybe it's the cannabis,' Quentin quipped. 'He's got withdrawal symptoms.'

'That's not funny, Quentin. Anyway, we'd better get on to Suffolk.'

'I think not,' Quentin said, shaking his head.

'Not? Why not?'

'Because Cultured Voice said to try closer to home.'

'Closer to home? You mean we've come all this way just to go back to London?'

'Looks like it,' Quentin said, starting the engine. 'Why couldn't he have said that in the first place instead of making us chase our tails?'

'What I can't understand,' Wanda said, 'is why he's getting us to find the Maserati if he already knows where it is; and if he knows, how does he know?'

Quentin shrugged. 'Maybe the Chandlers told him, or maybe he's just making an educated guess.'

'It doesn't make sense,' Wanda replied. 'But then nothing he gets us to do makes sense. Not at first anyway.'

They were approaching Chelmsford before Wanda received a call from Tina Patterson.

'Hi, Tina. Everything all right?' she asked, switching to loudspeaker mode.

'Yes. Adam's here covering for Philip. He's just nipped out to get us some doughnuts.'

'Really? Did you call Adam in or did he hear from Philip?'

'I called him. I tried calling Philip but no answer. I couldn't go on running the place on my own, and I didn't know whether to call Adam or shut up shop, so I called him. That's not why I rang, though. I thought you'd like to know that Philip's son rang here earlier.'

'Did he? What for?'

'Apparently Phil's not answering his mobile or his home phone. Lewis, that's Phil's son, said he needed to contact him and asked if I knew where he was.'

'OK,' Wanda said. 'Did he say why he needed to contact him?'

'No, but I'm guessing he wanted money. Phil was always moaning that the only time he ever called was when he after money. Anyway, I said I hadn't heard from Phil since yesterday morning. He muttered something about trying his mother instead. Then he said that was no good because his mother was in France with her new boyfriend.'

'By his mother, you mean Philip's ex-wife?'

'Yes. Her name's Martha. I just thought, you know, even his own son doesn't know where he is.'

Bells clanged in Quentin's brain. *Closer to home.*

'Tina,' he practically shouted. 'Do you know where his ex-wife lives?'

'Yes,' came the answer. 'She lives in Putney.'

* * *

It took them another two hours to get to the address Tina had given them. The houses in the short avenue were detached, built in the large, 1930s style, set back behind wide front gardens. Martha Chandler's was the last property in the avenue, and backed onto a green park area. Its driveway ran along the avenue side of the premises to a brick garage at the rear. Beyond the enclosing garden wall, there were trees, both behind and on the park side.

'This is tricky,' Wanda said. 'This place isn't secluded like the others we've been to. If Lorna was held here, I suppose it was convenient for Philip in the first instance, but I can see why he couldn't keep her here.'

Quentin picked up the story. 'He had to get her out before his ex came back or a neighbour got suspicious. So he had her moved to a more isolated place, The Hacienda. Too risky to keep a person in Putney, but a perfect place to keep a conspicuous car,' he finished triumphantly.

'That's probably it,' Wanda said. 'I'm sure we could get to the garage without being seen by neighbours, but anyone inside the house would see us. We need to know it's definitely empty.'

'I'm getting a feeling of déjà vu,' Quentin said with a shake of his head. 'I've spent most of this case either watching houses and garages or breaking into them.'

'As needs must,' Wanda murmured.

A woman in a flowing summer skirt and a fluffy cardigan came out of the neighbouring house, carrying a handbag and a huge bundle of flowers. As she neared the front gate and noticed Quentin and Wanda, a look of annoyance crossed her face, as though she objected to anyone except residents being parked in the avenue.

Quentin wound down the window and called to her.

'Excuse me. We're trying to contact the lady who lives in this house, but she doesn't seem to be in and I don't have her number. Do you know when she'll be back, by any chance?'

The woman stepped towards them. 'Martha? End of the week, I think.'

'Oh,' said Quentin, deciding to stick with this line of enquiry. 'It's just that her son is at university with my brother, and apparently he's trying to contact his father. He's worried that he can't get hold of him.'

'He would be,' the woman said, rolling her eyes. 'Always after something, that's Lewis. Well, he's out of luck. Philip was here last night, but he's gone now.'

'Really? Did he say where he was going?'

'No. Just a flying visit, he said. Didn't want to talk, couldn't wait to get away. I didn't know he still had a key. He hasn't been around much since the divorce. I'll tell Martha when she's back. She might not want him bringing other people into the house when she's not here.'

'I'm sure they'll sort it out,' Quentin said. 'Thanks for your help.'

The woman nodded, and carried on to wherever she was going. Quentin drove past her to the end of the avenue and round the corner, where he pulled over and waited till he saw the woman emerge, cross the road and disappear.

* * *

'So Cultured Voice was right,' Wanda said as they left the car and walked back to the house. 'The Chandlers used Philip's ex-wife's place as a temporary bolthole, but now the birds have flown.'

'Yes, but we still need to check that the Maserati's here.'

'Why? Surely sending you to find the car's just a means to get to the Chandlers, isn't it? That's what Cultured Voice really wants.'

'Maybe, but I'll look pretty silly if I say I found the Maserati here if he knows it's somewhere else. Come on, let's hurry. We don't want any more neighbours seeing us nosing around.'

The road was deserted. They saw no one on their way, nor any movement from any direction. The only sounds came from the general direction of the park.

When they walked along the side of Martha Chandler's house to the garage, they got a different perspective of the property. Across the width of the garden, on the park side, there was another brick structure. A workshop, Quentin guessed, and anyone held inside would have to shout very loudly for anyone to hear.

'It's quite private,' Wanda commented, looking towards the neighbouring house. 'No one could see into this garden from that house with those bushes there, unless they were on the roof, and there's nothing at the back or on the other side except trees and greenery. Let's check the garage first. There's a window.'

'Seems like there's something up against it,' Quentin said as he approached the window. 'You can't see in.'

He retraced his steps and examined the garage door. 'This looks like it's electrically operated.'

'What a nuisance,' Wanda said, pulling a face. 'Still, you must be able to override the electrics and open it manually.'

'I expect so, but I don't know how.'

'Nor do I,' Wanda admitted, 'but I know a man who will.'

'Really? Who?'

'Colin.'

'Colin's got electric doors on his garage?'

'Don't sound so surprised. Why wouldn't he have electric doors? He lives in Wanstead, not Wormwood Scrubs.'

'I know that,' Quentin said, exasperated. 'I've never noticed, that's all.'

'He only had them fitted recently. Anyway, I'm asking him.'

'Well, don't take too long,' Quentin said. 'It may be secluded but we don't know when Mrs Flower Lady will be back.'

The process of overriding the electrical mechanism proved awkward and, according to Colin, only worked because the one they were tackling was an older type. Quentin held his breath as he swung the door up. He let out a low whistle as a gleaming red Maserati filled his vision.

He exchanged a triumphant glance with Wanda.

'I'll stand guard in case anyone comes while you check it over,' she said.

Quentin slid along the side of the car and pulled the driver's door open. More than a hundred grand of sports car and it wasn't even locked!

He slipped into the driver's seat and switched on the interior light. There was the remainder of a packet of mints in the central well. A chamois protruded from the side pocket and there was a pair of leather driving gloves on the passenger seat. Swivelling round, he saw a book of road maps on the back seat, along with an A-Z of London. He opened the glove compartment and found a torch, a magnifying glass, some tissues, a pen and a few sheets of blank paper. Nothing to give them a clue as to where the Chandlers had gone. He went to the boot and looked inside. A spare wheel, a box of tools, a travel blanket and a tow rope.

Bloody hell, Quentin thought. Hopefully no one would need a tow rope in a car this expensive. He got back into the car, this time on the passenger side, and sat for a while, gazing around him in case he'd missed anything. Nothing. He felt cheated. The Chandlers had eluded him and the Maserati told him nothing. As if expecting a clue to magically appear, he checked the glove compartment again. Everything was the same. He picked up the sheets of paper. They were still blank. No invisible hand had written any vital information for him to find, no divine inspiration came to him. He stared at the top sheet. Something made him run his fingers over the smooth surface. Mainly smooth, but he felt indentations at the top of the page, impressions from the tip of a pen or pencil writing on a piece of paper on top of it. Folding it carefully, he placed it in his pocket and returned the rest to the glovebox.

'Anything?' Wanda asked when he joined her.

'Probably not,' he said. 'Let's check the workshop.'

'I had a quick look when you were in the garage,' Wanda told him. 'It's locked and you can't see in.'

Using his Swiss army knife, Quentin managed to get the workshop door open. It was dark inside, so he switched on his phone torch and shone it round. A workbench ran along one wall, though there were no tools in sight. Unlike The Hacienda's cellar, there were no visible signs that anyone had been held captive there. He saw a bottle of water and a cup half filled with cold coffee, but that could have been left there at any time. Coming out and closing the door, he went back to Wanda.

The light was beginning to fade as they walked back to the car. Once inside, Quentin rummaged around for a pencil. Then, placing the sheet of paper from the Maserati on his notebook, he passed the pencil lightly over the indentations to reveal the wording.

'Code 1805,' he read aloud.

'Probably the code for the garage door,' Wanda suggested.

'Yeah,' Quentin said, disappointed and suddenly tired. 'I think I've had enough for one day. Let's go home and get something to eat.'

Chapter Thirty-two

It was six o'clock the following morning when Quentin's mobile woke him. Struggling onto an elbow, he grabbed the phone with his free hand.

'Yes?' he said, seeing that the number was withheld.

'You're awake then, Mr Cadbury. How did you get on yesterday?'

'All right, I suppose,' Quentin answered, blinking the sleep from his eyes. 'I found the Maserati, if that's what you mean.'

'Good. Is that all you found?'

'Yes. Apparently the Chandlers had been there, but they're not there now.'

There was a pause. 'What a pity,' Cultured Voice said at last. 'Did you find out where they went?'

'Not yet, but I'll be back on it today.'

'One more day, Mr Cadbury, then I'll have to consider an alternative method for dealing with them. That's after I've found them, of course. For some reason, they're not taking my calls. Really, after all I've done for them. I can assure you Philip Chandler wouldn't be driving a Maserati without my money, nor would William have been lording it up in Barcelona for the last five years. Most ungrateful, don't you think?'

'If you say so.'

'I do, and so should you. After all, if they'd handled the situation properly, you wouldn't have had the unfortunate experience of finding a body.' The cultured tones became clipped. 'I'll put feelers out for the Chandlers. If I find them before you, and I suspect I will, I'll hand them to you on a plate to pass safely into police hands. I'm sure that would please your friend in the Metropolitan Police Force. Last chance, Mr Cadbury. Goodbye. Have a productive day.'

'Have a productive day!' Quentin mimicked when the line went dead. He swung his long legs out of bed just as the door was pushed open and Magpie came in, sprang onto the bed and settled into the warm patch that Quentin had just vacated.

'It's all right for you,' Quentin told him. 'We don't all have the luxury of a lie-in. Some of us have to run all over the country on a manhunt without a clue where to start looking.'

Magpie turned green eyes on him, mewed, then stretched out as if ready for sleep.

'No sympathy from you, then,' Quentin grumbled, and went downstairs for a shower.

* * *

Quentin had barely finished his ablutions when he heard a knock on the front door. After unbolting it, he opened it to find Wanda and Colin.

'Hello. How come you're so early?' he asked, eyeing Colin with suspicion.

'I called Colin after I left you last night,' Wanda explained. 'We need as much help as we can get to track the Chandlers down.'

Unease crept into Quentin's mind. Colin had been up at the crack of dawn, driven from Wanstead and was here already? Or… had he driven to Wanda's last night and–

'Wake up, Quentin,' Wanda said, interrupting his maudlin thoughts.

Realizing he was blocking the doorway, he stood aside to let them in, annoyed with himself for letting old jealousies distract him from focusing on the task in hand.

'I'll make us a drink and a bacon sandwich while we think about where to start,' Wanda said.

Forty-five minutes later, they'd finished breakfast but no one had come up with an idea.

'We have to do something,' Wanda said.

'We can't get to all the remaining empty properties on Property Perfections list in one day,' Colin said.

'We know that,' Quentin said irritably. 'We've already said they're unlikely to use those anyway, so why state the obvious?'

He went quiet when Wanda looked at him, raising a perfectly arched eyebrow. He read the warning in her eyes. *Stop*, it said. Jerking himself upright, he reached for his phone and punched the keypad.

'Who are you ringing?' Wanda asked.

'Lorna. Just before she was kidnapped, she said she'd been doing some digging into Property Perfections. I'd forgotten about it.'

'If she'd found out anything, she'd have told Philmore, wouldn't she?' Colin asked.

'Got a better idea, Col–' Quentin broke off when his call was answered. 'Lorna? Hope I didn't wake you. Listen, remember just before you were kidnapped, you were on the phone to me and you said you'd been doing some digging into Property Perfections? What was it you were going to tell me?'

'Oh yes, I remember,' Lorna replied. 'It doesn't matter now, though.'

'Tell me anyway. It sounded important at the time.'

'Well, one of my sources found out that William Chandler's got a private plane at Loddonfield airfield near Basingstoke.'

'Really?' Quentin gave a low whistle. He had visions of the Chandlers waving from the cockpit as their plane climbed into the air. The image was dispelled at Lorna's next words.

'I've told DCI Philmore though, and he said he'd arrange surveillance and tell the airport authorities not to clear the plane for take-off.'

'Oh,' said Quentin dejectedly. 'OK, Lorna. How are you feeling?'

'I'm all right. I'm supposed to be taking the rest of the week off, but I might go in this afternoon.'

'I shouldn't rush it,' Quentin advised. 'I know you love your work and you want to break this story, and I promise to share anything that will help you do that, but you've had quite a time of it, so look after yourself.'

'Well?' Colin demanded when Quentin had rung off.

'Will Chandler's got a private plane near Basingstoke, but Philmore's got it covered.'

'Interesting,' Wanda said thoughtfully. 'So they could be making for there.'

'It won't do them any good. They'll be nabbed,' Colin pointed out.

'Yes,' Wanda countered, 'but they don't know that. How would they?'

Colin shrugged. 'Why didn't they go straight there, instead of going on the run? And if this Henry Lawson is your cultured friend, why doesn't he know about it?'

'He might,' Quentin said, feeling slightly guilty for the way he'd snapped at Colin when he was trying to help. 'It was probably his money that paid for it. There might be a reason they didn't go straight there. Maybe they're lying low for a while, before they try that avenue of escape. When I heard the Chandlers talking, Will said he had a return flight booked. He won't risk that now though – he'll guess all flights to Barcelona will be checked.'

'All the more reason to go straight to Basingstoke,' Colin said.

'Right,' Quentin said, feeling suddenly decisive. 'All this speculation's getting us nowhere. Wanda, please can you look up the number for Loddonfield airfield?'

Without asking why, Wanda did as she was asked.

'Thanks.' Quentin rang the number and waited. 'Hello? Good morning, this is William Chandler ... Fine thank you, but I need my aircraft urgently ... What? Another two days ... Sorry, I just thought you might have got it from another supplier ... OK, thank you.'

Quentin turned to Wanda and Colin. 'Engine trouble,' he said, lowering the phone. 'They're waiting for a part. I nearly came a cropper though. The bloke said he told me yesterday that it would be a few days. If Will rings today and they ask him why he's ringing twice in one day, he'll smell a rat.'

'I should think he would,' Wanda said. 'And if Will speaks to the same guy, he might notice the difference in your voices. Which means the Chandlers might not go there at all.'

'Blast it,' Quentin growled, not relishing another day, possibly more, looking for the Chandlers. 'If we don't track them down before Cultured Voice, he might have them killed.'

Colin looked surprised. 'Would he? He's been working with the Chandlers for years, hasn't he?'

Quentin snorted. 'Oh, he would if he had to, believe me. That's another reason I want to find them before he does. I don't like them, and I know they're crooks, but I don't want their deaths on my conscience.'

'Well,' said Wanda, 'Philmore will have the ANPR unit on the lookout for the Lexus, so that's something.'

Colin raised his eyebrows. 'Unless they've changed it.'

'Bloody hell!' Quentin said, bringing his fist down on the table. 'At this rate, I'll still be sitting here when Cultured Voice rings again!'

It was Wanda who took the next positive action. Leaving Quentin and Colin trying to work something out, she retreated to the kitchen with her mobile. She returned five minutes later, her generous mouth set in a grim line.

'The Lexus is in Property Perfections' car park,' she told them. 'Tina says Will had been using it during his stay here. He turned up in it to see Philip not long after he rushed out on Monday. When she told him Philip wasn't there, Will rang him. He seemed shocked at whatever Philip said and left in a hurry, but left the Lexus behind.'

'So now we don't know what car they've got. Very helpful,' Colin said.

'Just a minute.' Wanda held up her hand, then closed her eyes. 'Let's think about this. When we were at The Hacienda, Philip drove away in the Maserati, right? He drove it to his ex-wife's garage. He must have picked Will up somewhere on the way because, according to Martha Chandler's neighbour, Philip had someone else with him. So—'

'So,' Quentin interrupted, 'if the Maserati's in Martha's garage, what car did the Chandlers leave Putney in?'

'Martha's car?' Colin suggested. 'She wouldn't necessarily take her car to go on holiday.'

There was a silence while the implications of this sank in.

'I don't suppose,' Quentin said at last, 'there's the remotest possibility that there's a way we can find out what that registration number is?'

'There's one way to find out,' Colin said. 'Ask Martha. Don't look at me like that. Tina might know Martha's number, or if not, she might have the son's number from when he rang the office. He might know the car reg, but if he doesn't, ask for his mum's number.'

'Yeah right,' Quentin scoffed. 'And what would we say? Hello Mrs Chandler, can we have your car number plate to track down your ex-husband?'

'Actually, Colin, that's not a bad idea,' Wanda commented. 'And as it's the only one we've got, we might as well use it. I'm sure we can think of some excuse for wanting to know.'

It took five minutes to get the son's number from Tina, and a further two for Wanda to set the number withheld facility on her mobile. Quentin and Colin listened in awe as she spoke to Lewis Chandler without hesitation when he answered her call.

'Is that Lewis? Lewis Chandler? … Oh, hi Lewis. I hope you don't mind but I got your number from your dad's office … No, he wasn't there, that's why I'm ringing you. I'm a friend your mum's neighbour and she says she thought she saw someone driving your mum's car away … Yes, she knows your mum's away so she wanted to make sure it was her car, and if it was, whether she should report it to the police.'

Wanda paused, then resumed. 'Well, you shouldn't report it until you're sure it's her car … Do you know the make of your mum's car, and the registration, by any chance? She said she couldn't be sure of the colour, it was getting dark … Your mum's is silver? What's the number? Just a minute, I'll check it against the one she gave me … Oh no, it's all right, it's not the same so it can't have been your mum's. Panic over. Sorry to have troubled you.'

Ending the call before she had to give any further explanation, Wanda lowered the phone.

'A silver Mondeo,' she said with a triumphant grin, and added the registration.

'You know, Mrs Merrydrew, you're a pretty good liar,' Quentin said.

'Thanks. You're not so bad yourself.'

'Don't mind little old truthful me,' quipped Colin. 'Let's hope I never get called as a character witness for either of you.'

* * *

When he rang Philmore and asked him to alert the ANPR unit to look out for the Mondeo, Quentin was surprised that Philmore didn't even ask how he'd found out about the Chandlers using Martha's car.

'He's probably past caring how we know,' Wanda said after the call. 'Let's hope we're right and they have taken her car. Still, Philip's car is in her garage and hers isn't, and according to their son it should be, so it's a fair assumption.'

'OK, we know what car the Chandlers are in, but they could be anywhere by now,' Colin pointed out. 'So what can we do?'

Quentin sighed. Less than two weeks ago all he'd had to worry about was getting fit for the Tresco marathon. If only he hadn't taken that particular route that morning… If only he hadn't found Dave's body slumped against the wall in that alley, streets away from where he lived…

The thought hit Quentin like a thunderbolt. 'Bloody hell!'

'What?' Wanda and Colin chorused.

'Dave's house.'

Colin stared at him. 'What about it?'

'It's empty, and the owner isn't going back.'

Colin shook his head. 'They wouldn't dare. Hide out in a dead man's house, a man who was killed because he found out about their little game? Never.'

'I don't know,' Wanda said slowly. 'It's a pretty safe bet. They know the police have already been over it, so they probably won't be going again. Philip might know there's a sister, but Anne Roberts lives in Newcastle and access is still being refused anyway. Hiding in plain sight. If that's where they are, it's brilliant.'

198

'But it's a terraced house, isn't it?' Colin said. 'What about the neighbours?'

Quentin shrugged. 'They could have gone in at night and kept quiet. Or they could tell any curious neighbours they were relatives. His sister told me they only kept in touch by phone after he left Newcastle, so I doubt the neighbours know much about her. The Chandlers could be cousins sorting the house out. I'm sure they'd have a story ready. They're not exactly stupid. They've been running a successful, shady business for years, and getting rich on the back of it.'

Colin nodded. 'Can't argue with that.'

Wanda stood up. 'Well, come on, you two. What are we waiting for?'

Chapter Thirty-three

As usual, they agreed to take two cars, with Colin to follow Quentin and Wanda in his Honda Civic. At the last minute, Quentin decided to take Victor.

'You never know,' he said, 'Victor might sniff out something we don't know about. It was his home after all.'

With the case so far having proved unpredictable, Quentin filled Magpie's automatic feeder and Wanda took food for both dogs, as well as some snacks and a flask of coffee. At Quentin's insistence, Mozart travelled with Colin.

'They'll be better apart,' Quentin said. 'We don't know how Victor will react when he sees his old home.'

'How will he get a chance to react at all?' Colin asked. 'If the Chandlers are there—'

'Don't know,' Quentin admitted. 'We'll have to wait and see. Play it by ear.'

Expect the unexpected. The phrase ran around Quentin's head as he recalled it being said to him by Cultured Voice on several previous occasions.

As they neared the road where Dave Brown had lived, Colin found a parking space in an adjacent street while Quentin and Wanda drove slowly along the road. Victor, his nose pressed up against the back window, gave a sudden bark.

'It's that one,' Quentin said, recognizing the letter box on the wall. 'Victor knows where we are.'

They drove by slowly, then back again, searching for a sight of Martha Chandler's car, but there was no silver Mondeo to be seen.

'That doesn't mean they're not here,' Wanda said. 'There's not much parking so they could have parked round the corner like Colin, or abandoned the Mondeo and hired a car.'

'I feel like we're going round in circles,' Quentin complained.

'That car's pulling out,' Wanda said, pointing ahead. 'Park there.'

Quentin knew from his previous visit that residents' permits were meant to be displayed on parked vehicles, but as he'd often done before, he ignored the rule and slipped into the vacant space immediately after the departing car was out of sight. As he killed the engine, Colin walked nonchalantly up to them.

'What was the Mondeo's number?' he asked when Quentin wound down the window.

Wanda told him and a broad grin appeared on Colin's face. 'It's in the next road,' he said.

'Right,' Quentin said, pleased that his idea had paid off. 'That means they haven't been out in it today, or at least not since I rang Philmore, or they would have been spotted on ANPR.'

'OK,' Wanda said, running her hand over her fair hair. 'It looks like we've found them. Well done for thinking of this as a hiding place, Quentin.'

'Thanks,' Quentin replied, grateful for Wanda's praise. 'The question is, what do we do now?'

'Ring Philmore, of course,' Colin said at once.

Quentin and Wanda exchanged glances.

'What?' Colin looked at each of them in turn, suspicion in his tone. 'You're not thinking of tackling them yourselves?'

'Of course not,' Wanda said, 'but we need to be sure they're definitely in there.'

'Yes, we do,' Quentin said. If the Chandlers were just yards away and they could get to them before Cultured Voice could intervene, as well as getting justice for Dave, his sister and Lorna, and garner credit from Philmore for handing them over as a fait accompli – well, the idea was hugely appealing.

'Why don't we go through the alley to the back,' Wanda suggested. 'We might be able to see if there's any movement through the windows. Colin, you could sit here in the car and watch the front. Ring if you see anything.'

'OK.' Resignation sounded in Colin's voice. 'But any problem and I'm ringing Philmore.'

'Of course,' Wanda said, giving him a beguiling smile.

'It'll be all right,' Quentin said. 'It's not as if the Chandlers are armed. They may be clever, but they're pussycats next to those roughnecks, the ones who kidnapped Lorna.'

Colin stepped back while Quentin and Wanda climbed out from the car.

Before Quentin could stop him, Victor clambered down via the front seats, pushed past Quentin's legs and ran up to his former home and into the forecourt. It was the fastest Quentin had seen him move since he'd found him.

'Victor!' he shouted. 'Vic–' His voice was drowned out by Victor's barking, loud and incessant. He looked at

Wanda and Colin, wondering what to do. If he went to get Victor, the Chandlers might see him, and if he didn't, a neighbour might come to see whose dog was making so much noise.

'I'll go,' Wanda said. 'They might not recognize me.'

She hurried away, and soon Quentin heard her talking, as if trying to persuade Victor to return to the car, although what she said was indiscernible over Victor's frantic barking. She succeeded in dragging the dog by his collar, getting him through the gate and onto the pavement before he broke away, ran back to the door and resumed his constant barking. The door of the adjoining house opened and a woman emerged into the forecourt. Quentin moved forward, intending to give Wanda some support.

'Sorry,' Wanda said to the neighbour, gripping Victor's collar again. 'I don't know what's wrong with him today.'

'Goldie?' the woman called, and Victor stopped barking, his ears twitching.

'His name's Victor,' Wanda said.

'Oh,' the woman said. 'He's just like Goldie.'

At the mention of his previous name, Victor pulled against his collar as though trying to get to the woman.

Quentin stepped forward and intervened. 'He's a rescue. We haven't had him long. Come on, Victor,' he cajoled, grasping the other side of Victor's collar.

As if realizing he wasn't going to get inside the house, Victor allowed himself to be led the few yards back to the car. As they neared it, Quentin relinquished his hold on the dog's collar to Wanda and looked back at the house. An upstairs curtain was pulled open, then quickly closed again, but not before Quentin found himself looking directly into the eyes of Philip Chandler.

'They're in there and Philip's seen us,' Quentin growled. His delight that his reasoning about the Chandlers being there had been correct was dowsed by the knowledge that their chance of surprising them had been foiled.

'Where's Colin?' he asked Wanda as they manoeuvred Victor into the car.

'I don't know.'

'What a fiasco,' Quentin said. 'They must know they've been rumbled. I'll bet they're planning to scarper. You stay here and if they come out the front way, drive after them. I'll go round the back.'

Without waiting for an answer, Quentin sprinted along to the alleyway and ran to the end, then turned onto the path that gave the houses rear access. He got to Dave's back gate just as it was flung open and Philip Chandler came tumbling out.

'Oh, no you don't,' Quentin muttered, throwing himself at Philip and stopping his progress.

Philip rebounded and dodged sideways, bringing his arms up in defence. Quentin prepared to lunge at him, but felt himself being pulled backwards. Will Chandler was stronger than his brother. His grip on Quentin's arms was vice-like, and Quentin felt fingers digging deep into his flesh. Philip recovered, moved forward and caught hold of Quentin's shoulders. With an almighty shove, they pushed Quentin over, his head grazing the wire fencing that bordered the path.

Winded and struggling to get up, Quentin looked round to see Will's hand, gripping a lump of wood, raised ready for a swipe at his head. Before Will could strike, he was thrown off balance by someone barging into him, sending him reeling into Philip and dropping the piece of wood in the process.

'Leave it, Will,' Quentin heard Philip say. 'Let's get out of here.'

Then the brothers were running, their footsteps resounding on the concrete path.

'Thanks,' Quentin gasped as Colin helped him to his feet. 'Never mind me. Get after the Chandlers.'

Colin did, but Quentin knew he wouldn't catch the fleeing men. He held on to the fence and pulled himself up, drew in several deep breaths, then began the chase. In a few minutes, he drew level with Colin.

'They turned right,' Colin panted as Quentin sped past him.

Quentin kept on, turning right at the next corner. The two men were halfway along the road, though Quentin could see they were flagging. Given another hundred yards, Quentin knew he would catch them, but he didn't have a hundred yards. The silver Mondeo came into view and the Chandlers reached it. Minutes later, Quentin stood panting as he watched the Chandlers drive past him and disappear round the corner.

'Bugger it!' he yelled, collapsing against a garden wall.

'Are you all right?' a pedestrian asked him.

'Yes, thanks,' he lied, and walked slowly back to meet Colin, whose run had diminished to a slow jog.

'They got away,' Colin said, unnecessarily.

'Yeah.'

Too tired to talk, they went back to Wanda, who was standing by the car. Victor's nose was pressed up against a back window.

'I called Philmore,' she told them. 'I'll call him back and tell him the Chandlers are on the move. It's pointless him coming here now.'

'Yes, I suppose,' Quentin said miserably. 'Still, at least I didn't get my head bashed in, thanks to Colin.'

'What *I* want to know,' Colin said, 'is why we chased them. I couldn't have caught them, and if you had, what would you have done? Sat on both of them in the street until the police turned up?'

Quentin shrugged. 'I'd have thought of something.' Would he, he wondered. OK, so he was younger and fitter than either of the Chandlers, but two against one?

'Cheer up, Quentin,' Wanda said. 'It was a good plan. It's not your fault they got away, and Victor didn't know what he was doing. Maybe he thought Dave was in there waiting for him. Anyway, as we're here, I vote we go in anyway. We may find something useful.'

Colin made a face. 'Such as?'

'We won't know unless we look,' Quentin said, warming to the idea. 'We'll go in the back way. The Chandlers left in a hurry. I bet they didn't stop to lock the back door.'

Quentin was right. Not only was the back door not locked, it was wide open when Quentin and Wanda got there, leaving Colin to comfort Victor and fend off curious neighbours.

'They've cleaned up a bit,' Quentin said as they went through the ground floor. The detritus that had littered the floor was still there, but it had been pushed into several heaps on either side, leaving a space in the middle and a pathway to the hall and stairs. In the kitchen, evidence of recent occupation remained on the counter, and the kettle was still warm. Upstairs, not much had been moved, except the mattress had been straightened and the quilt put in place. The things Quentin remembered seeing on the floor had been pushed aside.

'They didn't have time to take everything,' Wanda said, picking up a suit jacket and a tie from a bedroom chair. 'They just panicked and ran. Who do you think they recognized, you, me or Colin? I mean, they could see us all from that window, couldn't they? When Philip last saw me, I was disguised, so were you, but Colin was pretty much himself when we met Philip in Devon.'

'Dunno. I expect Victor spooked them first. Whatever, they know we're onto them. Better bring that jacket and tie, hand it over to Philmore as evidence that they were here.'

'You think we should? We'll get a right rollicking if he knows we've been in here.'

Quentin wasn't listening. His gaze had settled on something on the bedside cabinet, something he remembered from the last time he'd been here. He moved towards the cabinet and picked it up.

'A crossword book?' Wanda said, eyeing it curiously. 'The Chandlers were so sure they were safe here, they were doing crosswords?'

'No, Dave was. This was here before.'

'And? Is that significant?'

Quentin shook his head. 'Probably not. It's just… this page, the last crossword Dave was doing, it's only got two clues filled in.'

'So he fell asleep before he could finish it,' Wanda said, taking the book from him. 'Or perhaps he couldn't do the rest of it.'

She looked at the black and white grid on the page. 'Code,' she read aloud. 'And Trafalgar. They're just answers to clues. What are you thinking?'

'I'm not sure, but…' Quentin broke off. Something was tugging at his memory, nagging at it, but he couldn't think what it was. *CODE*. He'd seen that written somewhere recently. Where? He dredged his memory, going over the events of the last few days then shook his head.

'The Maserati!' Wanda cried out. 'The piece of paper you took from the glovebox. Didn't that say Code something?'

'Yes, that's it, Wanda, but I can't remember the rest and I've left it at home.'

Wanda pursed her lips. 'You think it's connected?'

'Could be. I mean, the clues are just random, but they would have jumped out at Dave if he'd sussed something on Property Perfections' system. Maybe there's a code to get into a certain computer or a file, and somehow he discovered it.'

Taking out his phone, Quentin photographed the page, berating himself for not doing so the first time he'd been there.

'Do you think we should bring Victor in?' Wanda asked. 'That was your original idea, to see if he sniffed anything out. It might help settle him too. He's pretty agitated; he might calm down when he sees Dave's not here.'

'It's worth a try, as we're here. It's not as if we're disturbing anything, or contaminating the scene. The Chandlers have already done that.'

Quentin left and returned with the retriever, who rushed in excitedly, going from room to room and sniffing at various things. He finished in the hall, where a lead hung from a hook by the door. He sat on the floor, looked up at Quentin and whined.

'Sorry, Victor old boy,' Quentin said, moved by the dog's pathetic whimpering. 'Your master's not here. Come on, let's go before the whole street wants to know what's going on.'

* * *

They were all back at Quentin's before his mobile rang.

'It's Philmore,' he said, raising his hand to stop them talking. This is it, he thought. They've spotted the Mondeo and arrested the Chandlers. So, after all he, Wanda and Colin had done, they wouldn't get the glory or the recognition they deserved. But if the Chandlers had been caught...

'We've got the Mondeo,' Philmore barked. 'It was abandoned outside Greenwich tube station. There's no sign of the Chandlers.'

Chapter Thirty-four

'So we're back to square one,' Colin said. 'The Chandlers probably jumped on a tube to who knows where. They could be miles away by now.'

'Yeah,' Quentin said. His disappointment that the brothers had got away had been eclipsed by apprehension.

How would Cultured Voice react when he learned that Quentin had found the Chandlers and let them get away?

The call came an hour later. Quentin was in Greenwich Park trying to clear his head when his mobile trilled. His spirits dipped further when he saw the number was withheld. So much for giving me another day, he thought. He considered not answering, ignoring this and all future calls from the man who, at the moment at least, was controlling his life. Knowing the risk was too high, he pressed the answer button.

'Yes?'

'Well, Mr Cadbury, did you find my former colleagues?'

'I did, yes.'

'Excellent–'

'But–' Quentin interrupted.

'Ah, there's a "but". How predictable. So what have you got to tell me, Mr Cadbury?'

'I tracked them down and almost got them, but…'

'They outwitted you and got away?'

'Not exactly.'

'How, exactly?'

'They didn't outwit me.'

'But they still got away?'

'Yes,' Quentin confessed, unwilling to reveal that it was a dog who'd ruined his plan.

'How disappointing. Well, I'm afraid I can't wait any longer. I'll have to make alternative arrangements to deal with the Chandlers. They still haven't had the courtesy to inform me what's happening or where they are. It just proves that you can't rely on anyone but yourself. And I think the truce between us is at an end. Watch yourself, Mr Cadbury, and the delectable Mrs Merrydrew.'

Quentin held on to the phone long after the conversation had ended. His heart pounded, his thoughts raced and his determination to find the Chandlers was renewed. He felt the urgency of the situation. He must find the Chandlers and bring them to justice, if only to get his nemesis off his back. A pang of guilt stabbed at him, and he cursed the man who had changed his need to find Dave Brown's killer into a need to protect himself and Wanda.

Colin was right, he realized with a heavy sigh. They were back to square one.

* * *

'It's all right, Quentin,' Wanda soothed when he gave her the gist of the conversation. 'We'll figure something out.'

'Yeah. Colin gone home?'

'Yes. He said to ring him if we have a lead on the Chandlers' whereabouts.'

Quentin felt a fresh cloud of gloom settling on him. Bloody hell, he thought. They were there, right in front of me, and they got away. So close, yet they might as well have been a million miles away.

'I must be losing my touch,' he mumbled, more to himself than Wanda. 'I mean, I've tackled villains before and won, but I couldn't even floor a couple of middle-aged men.'

'Stop it!' Wanda commanded. 'There were two of them, and they were desperate. Desperation makes people stronger. Stop feeling sorry for yourself and concentrate on our next move.'

'Where do you propose we start?' Quentin said bitterly. 'We haven't even got a car to track. Those two could be abroad by now.'

'No, they couldn't. They haven't had time, and all the airports and ferry ports are being watched. Anyway they'll need passports. Will may have had his with him, as he only came into the country recently, but Philip probably won't. He was already at work before he rushed off to The Hacienda and discovered that Lorna had escaped. We know he didn't go back to the office, and he wouldn't have risked going home knowing he'd been rumbled; so, as far as we know, he went straight to his ex-wife's. He may have picked Will up on the way.'

As far as they knew. Quentin thought there was probably a lot they didn't know, like whether Philip had been able to slip back to Chelsea to get his passport at any time. He didn't feel inclined to argue the point, and in his heart he knew Wanda was right. They should be trying to find a way forward.

But how?

* * *

After what seemed an age but was actually only fifteen minutes, Quentin's phone rang again. He brightened when he saw Tina's number.

'Hi, Quentin,' Tina said when he answered. 'Listen, I'm sorry I didn't tell you about Will Chandler coming here and leaving the Lexus in the car park. I honestly didn't think it was important.'

'It's all right, Tina. You've been a great help, really.'

'So are you any nearer to getting Philip?'

'No,' Quentin said, unable to face admitting, for the second time in a few hours, to letting Philip slip through his fingers. 'We're still working on it.'

'OK. Well, at least your journalist friend is OK. Such a shame about poor Dave. The more I think about it, the more I want his killer caught. Keep looking, won't you? Let me know if there's anything I can do.'

Her words rekindled Quentin's desire to see the killers and kidnappers brought to justice, if they were one and the same. Even if they weren't, Philmore had the photo of the kidnappers' car taken at The Hacienda. All Philmore had to do was alert the ANPR unit, so unless the two thugs who'd kidnapped Lorna hadn't used the car since then, they should have been picked up by now.

'They could have changed cars,' Wanda said when he voiced his thoughts. 'And just because they were hired to kidnap Lorna doesn't mean they're the ones who murdered Dave. Lorna may have got the wrong end of the stick when she heard them talking.'

Placing his hand on his forehead, Quentin gave a long moan.

'Bloody hell!' he almost yelled. 'I'm getting brain-ache, with all these suspects. Boatman, the Chandlers, the kidnappers and possibly separate murderers as well.'

'You forgot Cultured Voice,' Wanda reminded him. 'Perhaps we should have stayed in the Scilly Isles.'

Quentin knew she didn't believe that any more than he did, but her slightly scathing tone jerked him out of his self-absorption.

'OK, ma'am,' he said with false cheeriness. 'Let's get our thinking caps on.'

* * *

Thirty minutes later, Quentin rang Philmore. 'Any developments?' he asked.

'Not really,' Philmore replied, sounding fraught. 'We traced the Vauxhall you photographed on Monday. Officers have been to the registered owner's address but nobody was there. I've applied for a search warrant. The car's parked nearby, so either the guy's walking or using another car. Maybe he's using his mate's car, the bloke who was with him at The Hacienda.'

'Right,' Quentin said, seeing another brick wall appearing to block his chance of catching any of the criminals. 'I don't suppose you're going to share the address?'

'No. And I've got to go.'

The call was cut off and Quentin felt a stab of annoyance. He realized that though the police were grateful for any information the public could give them, this arrangement was strictly one-way. Philmore would be in trouble if he was heard discussing an ongoing case with anyone outside the force. But to cut him off so abruptly…

He flung the phone down just as it rang again. He didn't recognize the number.

'Quentin? It's DS Francis. The chief's been called away. I'm just letting you know the Vauxhall's registered to a Joseph Walters.' Francis's tone was curt. Quentin knew she didn't believe in giving information to a private investigator, no matter how helpful they'd been. Reading between the lines, he guessed Philmore had given his approval.

'It's a flat in Peckham,' Francis went on. 'The owner of the music shop underneath says Walters hasn't been there since Monday afternoon. He says he'll let us know if he comes back, but we're not holding our breath. Chances are he's done a runner, perhaps his mate as well, if they've found out Lorna's escaped. She's seen them so she can identify them. She's coming in later to look at our mugshots, see if she can ID him and spot the other guy who took her to The Hacienda.'

'Can you tell me the name of the music shop owner?'

Silence.

'Come on, Debbie, you should know you can trust us by now.'

'It's Mustafa,' Francis said after a moment's hesitation. 'Mustafa Mamet.'

'Thanks. Don't worry, no one will know where this information came from.'

'Yes, well, we're short-handed as always. Get back to us immediately if you find anything, and I do mean immediately.'

'I will. Anything on the Chandlers?'

'No.'

'OK, Debbie, thanks.'

As the call ended, Quentin realized she hadn't given him the full address. Perhaps she thought that was a step too far.

'Joseph Walters,' he told Wanda. 'A flat above a music shop in Peckham, and the owner's called Mustafa Mamet.'

'I'll check it out,' Wanda said, going to Quentin's computer. It was several minutes before she looked up.

'This must be it. Mustafa's Music Emporium. Doesn't sound as though they sell grand pianos.'

She jotted down the address then glanced at her watch. 'The shop'll be closed by the time we get there, and the owner obviously doesn't live on the premises if Joe Walters lives in the flat above.'

'Yeah. Anyway, I'm supposed to be looking for the Chandlers.'

'I know, Quentin, but we've got no clue as to their whereabouts, and even if the kidnappers aren't important to Cultured Voice, they are to us and Lorna, especially if they're the ones who killed Dave.'

'You're right, Wanda. But if they've done a runner, we could be heading into a dead end. Still, I suppose we might learn something if we talk to the shop owner, or...'

Quentin tailed off, recalling the detective sergeant's words. *We're short-handed as always. Get back to us immediately if you find anything.* Was she suggesting that she, and possibly Philmore, were expecting him to act on the information about Joe Walters? Of course, she'd deny it, but as far as Quentin was concerned it was a green light. His ego swelled. The Metropolitan Police needed their help.

'Come on,' he said, jumping up. 'We'll go and find this place. It'll be better than sitting here doing nothing.'

'Now? We've been on the go since six o'clock this morning. I thought we agreed the shop would be closed when we get there?'

'What else can we do at the moment? The Chandlers disappeared at a busy underground station. They could be in John o'Groats by now, or on a yacht in some secluded marina. I should be tired, but being so close to them and letting them slip away is still bugging me. You don't have to come with me, but I'm going.'

Wanda stood up. 'We'd better take the dogs then. Anything could happen when you're in this mood.'

Chapter Thirty-five

It was nearly seven o'clock before they arrived at the music shop. There were posters of old pop stars and bands in the window, and through a gap between them, in the street lamplight, they could see racks of CDs, although most of the space was filled with records, mainly LPs.

'Very retro,' Quentin muttered as they walked back over the road to their car.

'Yes. Vinyl's getting very popular. Collectors pay a lot for it if it's in good condition.'

'Do they?' Quentin thought of his mother's collection of records, left with him when she'd emigrated and still languishing in a corner of his second bedroom. He hadn't had the heart to get rid of them. Truth be told, although he had no means of playing them, he remembered with affection the many times he'd heard them during his childhood.

'OK,' Wanda said, breaking his reverie. 'So now we know where Joe Walters lives, but he hasn't been here since Monday afternoon. That's two days. What are the chances of him coming back now?'

Quentin shrugged. 'Depends how much he knows. I mean, if he knows Lorna's escaped, practically no chance. If he doesn't, why would he worry? After all, even if she was released and gave the police his description, he wouldn't necessarily be found in a city the size of London. Neither of the kidnappers know I took their number plate, and as far as we know, they don't know they nearly set The Hacienda on fire. As far as they're concerned, they were paid to do a job and they've done it.'

'Well,' Wanda said, 'the place is in darkness so there's obviously nobody here. I vote we get a takeaway and go to Colin's. It's not too much further than going home. We'll come back in the morning and speak to Mustafa, or whoever's running the shop. We can—'

Wanda stopped, grabbed Quentin's arm and nodded towards the music shop. A light had come on and a man stood framed in the open doorway.

They leapt simultaneously out of the car and dashed across the road, eliciting an angry toot from an oncoming vehicle. They were behind the emerging man before he had time to walk away after locking the shop door.

'Excuse us,' Quentin said, judging him to be in his early fifties. 'Are you the owner or manager of this shop?'

'Yes,' said the man, eying him warily. 'I don't keep cash on the premises.'

Mustafa, if that's who this was, may have had a Middle Eastern name and dark-eyed Middle Eastern looks, but his accent was pure London.

Wanda stepped forward, smiling at him. 'Sorry, we didn't mean to startle you. We're looking for Mustafa.'

'Why?'

'We just want to ask him about the man who lives upstairs.'

'Ah.' A look of understanding settled on the man's face. 'I'm Mustafa, and I don't know where Joe is.'

'OK,' Quentin said, 'but we just wondered if you knew somewhere he might go, you know, any of his usual haunts, or a friend or relative he might be staying with.'

'No, I don't. If I did, I'd have been after him myself. Owes me six months' rent. What's it got to do with you?'

'We're friends of someone who's anxious to find him,' Quentin said.

'Why?' Mustafa asked again. 'What's he done? The police have been asking about him too. They're getting a warrant to search the flat.'

'We think he hurt a friend of ours,' Wanda ventured.

'Hurt? You mean he duffed somebody up?'

'Yes, our friend Lorna.'

'He hit a woman?'

'Yes,' said Quentin, thinking of Lorna's bruised eye and swollen face.

'Always was a vicious bastard,' Mustafa said vehemently. 'Bashed the kitchen door in during one of his rants. Should have evicted him months ago, but...' Mustafa shifted uncomfortably. 'Well, he's bigger than me, and eviction orders take forever. Bloody thug.'

My sentiments exactly, Quentin thought. 'You have keys to the flat, presumably,' he said.

'So? I'm not letting you in there before the police. Can't afford to get on the wrong side of the law. It's hard enough trying to make an honest living round here as it is.'

'The police needn't know,' Wanda said. 'Who's going to tell them? If they find out, you can say we took the keys and let ourselves in when you weren't looking.'

'I don't know,' Mustafa said, uncertainly.

'Can we talk inside?' Wanda asked, smiling at him again.

After a moment's hesitation, Mustafa unlocked the door and gestured them in. The shop smelled musty, and several piles of long-playing records were gathering dust on a cabinet.

'Look,' Quentin said, deciding to come clean, 'the truth is we're private investigators and we're trying to help the lady who Joe hurt. We know you shouldn't let us in there and we don't want to get you into trouble. Why don't you leave the keys on the counter and nip to the loo? We'll pinch the keys and have a quick look round upstairs. Or come with us if you like. It's your property after all. We'll cooperate fully with the police when we need to, but why wait when we might find something to give us a clue as to where Joe is?'

Mustafa looked from Wanda to Quentin and back to Wanda, as if trying to decide what to do.

'I'll take the lady up,' he said to Quentin when Wanda produced a business card. 'You stay here.'

Quentin was about to protest, but a look from Wanda stopped him.

'It's all right,' Wanda said. 'Thank you, Mustafa, that'll be fine.'

Quentin handed her a pair of the surgical gloves he'd brought with him and watched as she followed Mustafa to the back of the shop and through an archway, then heard them climbing the stairs. Honestly, he thought, do I look like I'm about to trash the flat or steal something? Still, can't be too careful, I suppose. Maybe he's had trouble before.

Perching on a stool, he glanced around him. The place was painted in cheerful colours, mainly orange and green, though its brightness was dimmed by at least several years of wear and tear as well as dust. The paintwork was pitted in places and the flooring was worn. Quentin wondered if the flat was in a similar condition.

Wanda returned first, while Mustafa locked up the flat.

'Anything?'

'Not much, but I photographed a few things. I left everything exactly as I found it.'

When Mustafa joined them, Quentin shook his hand and Wanda gave him her warmest smile.

'That's been a great help,' Quentin told him, though he had no idea whether it had or not.

'And,' Wanda said, 'there's no need to mention this to the police, is there? We'll tell them if we need to, and we won't implicate you.'

'I hope not,' Mustafa said.

'You should let the police know immediately if he comes back, but please would you ring us too?' Wanda added. 'You've got our card.'

Mustafa gave an acquiescent nod.

'Poor guy,' Wanda said when they were back in the car. 'It can't be easy for him.'

'No, probably not. Let's get some food. I'm starving.'

Chapter Thirty-six

'So fill me in on what you found at the flat,' Colin said, helping himself to a plateful of tandoori chicken. 'Makes a change for you to keep me in the loop. Glad you brought this in. I couldn't be bothered to cook.'

Twenty minutes later, they were on Colin's settee, scrolling through the photos Wanda had taken in the flat.

'I couldn't find a passport or a driving license,' she said.

'He may not have a passport,' Colin pointed out. 'At least not a current one.'

'There's this, though,' Wanda said, jabbing a finger at an image and enlarging it. 'It's his rent book. Mustafa was right – he hasn't paid his rent for six months. Looks like he was short of money.'

'He wasn't short of money when he went back there on Monday,' Quentin said darkly. 'I saw Will Chandler pay him, and his mate.'

'Well,' Colin put in. 'If he can deprive Lorna of her freedom, then six months' rent is hardly going to worry him.'

'Then there's this,' Wanda said swiping across to the next picture. It was a court summons, issued to Joseph Benjamin Walters for non-payment of maintenance to his ex-wife for the care of their son.

'Crikey,' Colin said. 'Looks like he owed money all over the place.'

'That's about it, except for this,' Wanda said. 'It's a telephone number.'

Quentin stared at the image. It was a London number, with the name Lauren written next to it.

'Lauren,' Quentin mused. 'A girlfriend, do you think?'

Wanda gave a derogatory laugh. 'Well,' she said, 'any woman going out with him must be either as bad as he is or blind to his actions.'

'Hmm. What do we reckon then?' Quentin asked after several minutes' silence. 'Is he staying with her?'

'There's only one way to find out,' Wanda said.

'What?' Colin demanded, looking from her to Quentin. 'Are you thinking what I think you're thinking?'

'Why not?' Quentin said. 'We've taken a gamble on a random phone call before and it's paid off.'

Colin removed his glasses and cleaned them with the bottom of his shirt.

'It won't work,' he declared, shaking his head. 'What can you say to her? "Sorry to trouble you, but have you got a kidnapper, possibly even a murderer, living with you?"'

'We'll think of something,' Quentin said unconvincingly.

'I already have,' Wanda said.

Colin eyed her quizzically. 'Come on then, spill.'

'Well,' Wanda began, 'we know he's divorced, probably because his wife had the sense to get rid of him—'

'Oh no,' Colin interrupted, closing his eyes as if in despair. 'You're not going pretend to be his ex-wife.'

'Not many people have a voice like yours, Wanda,' Quentin said. 'He'll know his wife's voice. Even if they've not been together for years, he'll recognize her voice.'

'*He* will,' Wanda agreed, 'but it's Lauren's number. She might not even know his wife. Let's face it, if he hasn't paid her maintenance for months, he's probably trying to avoid her. I could be his wife ringing to chase it up.'

'But his wife might not know about Lauren,' Colin said, 'so how would she know Lauren's number?'

'I know it's a gamble,' Wanda said. 'But I think it's worth a try.'

She looked at the photo of the court order again. 'Non-payment of maintenance to Jane Margaret Walters in respect of their son Bradley Kevin Walters. Jane. That's a good name – no abbreviations usually. Let's hope she hasn't got a nickname or something.'

Ignoring Colin's hostile expression, she picked up her mobile and punched in the number.

'I've still got the number withheld setting on,' she said, switching the phone to loudspeaker as she pressed the call button.

It was several seconds before a female voice said, 'Hello?'

'Lauren?' Wanda lifted her voice above its usual low tone.

'Yes. Who's this?'

'It's Jane. Is Joe with you?'

'Why?' Lauren sounded enraged. 'You're divorced, in case you've forgotten.'

'I haven't forgotten.'

'Well, he's not here, and he wouldn't want to speak to you if he was.'

'Look, Lauren, he hasn't paid my maintenance for months, and Brad–'

'You're lying. He's up to date with the payments. I should know – I gave him the money.'

Wanda feigned a coughing fit. 'Sorry,' she said. 'I've got a cold. Did you say you gave him the money?'

'Yes, and I didn't do it for you, I did it for his son.'

'Well, we didn't receive it and the court has issued a summons.'

They heard the sharp intake of Lauren's breath. 'I don't believe you. You're just trying to get more money out of him, you greedy bitch. Why don't you leave us alone?'

'Listen, Lauren, I don't want you to go through what I went through. Can I come and see you and we can talk this over, woman to woman.'

'No you bloody well can't!' Lauren yelled. 'Don't come anywhere near here.'

Wanda gave an exaggerated sigh. 'Well, it's up to you, but he's lying to you and I can prove it.'

There was a moment's silence. 'What do you mean?'

'I've got a copy of the court summons. I can bring it over and show you. I mean, if he didn't use your money to pay the maintenance, what did he use it for?'

Another silence.

'I know Joe,' Wanda went on in the same false voice. 'If you ask him about it, he'll deny it, but if I bring the court summons over, he won't be able to deny it.'

'You can't come here.' Lauren's voice quavered a little.

'No, of course not. I'll meet you somewhere nearby. Is there a café or somewhere we could talk?'

There was a pause, as though Lauren was considering this. 'I work at the Blue Tomato,' she said at length. 'You could meet me there. It's in Basin Street.'

'Basin Street?'

'Yes. Lewisham.'

'OK. Can I come tomorrow?'

'I start at eleven. Come before the lunchtime rush.' Lauren's tone hardened. 'And if I find out you're lying, I'll have the law on you.'

'I'm not lying,' Wanda assured her. 'Bye, Lauren. See you tomorrow.'

Both Quentin and Colin looked at her in admiration as she hung up.

'You should be a politician, Wanda, making up things like that on the spot,' Colin told her.

'Give me a few years,' Wanda teased. 'You might see me in parliament yet.'

* * *

Having accepted Colin's offer to stay, Quentin woke the next morning disorientated by his surroundings. Wanda wasn't there, and when he'd blinked the sleep from his eyes, he sat up and checked his phone. He'd half-expected a call from Cultured Voice to brag that he'd found the Chandlers and dealt with them, but to his relief, there were no missed calls.

'I'm coming with you,' Colin informed them when they were ready to leave. 'No arguments. I spent hours cramped up in a car thanks to this bloke and his kidnapping, not to mention creeping round The Hacienda in the dark. If there's a chance of catching him, I want to be there.'

'In that case, we might as well take your car,' Quentin said.

Having found the postcode for the Blue Tomato online, they left Wanstead and reached Lewisham just after ten-thirty. They found the café and parked nearby.

'Stay here for a bit,' Quentin said to Wanda and Colin. 'I want to check the place out.'

'Why?' Wanda asked. 'Lauren won't be there yet. She doesn't start till eleven.'

Quentin shrugged. He didn't really have an answer. He just had an uneasy feeling that the meeting wouldn't be straightforward.

'Lauren may have told Joe about your call, Wanda,' he said. 'Better safe than sorry, and I want to get the layout of the place in case we have to leave in a hurry.'

He walked the few minutes to the Blue Tomato. An aroma of frying bacon emanated from it as he approached. He stopped, ostensibly to read the menu, which boasted morning coffee, snacks, light lunches and afternoon teas. Surreptitiously, he glanced through the window, noticing a young man and a girl who looked to be no more than teenagers behind the counter. He swept his gaze around the various tables. There was no one he thought resembled Joe Walters. He checked again, realizing he'd only seen him from a distance and in the half-light of dawn. He turned to go back to the car, then froze. Coming towards him was the man he'd seen at The Hacienda.

Chapter Thirty-seven

Despite the distant view he'd had of him, Quentin recognized Joe Walters immediately. It was the same muscular build and loping stride. He quickly swung round and darted into the nearest doorway, a florist next to the café, and then wondered why. Joe Walters wouldn't know who he was. He'd never seen Quentin. Nevertheless, Quentin remained still until Walters was inside the café. Why is he here, he thought. Had his hunch been right? Had Lauren let on that, as she thought, she was meeting Joe's ex-wife? Or had Joe got it out of her somehow? He pictured Lorna's bruised face and wondered if Lauren had been subjected to the same treatment.

Torn, he tried to think what to do. Would the man stay in the café? Venturing past the window, he saw Walters take a seat at a rear table. Quentin whipped out his phone and texted Wanda.

Joe Walters just gone into café. No sign of Lauren.
Going in.

Taking a deep breath, he pocketed the phone and pushed the café door open. He took a seat where he could see Walters and studied the menu. The young man he'd seen behind the counter went to Walters' table.

The place was quiet, and Quentin could hear what was being said above the hiss of the coffee machine.

'What can I get you?' Quentin heard the young man ask Walters.

'Nothin' yet, I'm waiting for someone,' came the surly reply. Walters sat, tapping his fingers on the table, a dark expression on his hard face and his eyes fixed on the door.

The young man approached Quentin.

'What would you like?' he asked.

'Just coffee for the moment, please.'

Quentin watched as the young man moved back behind the counter, spoke to his colleague, then attended to another customer who was waiting to pay his bill. As he handed the customer his receipt, the phone rang, and the young man went through a swing door, which presumably led to the kitchen. A few minutes later, he reappeared.

'Lauren's not coming in,' he said to the girl who was dispensing coffee from the machine. 'I've called the boss. She'll have to come in or we won't be doing lunches.'

Quentin frowned. Lauren wasn't coming in, but Walters was here. It confirmed Quentin's hunch that Walters had found out about the phone call, supposedly from his ex-wife, and had come to confront her.

Quentin wasn't sure whether to wait until Walters realized that she wasn't coming, and follow him home before calling Philmore, or call Philmore now. After a short deliberation, he texted Wanda.

Lauren not coming. Walters waiting for his ex. Call Philmore. I'll follow Walters if he leaves.

There was a selection of newspapers by the counter, and after his coffee arrived he collected one and made a show of reading it. Between sips of coffee and turning the pages, he glanced at Walters. Eleven o'clock came and went. By twenty past, Walters was getting visibly agitated.

A few more customers came in, and after taking their orders, the young waiter asked Walters again if he wanted anything.

'Coffee!' Walters barked, drawing surprised looks from the people at the next table.

The front door opened and Walters stared at it as if in anticipation. He brought his fist down on the table when he saw an older woman enter and go straight behind the counter. The boss, Quentin assumed.

Walters stood up, strode to the door and went out, not bothering to cancel his order for coffee. He stopped on the pavement, and Quentin saw him punching a number into a mobile phone. The call apparently wasn't answered, because Walters' lips didn't move and he lowered the phone and resumed his striding.

Quentin threw a five-pound note on the counter and flew out the door. Seeing Walters ahead, he followed, praying that his quarry was going to Lauren's and that she lived close by. If Walters was heading to a vehicle, he'd lose him. Quentin kept a discreet distance while Walters, seemingly deep in thought, strode purposefully along, away from the main road and into the side streets. After several turns, he stopped, then went into a house halfway down a road without looking in Quentin's direction.

Breaking into a run, Quentin raced to the house he thought Walters had gone into. The one with the lamp post outside, he told himself. He stopped at the lamp post and gazed at the house. Was it this one? The houses were flat-fronted, in long terraces, broken by narrow walkways for rear access every so often. Edging towards the house nearest the lamp post, he could hear raised voices from inside. He couldn't make out what was said, but one was definitely a woman's and the other sounded like Walters' had when he'd shouted from the steps of The Hacienda.

Quentin pulled out his phone and called Wanda.

'The police are on their way,' she told him when she answered. 'Philmore's trying to get here–'

'He's left the café,' Quentin interrupted, looking at the number on the door in front of him. 'I think he's with Lauren. 37–'

He broke off, realizing he hadn't noticed the name of the road.

'Hold on a minute,' he said, running to the nearest corner. 'It's 37 Walnut Road. Tell Philmore.'

Not waiting for a reply, he sprinted back to number thirty-seven. A few pedestrians passed him, and he walked on a little, thinking it might look odd hanging around in the same spot. He turned and walked back, passing number thirty-seven and hoping Walters wouldn't come out again before the police arrived. He paced up and down, wondering whether he should take action now, but at that moment, he saw someone overtake another pedestrian and come towards him. Wanda. His heart lifted as she reached him. He nodded to number thirty-seven, and was just turning to face her when he saw the blue and yellow markings of a police car as it nosed its way onto double yellow lines by the corner of the road.

'I'll go and find out if they're here for Joe and if they're going in straight away,' Wanda said, and walked briskly up to the police car.

When she didn't return, Quentin guessed she was trying to explain their connection to the case. The tide turned when a dark-blue Audi drew up and Philmore and DS Francis got out.

Quentin flinched as a scream from number thirty-seven filled the air. Without waiting for Philmore, Quentin rushed forward and knocked on the door as hard as he could. Then everything happened at once. The police car hurtled down the road, blue lights flashing, and stopped directly opposite number thirty-seven. Four uniformed officers spilled out onto the pavement.

'The woman's screaming,' Quentin told Philmore as he came running up to him.

Philmore immediately ordered two of the officers to cover the rear of the premises, then gestured to the others to stand by. The screaming had ceased, and Quentin could no longer hear raised voices. He prayed that his knocking had stopped whatever Walters was doing to Lauren. He stood back as Philmore gestured to the two remaining officers to break down the door. They'd only managed one charge before Walters came racing out of an adjacent walkway and fled down the road, followed by the two uniformed cops.

While Philmore cursed, Quentin took off in pursuit, his long legs and running experience enabling him to overtake the pursuing officers in minutes. Walters had reached the corner before Quentin caught up with him. Felling him in a rugby tackle, Quentin felt a sharp pain shoot up his thigh as his knee hit the concrete. Walters was strong, though, and he threw Quentin off and made to get up. Too late. The two cops were there, either side of him, catching hold of his arms and holding him fast. Philmore came up behind him with the two remaining officers. They hoisted the wanted man to his feet as he struggled to get free of his captors.

'Get off me,' Walters snarled.

Philmore rounded on him.

'Are you Joseph Walters?' he asked.

'Yes, he is.'

Quentin looked at the woman who'd come up beside Philmore. The cut on her face was still oozing blood. Lauren, Quentin assumed.

Philmore looked directly at the man Lauren was glowering at. 'Joseph Benjamin Walters, you're under arrest for the kidnapping of Lorna West and on suspicion of the murder of David Brown.'

At the mention of Dave Brown's name, Walters stopped struggling, his eyes widening.

'Rubbish!' he spat. 'You can't prove I killed that bloke.'

The fact that Walters knew who Dave Brown was, and because he didn't immediately deny it, was proof enough for Quentin.

A small knot of onlookers had emerged from nearby houses, and were gathered a short distance away. They parted as a thin, balding man with dark-framed glasses, being pulled by two dogs, pushed through them.

'Get your filthy 'ands off me, friggin' coppers!' Walters shouted, pulling against the hands that held him. Then he recoiled as a golden retriever loped up to him, growled and began barking.

'Victor!' Quentin called.

Victor carried on barking and growling, baring his teeth in a way Quentin had never seen before. Walters kicked out at him, catching Victor on his injured leg. Victor yelped in pain but didn't move. He resumed barking and growling, and Quentin knew without a doubt that this man had been there when Dave was killed. Whether it was him or his mate who had wielded the knife was yet to be proven, but from the way Walters had kicked out so brutally at Victor, Quentin was willing to bet it was him.

'There's your proof,' Quentin said to Philmore.

It was Debbie Francis who answered. 'Shame he can't talk,' she said. 'But if there's any more evidence to find, we'll find it.'

'All right, Sergeant,' Philmore said to Francis. 'Let's get him back to the station where we can question him properly.' He turned to one of the uniformed officers. 'Read him his rights and take him in.'

Chapter Thirty-eight

'Lucky you brought Victor along,' Quentin said when they were back at Colin's. 'Just at the right time too, Colin.'

'Oh yeah,' Colin said, his voice heavy with sarcasm, 'Mr Just-in-Time, that's me. Anyway, luck had nothing to do with it. Dogs have an amazing sense of smell and long memories. I knew that if Walters was there when Dave was killed, then Victor would sniff him out. An educated calculation, you might say.'

'Ahem.' This came from Wanda, who said no more but looked askance at Colin.

'Oh, all right,' Colin continued. 'It was Wanda's idea. She texted me and told me you'd found Walters and to bring Victor. But if I hadn't insisted on going with you this morning, Victor wouldn't have been there.'

'Joint effort, then,' Quentin said, deciding to be magnanimous now that they'd had at least one good result from their efforts. 'Lorna was over the moon when I told her we'd caught one of the kidnappers.'

The conversation dwindled as they finished the fish and chips they'd bought on the way back from Lewisham. Quentin dowsed his few remaining chips with vinegar, his mood alternating between elation, disappointment and apprehension. In spite of the successful capture of Walters, he was disappointed at their failure to track down the Chandler brothers, and apprehensive about the possible backlash from Cultured Voice.

'Where the hell are they?' he mused aloud.

'Who?' Colin asked.

'He means the Chandlers,' Wanda said.

Colin pushed away his empty plate. 'We've been through this a thousand times. They could be anywhere.'

'Hmm.' Quentin looked at Wanda. 'Any ideas, Wanda?'

'Yes. I vote we go home and leave Colin in peace.'

'You can stay if you like, Wanda love,' Colin assured her.

'Thanks, Colin, but we've invaded your space for long enough. We'll go home. It doesn't look as if there's anything else we can do at the moment. We'll ring you if anything comes up.'

'OK,' Colin said. 'But make sure you do.'

* * *

Back in Greenwich, Quentin's feeling of incompleteness persisted. His mind kept straying to places he thought the Chandlers could be hiding out and coming up with nothing. The only possible escape route he knew about was the plane at Loddonfield airfield. Was it really only yesterday that they'd been told the aircraft would be out of action for at least two days? Two days. That would make it tomorrow, Friday, before it could be flown. Could the Chandlers wait that long? Or would they decide to risk staying in Britain until the heat was off?

'Bugger it,' he muttered, pouring himself a whisky. Magpie strolled in from the kitchen, his attitude still lukewarm after Quentin's recent spell of absences. He stared at Quentin haughtily when Quentin cursed again.

'No need to get on your high horse, boy,' Quentin told him. 'How would you feel if you caught all the baby rats but you knew the king rat had got away? Anyway–'

The ringing of his phone made him stop. 'Hello,' he said gruffly, not bothering to check the display.

'Quentin, it's Lorna. Someone's just sent our newsdesk footage of a small plane trying to take off from Loddonfield airfield. They didn't make it – they crashed into the perimeter fence. The footage shows two men abandoning the plane and running towards the trees. The thing is, it was still semi-light, but Loddonfield's not manned after sunset, so they had the place to themselves.'

'Bloody hell!' Quentin gasped, his brain working overtime. 'Have you told Philmore?'

'About to, but I thought I'd let you know first, seeing as you're the one who tracked down one of my kidnappers. Now that the villain's been caught, it might be easier to flush out the other one.'

'Yes, maybe. Why are you working when you should be taking it easy? I know – journalists are always at work. How long since the plane crash?'

'Not long. It was taken on a mobile phone. The covering message said "a few minutes ago" and it was sent in at eight-twenty.'

'So they could still be in the area. OK, Lorna, thanks.'

Setting down his untouched whisky, he called Wanda.

'Hope you weren't planning on an early night,' he said when she answered. 'We're off to Basingstoke.'

* * *

'Why are we going to the airfield?' Wanda asked as they left Greenwich in Quentin's BMW. 'It's two hours to Basingstoke. Anything could happen in that time.'

'I know, but…'

'You'd rather go on a wild goose chase than sit at home doing nothing?' Wanda suggested. 'How do we know it's definitely them? I mean, their plane was out of action, wasn't it?'

'It's got to be them. It's too much of a coincidence. And we don't know what part the engineers were waiting for. If it could still fly, the Chandlers may have decided to risk it. Or maybe they stole someone else's plane. They only need to get across the Channel, then they can disappear. Given that they dumped their car at the underground, they could have taken the train to the airport.'

'Philip Chandler on a train, after his Maserati and Lexus? Still, any port in a storm.'

'Exactly. Then again, they might have hired a car. Are those two all right in the back?'

'Yes. Mozart wasn't impressed – he'd just settled down for the evening – but Victor's OK. I think he's used to going out late at night.'

'Yeah, probably,' Quentin said, remembering that it must have been very late when Dave was killed. 'Anyway, for goodness sake, ring Colin, or he'll accuse us of leaving him out again.'

There was no reply to Wanda's call, so she sent Colin a text instead.

At this time of evening, the M25 was reasonably quiet, and they made good time. It was nearly ten-thirty when they got to Loddonfield. In the airfield lights, the scene was clear. The stricken plane stood askew at the end of the runway, one of its wings partially torn off. The local police were in evidence, as were some airfield staff, presumably still on the premises or called back after the crash. A knot of local journalists, cameras and phones at the ready, stood a way off.

They approached a journalist, a middle-aged man with a tired look about him. Wanda gave him one of her special smiles.

'Hello,' she said easily. 'Lily North, Associated Press. I was in the area when I heard about this. What happened?'

'Not sure exactly,' the reporter replied. 'They think joyriders. They chose the wrong plane though. One of the airport staff said it wasn't airworthy, and they were keeping it grounded until they'd fixed it.'

'Joyriders? They'll have them on CCTV, won't they?'

'Hopefully,' the man said, shrugging.

'How did they start it?' Wanda persisted. 'Wouldn't they have needed a key or something?'

The reporter looked at her. 'I can see you haven't covered this sort of thing before. It's a Cessna single-engine, so yes, it needs a key to start it.'

Wanda fixed an innocent gaze on him. 'You've got me, this *is* my first time covering an air incident. Don't you have to have permission to take off and land? Obviously not joyriders, but if you have a plane here?'

'Qualified pilots can come and go in their own plane when they like, but they're supposed to let the staff know beforehand.'

'Oh.' Wanda nodded towards the broken aircraft. 'What about the pilot?'

'Two blokes, apparently, but some guy who filmed it said they didn't look like kids.'

'So where are they now? Hospital?'

The reporter rolled his shoulders. 'They couldn't have been hurt much. Ran off, apparently. The cops have mounted a search but no news on that front as yet.'

'Just a question of wait and see then. OK, thanks. I'll call this in.'

She took out her mobile and photographed the plane, then she whirled away, punching random keys as though making a call.

The journalist stared after her, then gave Quentin a questioning look.

'Women!' Quentin said, shaking his head. 'We're supposed to be on holiday, but you reporters are always working, aren't you? Can't leave it alone.'

He swung round and trailed after Wanda. 'Was that really necessary?' he queried when he caught her up. 'You could have charmed the information out of him without pretending to be the press.'

'I thought he'd speak more freely to a fellow reporter,' she explained. 'It worked, didn't it?'

'Yeah. So either Will Chandler had a spare aircraft key or he somehow got it from wherever it was kept here. Or maybe Philip had a key.'

'Well, it didn't do them much good. Now they'll be on the police radar for taking an aircraft without the proper protocol or precautions. They've done exactly what they didn't want – drawn attention to themselves.'

'Yeah,' Quentin said again. He wondered if Philmore would turn up, then decided he wouldn't. There was no point now the Chandlers had done their disappearing trick again. The local police were already making a search.

'They must be desperate,' he carried on. 'Lorna said the footage was sent in at eight-twenty. So say the crash happened at about eight-ten – that's over two and a half hours ago. They'll be long gone if they hired a car, but on foot… I mean, they were seen running into the trees, so if they couldn't find their way back to the car before the police arrived, they may not have gone too far.'

'Hmm. Well, come on, clever clogs – you brought us all the way down here. Now what? I don't feel like a two-hour drive home.'

'Nor do I,' Quentin admitted. 'We'll get a hotel for the night.'

The journalists were beginning to trickle away and uniformed police officers were sectioning off the affected area with tape. Realizing there was nothing else they could do that night, they went back to the car, which they'd parked next to one of the police vehicles. They were just trying to decide where to look for a hotel when two police officers walked up to the car next to them.

'Oh good,' Wanda said, winding down the window. 'Excuse me, officer, can you tell me where would be the best place to find a hotel for the night?'

'There's plenty in Basingstoke,' said the nearer of the two. 'There's definitely a Premier Inn. You could try that.'

'Thank you,' Wanda said.

The young officer turned as his colleague, a WPC, looked up from her police radio and called to him.

'Forget about going home, Paul. Looks like it's a night for joyriders. We've just had a report of a boat being stolen from its mooring on the riverside.'

'That's not on our patch,' the young officer complained, then gave a resigned sigh as he fell into the police car.

Chapter Thirty-nine

'Don't make it too obvious,' Wanda said as Quentin floored the accelerator and they hurtled after the police car.

'Why not? You're from the press aren't you? Why wouldn't you go after another story?'

'Ha ha. I don't think I'll say that, not to the police.'

'Anyway,' Quentin said, 'it might not be the Chandlers. It could really be joyriders this time.'

Wanda shook her head. 'If you believed that, you wouldn't be following a police car in a strange place at eleven o'clock at night. Better ring Philmore.'

Before Wanda could place the call, her mobile rang.

'Hello, Colin ... No, they'd fled the airfield by the time we got there ... We're en route to a river near Basingstoke ... A boat's been reported stolen ... The map says the River Loddon ... Yes, Old Basing, apparently ... Not really, just following our noses, but we think it's them ... OK, Colin. Bye.'

Keeping hold of her phone, Wanda rang Philmore. Quentin listened as she explained where they were going and why, as well as promising to contact him as soon as they were sure it was the Chandlers who'd taken the boat.

When the police stopped outside an expensive-looking property, exited the car and went to the front gate, Quentin and Wanda pulled up a little way behind them. As if waiting for the police to arrive, a man was at the gate and opened it for them. A woman joined them, and the four of them walked around the side of the house to the back. The houses here were well-spaced, and from where he'd parked the car, Quentin could see a path at the side of the property. Minutes later, he and Wanda were walking down the path which, as Quentin had suspected, led to the water. The gardens of the houses sloped down to the riverbank, and at this moment were lit by a security light activated by the couple they'd seen, accompanied by the two police officers.

It was quiet and the night was still. The woman's voice, raised in obvious agitation, carried through the air.

'...thought we saw the security light go on,' she was saying, gesturing vaguely above her head. 'We thought it might be a cat, or a fox, so we didn't rush out.'

'That's right,' the man boomed. 'Looked out from the bedroom window later and saw the boat wasn't there. Blasted yobs. Hope they fall in the river and drown!'

Unobserved, Quentin and Wanda stood stock-still, watching and listening. The two cops looked to where the man pointed. The male officer gripped a pole and peered down the slight incline into the river, as if expecting to see the imprint of the boat's keel on the water.

'So where would they go from here?' the female officer asked. 'Downstream?'

'Of course,' the man barked. He sounded impatient, as though he expected the officers to know the route of the river. 'The Loddon starts not far from here. It can only go downstream.'

'So where's the next place they could go?' the WPC persisted.

'How do I know? They could moor up anywhere, couldn't they?'

Quentin grimaced. The man's tone and turn of phrase reminded him of his own father's bombastic manner.

'I meant the next town on the river,' the WPC said.

'Fleet, I suppose,' the man went on. 'But the river runs into Berkshire, up near Reading, and loads of smaller places on the way. Why are we standing here talking about it? Shouldn't you be getting someone out there looking for my boat?'

'Let's go inside,' the young cop suggested. 'Then you can give us a description of the boat, and we'll arrange…'

The voices faded as the couple led the two officers through the garden to the house. After waiting a few minutes to give them time to get inside, Quentin moved forward, climbed over a low wall and walked through the garden, almost colliding with a post supporting a plaque. The security light snapped on, and Quentin dropped to the ground. Glancing up, he saw the plaque faced the river and declared the property to be "The Anchorage".

He looked down to the pole where the boat had been tethered, hoping that he hadn't been seen from the house. When nothing happened and the light went off, he slithered forward on his stomach towards the riverbank, hoping the security sensor wouldn't be activated again. Switching on his phone torch, he angled it down the bank by the pole. The ground was dry, with no visible footprints, but there was a definite indentation, as though something had been thrust into it. A pole or something to push the boat away from its mooring, Quentin assumed.

'Damn,' he muttered when he couldn't see anything to give him an idea of the thief's – or thieves' – identity. There was a trail of flattened grass, but no convenient clues or evidence.

'A waste of time,' he murmured. Of course it was, he reasoned to himself. This had to be a random boat theft. Why would the Chandlers choose to steal a boat from this property? How would they even know it was here?

Disappointed, Quentin rolled onto his side just as the security lamp flicked on.

'Bloody hell!' he exclaimed as two back-shoed feet appeared in his line of vision. He looked up to see the legs and the rest of the figure beside him clad in police uniform.

'Just what I was thinking, sir,' the young policeman said. 'Do you mind telling me why you're crawling about in the dark on private property?'

* * *

It was Wanda who explained why they were there. Seeing Quentin being approached by the young cop, she ran, climbed the wall and called to them.

'It's all right, officer, I can explain,' she said when she'd reached them.

The officer stared at her, recognition dawning. He produced a torch and looked from her to Quentin.

'You're the couple from the airfield,' he said accusingly.

'Yes,' Wanda said, smiling her most alluring smile. 'We should have known nothing would get past a smart young man like you. The truth is…' She glanced at Quentin, took a deep breath and carried on. 'The truth is, the two that crashed that plane, we think they're criminals we've been trying to track down—'

'What's going on out here?'

Quentin recognized the booming voice of the man whose boat had been stolen.

'I caught this man in your garden,' the young officer said.

The boat owner's eyes bulged. 'Huh! If you've come to steal my boat, you're too late! What…'

He tailed off as he caught sight of Wanda and blinked.

'We're so sorry to disturb you at this difficult time,' she gushed. 'We're private investigators and we're trying to find two criminals. We think they might have stolen your boat.'

'Private investigators?' the officer queried, sounding suspicious. 'How do we know you're not criminals?'

'Really, officer, do we look like criminals?'

'Just a moment, Wanda,' Quentin interrupted, the thought he'd had earlier still perplexing him. 'Can you tell me how long you've had your boat?' he asked the boat owner.

'Why?' said the man. 'What's that got to do with it?'

'Maybe nothing, but it might be important. Look, the Metropolitan Police are after these crooks too, and they know we're here. The officer here can check if you like, but while we're standing here, those thieves are getting away with your boat.'

'How do you know there's more than one of them? Oh all right, I bought the boat from the previous owners when we moved here, about eighteen months ago.'

'You've only lived here eighteen months?' Quentin said, excitement rising in his stomach. 'Do you remember the name of the person you bought it from?'

The man he'd questioned, the police officer, even Wanda, stared at him.

'Please,' Quentin urged. 'It could help the police with their enquiries.'

'Now just a minute,' the young officer began.

'Ford,' said the boat owner, ignoring the officer. 'Mr and Mrs Ford.'

Quentin's hopes came tumbling down. He exchanged a glance with Wanda and guessed at her thinking. Why had they rushed all the way from Greenwich, after a hectic day, in the vain hope of catching the Chandlers? His shoulders slumped in defeat. He turned to Wanda, about to suggest they call Philmore to get them off the hook then collapse in the nearest hotel bed, when she spoke to the boat owner.

'Who was the estate agent?' she asked.

'Perfect Properties – no, Property Perfections. How is that going to help find my boat?'

Quentin's hopes rose as Wanda flashed him a triumphant smile.

'What's going on?' the female police officer called as she came through the garden, followed by the woman Quentin took to be the boat owner's wife.

'Look,' Quentin said when the young cop had explained to the WPC, 'we really are private investigators and now we know for sure it *is* the people we're after who took your boat. Hold on and I'll prove it to you.'

He pulled out his phone and called Philmore, feeling slightly guilty because he hadn't yet replaced the one Boatman had stolen but glad he'd temporarily stored Philmore's direct number on this one. When he'd explained the situation, he passed the phone to the female officer, who, despite being the same rank as her partner, seemed to have more authority. After a short conversation, she turned to her colleague and shrugged.

'Looks like they're genuine,' she said. 'He wants to know the name of the stolen boat. What did you say it was, Mr Johnson?' she added, looking at the boat owner.

'The Drifter's Dream,' he said.

She relayed the information to Philmore, then handed the phone back to Quentin.

'We'll get on to Hampshire Constabulary HQ and the Marine Policing Unit,' Philmore said curtly. 'They should be able to do something. This boat can't have got far.'

The call was abruptly cut off.

'Thanks for the info, Quentin,' Quentin muttered as he lowered the phone. Philmore was right, though. *The Drifter's Dream* couldn't have got far. Did either of the Chandlers know how to handle a boat, especially in the dark?

'Right,' said the WPC, looking purposefully at Quentin and Wanda. 'The theft's being dealt with. It's in police hands.'

For God's sake, Quentin wanted to shout, this is more than a simple boat theft.

'All right, officer,' Wanda said, sending Quentin a warning look. 'I'm sure the detective chief inspector you spoke to will have it all in hand.'

The WPC exchanged a glance with her colleague. 'Yes, well,' she said, as though she realized she'd been outranked. 'We've got your statement, Mr and Mrs Johnson. We'll let you know if we need anything else. Come on, Paul, we're done here.'

When the officers had gone, Quentin turned to the Johnsons. 'Just one thing,' he said. 'How far could they have got since they took the boat?'

'Well, it only does about eleven knots, so maybe nine or ten miles.'

'OK, thank you. Oh, and how much fuel is there?'

Mr Johnson looked peeved. 'Enough for about thirty miles,' he growled.

'Don't worry, I'm sure you'll get your boat back,' Wanda told him as they turned to leave.

'Wait!' Johnson called after them. 'If you're going to find them, I'll come with you.'

'It's all right,' Wanda called back. 'We can handle it.'

As she and Quentin hurried back to their car, Johnson's voice bellowed through the night. 'I hope so, and you bloody well better find my boat!'

Chapter Forty

'Perhaps we should have let him come,' Quentin said as they studied the map. 'What I know about boats would fit in a thimble.'

'I know a bit.' Wanda traced her finger along the river line on the page.

'I thought you didn't like boats,' Quentin said.

'I don't, not on the open sea, but I did a bit of riverboating with my brother years ago. Put the torch closer. I really need to update my phone. You can get maps and GPS on mobiles now. Anyway, I think this is about eleven or twelve miles downstream from here. If we keep watch from there, we can wait for them.'

Quentin looked where she pointed. 'OK,' he said, 'let's go.'

* * *

When they'd found the place Wanda had indicated, they navigated their way to the river. Leaving the car, they found a spot on the riverbank where they settled down to wait, their phones and a torch beside them. Wanda had already rung Philmore and told him where they were headed and why.

'I'm on it,' was all he said when she rang again to let him know their exact location.

'We should be ahead of them,' Quentin said, wrapping Mozart's travel blanket around Wanda's shoulders.

'I hope we're not here all night,' Wanda said. 'I don't like the dogs being cooped up too long.'

'I'm sure they'll be all right. They've been fed and watered and you can let them out for a bit if need be.'

Quentin shone his torch along the bank. This stretch of the river seemed narrower, with just enough room for two boats to pass each other. On Quentin's left, there was nothing but grass and bushes for as far as he could see. On his right, there were a few large properties similar to the one the boat had been stolen from, the river making a natural boundary to the backs of the gardens. The moon had appeared from behind a ridge of clouds, lightening the view of the opposite bank. It showed the outlines of bushes and overhanging trees, their still bare branches bowing down to the water as if in subjugation.

Quentin stared in the direction that *The Drifter's Dream* should come from, wondering if they were wasting their time. Who was to say the Chandlers hadn't already abandoned it? They could have disembarked and stolen a car. But why would they do that so soon after taking the boat? They probably thought the boat wouldn't be reported missing until the morning. Maybe–

His chaotic thoughts were interrupted by the chugging of an engine. Quentin stiffened and Wanda gripped his arm.

'How will we know it's them?' she asked.

'I don't think many boats will be on the river at this time of night,' Quentin answered. 'It's not the Thames. And the timing's right.'

He wondered when the local police, or anyone from the Marine Policing Unit, would show. If they didn't, the boat would go on by. The police could intervene further downstream, but he and Wanda might miss the action then.

Quentin's mouth tightened. He thought of Lorna, kidnapped on the Chandlers' orders; he thought of Dave, killed because of the Chandlers' illicit money laundering racket, and Victor, left injured and bleeding beside his dead master; and he thought of Will Chandler, raising that lump of wood ready to strike him.

He leapt to his feet as the prow of a boat came into sight, a dark shape in the moonlight.

'Wanda,' he said urgently. 'Drive the car down as far as you can to this spot, but turn off the lights when you're here. Then as soon as they're level with us, put the lights on full beam and keep them on so I can read the name on the boat. If it's them—'

Wanda was gone before he finished the sentence, which was just as well, because he had no idea what he would do if this was the Chandlers. As the boat drew nearer, Quentin's stomach churned. The car pulled up about ten feet behind him, sidelights only showing. Then those lights were switched off. Quentin turned on the torch, went to the car and took out the binoculars.

'Keep the window down,' he told Wanda. 'I'll shout when to put the lights on.'

Returning to the riverbank, he crouched down. The chugging grew louder as the boat drew closer. Then it was there, directly ahead of him.

'Now!' he yelled.

Suddenly the water and the boat were flooded with light. Raising the binoculars, Quentin read the name of the boat's side. *The Drifter's Dream.*

'Gotcha!' he muttered. Then, as the boat seemed to slow, he saw someone on deck, shading their eyes from the light.

'Philip Chandler,' he whispered in triumph.

His thoughts whirled as he tried to think how he could stop the boat. Nothing came. Come on, Quentin, do something, he thought desperately. That triggered an unwelcome internal voice – a callous, cultured voice, sneering at his failed attempts to capture the Chandlers.

Something snapped in his head, and he did the only thing he could think of. He shook off his jacket, took off his shoes, jumped into the river, and swam.

* * *

The water was cold. Quentin gasped in shock but concentrated on getting to the boat before it was out reach. He'd been a fast swimmer in his youth, but he was out of practice. Nevertheless, he pressed on, all the time thinking how stupid he was trying to catch a moving boat in the dark and with no idea what he would do if he did. This quest seemed ridiculous, even to him, but every time he almost gave up, he heard that cultured voice mocking him, and it spurred him on.

Suddenly the sky was ablaze with light. From the riverbank came the scream of sirens and the pulsing of blue lights, but what really threatened the boat ahead was another craft fast approaching from the other direction, in the middle of the channel, its hooter blaring in a persistent warning.

The Drifter's Dream was obliged to either stop or collide with it. It slowed, and the chug of its engine ceased. Quentin had almost reached it when the hollow sound of a voice carried through the air. He couldn't distinguish the words, but guessed the voice was coming through a megaphone. He trod water, seeking a means of climbing aboard the boat. Before he had time to do anything, a loud splash sounded on the other side. Bloody hell, he thought, as he realized what had happened. Turning and striking out, he rounded the stern to see a man floundering in the water.

Quentin didn't know which of the Chandlers it was, but whoever it was and whatever they'd done, he wasn't prepared to let them drown. He increased his strokes, reaching the man just as his head disappeared under the water. It had been a long time since Quentin had done his life-saving course, but the basics came back to him as a flailing arm was flung up. Managing to grasp the collar of the jacket, he pulled the person to him face up, forced himself onto his back and, with an arm around the waterlogged body, began to swim towards the riverbank. The man he was holding kicked out, struggling against Quentin's grip.

'Keep still, unless you want us both to drown!' Quentin shouted. He spluttered as water slopped into his mouth, then turned his head and spewed it out. It wasn't far to the riverbank, but lugging a fully clothed deadweight hampered his progress. Relief swept over Quentin when his hand touched the bank. He hauled himself up, took in a few lungfuls of air and turned his attention to the man whose life he'd saved, dragging him clear of the water.

Pandemonium broke loose. Uniformed police appeared from nowhere, someone threw a blanket round Quentin's shoulders, Mozart bounded up to him followed by Wanda, and Philip Chandler sat up and was immediately arrested and handcuffed.

Will Chandler, it seemed, was still aboard the stolen boat. Two people, from the Marine Policing Unit, Quentin assumed, were going aboard *The Drifter's Dream*, shouting for Will Chandler to give himself up. After several minutes, a figure appeared from the cabin. Will Chandler, his shoulders slumped in defeat, stood before the two officers and allowed himself to be handcuffed. Quentin and Wanda watched as he was brought ashore. The two brothers, Philip still dripping river water and Will shaking his head as though in disbelief, stood side by side for a moment before they were guided to the waiting police cars.

One of the officers who'd brought Will ashore spoke to Quentin.

'Well done,' he said. 'Hope that bloke's grateful for you pulling him out. Stupid, jumping in like that. Shame we can't hold on to those two, but apparently they're wanted by the Met. They'll be transferred first thing in the morning.'

Quentin exchanged a look with Wanda. Philmore had acted on their information and put things in place. And, Quentin thought in an uncharacteristic fit of pique, Philmore would probably get all the credit.

Chapter Forty-one

'There's still something I don't understand,' Colin said the following evening back at Wanda's, where he had invited himself to dinner with her and Quentin. 'What happened to the evidence Dave had? The stuff he was supposed to give to Lorna? I mean, he was killed for it, and the Chandlers never found it or they wouldn't have kidnapped Lorna, thinking she had it. So where is it?'

'That's what's puzzled me all along,' Quentin admitted, 'until this morning. Anne Roberts rang.'

Colin's eyebrows lifted above his glasses. 'Dave's sister?'

'Yep. She received a flash drive in the post from Dave, with a note telling her to take it to the police if anything happened to him. The thing is, it was put through her neighbour's door by mistake, and the neighbour was away and only came back yesterday. The flash drive should provide enough evidence to make a case against the Chandlers,' Quentin said.

'There's something else,' Wanda said. 'The paper Quentin found with a number on it, well, the imprint of a number, in the Maserati – it turns out it was the code to get into a secret file on Property Perfections computer before it was wiped. Dave either sussed it or found it by accident. Philmore's going to produce it as evidence in court when the trial comes up.'

'Look at this,' Quentin said, bringing up the photo of the crossword he'd taken at Dave's house. 'Code, Trafalgar–'

'The Battle of Trafalgar, 1805,' Wanda interrupted. 'That's the number from the Maserati.'

Quentin recalled the understanding that had flooded him when he'd learned this. His instinct hadn't let him down. The words in Dave's crossword book weren't just random answers, and he'd done the right thing by keeping the paper he'd found.

'So what exactly was on the flash drive?' Colin asked.

'It hasn't been completely analysed yet, but according to Philmore, it shows a record of where any illegal money comes from and how it's fed through their system in various ways, via different businesses and investments, so its source can't be traced. Then the perpetrators, in this case Cultured Voice and the Chandlers, eventually end up with what looks like legitimate money.'

'Right. And the house where the boat was stolen from, the owners bought it through Property Perfections?' Colin asked.

'Yep,' Quentin said. 'And it wasn't that long ago. The Anchorage is quite a memorable name. If Philip handled the transaction himself, he'd likely remember that the sale included the boat and the mooring, so they took a chance that it was still there.'

'Right,' Colin said again. 'What did Philmore say about you cornering the Chandlers?'

'He was pleased, I think. You know Philmore, he doesn't say much.'

Philmore hadn't said much, Quentin recalled, but his heart had lifted at the DCI's last words.

'Well done, Quentin,' he'd said as though he meant it. 'We seem to make a good team, don't we?' Then, as if he'd realized he shouldn't encourage a member of the public to get involved with police business, he'd added, 'Unofficially, that is.'

'Debbie Francis rang later to say they've got the other kidnapper,' Quentin said now. 'Joe Walters gave him up for a deal. Walters said it was the other guy who killed Dave. And they found Lorna's DNA in the workshop at Martha Chandler's house in Putney.'

It had been a morning of phone calls, Quentin realized. His spirits had risen when Lorna had rung to congratulate him, and to thank him again for rescuing her.

'We'll meet up soon,' she'd said. 'I want to take you and Wanda for a celebratory meal.'

'By the way,' Quentin said, suddenly remembering something else that Anne Roberts had said. 'Anne's son has agreed to take Victor.'

'Oh. I'll miss him being around,' Wanda said.

'So will I,' Quentin admitted, 'but I think it's for the best. Apparently he's already got a dog, so Victor will have company.'

'The one I feel for is Tina,' Wanda said. 'She's out of a job – they all are at Property Perfections.'

'She's not worried about it,' Quentin assured her. 'I spoke to her this morning and she's already looking for something else. She wouldn't have stayed anyway.'

'Don't blame her,' quipped Colin. 'She's probably realized there's no such thing as the perfect property.'

'Oh, I don't know,' Quentin countered. 'I'm perfectly happy with my house.'

Except for one thing, he thought as soon as he'd said this. Cultured Voice knows where it is.

'Tell Colin our other news, Wanda,' he said, refusing to let Cultured Voice intrude on his euphoria.

'What's this then, Wanda?' Colin asked.

'Well,' Wanda began, looking at Colin as though she knew he would raise an objection. 'We're going back to the Scilly Isles tomorrow.'

Colin shot her an incredulous look. 'But Quentin can't take part in the race now.'

'Why can't I?' Quentin asked. 'I never withdrew my entry, and the run's not till Sunday. We've managed to get a flight to Newquay tomorrow, and we can go direct to Tresco from Penzance.' Quentin's enthusiasm faded a little. 'It's costing the earth, though.'

'I should think it would,' Colin said. 'Better hope for a lottery win. It's not as if you'll get paid for catching the Chandlers, is it?'

'No,' Wanda said. 'We've raided the piggy bank. I'm sure we'll get some paying clients once we've settled back into work.'

Colin pursed his lips and looked at Wanda, but said nothing to that.

'Oh well,' he said after a short silence, 'I suppose you both deserve a break after everything you've done.'

'You helped, Colin,' Wanda reminded him. 'We wouldn't have found out about The Hacienda if you hadn't rung Property Perfections when you did.'

Colin grinned. 'Yeah. I think I'm getting used to this detective malarkey. Count me out of the Scilly Isles though. If I want to see loads of people running their socks off, I'll watch the London Marathon from my own armchair, thanks very much. I'll look after Mozart and Victor though, as long as you're not gone too long.'

'Thanks, Colin,' Quentin said. 'We'll only be a few days.'

He wondered whether to mention the call he'd had from his parents late last night, but decided against it. They were coming over with his sister later in the year. A lovely family get-together, as his mother had described it. Despite the trepidation Quentin felt at seeing his father, with whom his relationship had never been easy, Quentin was delighted. Yet he felt he needed a break, time to distance himself from this latest case before having to think about anything else.

Yes, a break. A few days in Tresco with Wanda would do the trick.

Chapter Forty-two

The applause and shouts of encouragement from supporters along the Tresco marathon route filled Quentin's ears as the finish line came into view. He had been among the leaders for the first lap, but his run had slowed to a dogged trudge. His muscles protested against the vigorous pace he tried to put them through. The lapse in his training since his previous stay in the Scilly Isles showed itself in the most natural way – his legs refused to do what his brain told them to do, especially on the hills.

'Well done!' Wanda greeted him when he stood panting in front of her.

'I was rubbish,' he gasped between painful breaths.

'I'm surprised you even finished after what you've been through lately. That's a success in itself.'

After the post-event celebrations, with its carb-laden food, free-flowing drinks and friendly locals, Quentin felt better. They'd left it too late to find anywhere to stay, having cancelled their booking when they'd left the Scillies to pursue the case, but managed to get one of the tents on offer from the organisers.

'I've had more comfortable accommodation,' Wanda said as they hammered in the last tent peg. 'It's a long time since I slept in a tent. Still, this is nothing like the last time, thank goodness.'

'Really? Why, what happened last time?'

For a moment Wanda looked as though she would explain, but then a closed expression came over her face and she turned away.

'Not now,' she said. 'I don't want to spoil–'

She stopped at the ringing of Quentin's mobile, found the phone and checked the display. 'Number withheld,' she said, handing it to Quentin.

Not relishing another threatening conversation with Cultured Voice, Quentin took the phone tentatively.

'Yes?'

'You managed to get the Chandlers arrested after all, then, Mr Cadbury.'

'I did.'

'Just in time. I was about to take the matter into my own hands. Such a stupid risk, attempting to fly a plane that wasn't airworthy, don't you think? Still, I suppose they were desperate. People do strange things when they're desperate, don't they? Well, I don't know how you tracked them down, although I daresay the delectable Mrs Merrydrew helped.'

There was a pause, as though the caller was expecting Quentin to deny that Wanda was involved. Quentin said nothing, determined not to rise to the bait.

'So,' the cultured voice went on, his tone somewhat softer, 'I'm going to give you a second chance and repeat my offer of employment. You really should consider it, you know, Quentin. It would reap more profit than your quaint little detective agency. I could be persuaded to include Mrs Merrydrew on the payroll, if it would change your mind. I believe she's proven to be reliable and loyal, even if only to you.'

Heat suffused Quentin's neck and face as anger and disbelief swamped him.

'You– you… She… She's not interested. She'll never be interested.'

'Really?' The cultured voice resumed its hard edge. 'Perhaps you should let Mrs Merrydrew speak for herself. Just think of the luxuries you could both indulge in. You'd be able to supply her with the things she no doubt deserves, and reward her with rather better hotel accommodation than the cheap places you usually take her to.'

Stunned, Quentin gasped. He cast a look around the tent and thanked God that his nemesis couldn't see where they were sleeping tonight.

'One last thing, Mr Cadbury. This little escapade has cost me dearly. I assure you it won't take me long to make up the shortfall, but you owe me. So whether you take my money or not, you haven't heard the last of me. I'm still here, and I intend to stay around for quite a while, so watch your step. Goodbye, Quentin. Give my regards to your policeman friend, and Mrs Merrydrew of course.'

The words, and their inference, echoed in Quentin's head. Even though they had solved Dave's murder, had the killer and kidnappers arrested, identified a money laundering enterprise and captured the Chandlers, the real culprit, with his cultured voice and malicious insinuations, was still at large and had made Quentin feel like an under-achieving schoolboy.

'Giving you the benefit of his opinion again, is he?' Wanda asked brightly, as though she felt Quentin's discomfort. 'Did he threaten to kill you again?'

When Quentin shook his head, she continued. 'Well then, ignore him, Quentin. Come on, give me a hand with these bedrolls.'

Bedrolls! Quentin closed his eyes. For a horrifying moment, he imagined Cultured Voice in the opulent lounge of a swanky hotel with Wanda on his arm; a beautiful asset and an enchanting enhancement to his sophisticated lifestyle. He imagined…

'Hey,' Wanda said. 'Don't let him spoil the day. Come on. Camping will make a change and it'll be fun.'

'Fun? What, a groundsheet and public toilets? Wouldn't you rather be at The Dorchester or somewhere?'

'The Dorchester? Where did that come from? Oh, I'm not saying that wouldn't be nice, but you know, there are some things money can't buy.'

'Are there?'

Wanda unfurled the bedrolls, sat on one and patted the one next to her. Quentin sat down and she snaked an arm over his shoulders.

'I don't know what he said to you, but don't let him fool you. I remember what he told you that time – that he didn't get close to people, didn't have dependants and didn't want a family around his neck, but I bet he secretly wishes he had someone he could tell his troubles to at the end of a difficult day. I bet he's lonely.'

'Lonely!' Quentin had never considered that.

'I know one thing,' Wanda said, taking his chin in her hand and tilting his face to hers. 'I'd rather be in a tent with you than anywhere on earth with him.'

Quentin's depression fled and his spirits soared. Never mind Cultured Voice, with his threats and money and access to the higher things in life; never mind Colin, with his nice, comfortable house and generous pension; never mind any of the men who lusted after this beautiful woman beside him. Wanda was here, in a tent, in one of the most beautiful places in Britain. With him.

Nothing else mattered.

THE END

If you enjoyed this book, please let others know by leaving
a quick review on Amazon. Also, if you spot anything
untoward in the paperback, get in touch. We strive for the
best quality and appreciate reader feedback.

editor@thebookfolks.com

www.thebookfolks.com

More fiction by the author

THE MYSTERY OF THE HIDDEN FORTUNE

Book #1 in the Quentin Cadbury Investigations

Quentin Cadbury, a useless twenty-something, is left to look after his late aunt's London house when his parents head to Australia. But burglars seem determined to break in, and not even the stray cat he befriends can help him. As the thieves are after something pretty valuable, and illegal, he must grow up pretty fast to get out of a sticky situation.

THE MYSTERY OF THE LUCKY CAT

Book #2 in the Quentin Cadbury Investigations

Private detective Quentin Cadbury has his neighbour's recently demised cat in a holdall. Quite why, will be explained. But when he tackles a mugger, his bag gets mixed up with another. This has different contents – some very suspicious goods. Seeing an opportunity to catch a criminal, he blunders into a dangerous situation.

THE MYSTERY DOWN UNDER

Book #3 in the Quentin Cadbury Investigations

Evading a London gangster with a bone to pick, private investigator Quentin Cadbury and his sidekick Wanda Merrydrew decide to visit Australia to catch up with Quentin's family. Yet when they discover a burglar is causing upset in their quiet Sydney suburb, they can't help but get involved. Can Quentin catch a thief and prove his mettle to his ever-disappointed father?

THE MYSTERY ON THE CORNISH COAST

Book #4 in the Quentin Cadbury Investigations

Most people relish going to sunny Cornwall. Not so private investigator Quentin Cadbury, who is forced on a fool's errand by a career criminal who has his teeth into him. Tasked with delivering a package on pain of death, the hapless private eye is sent on a wild goose chase. Can he wrong-foot a master villain?

All FREE with Kindle Unlimited and available in paperback and hardback from Amazon.

Other titles of interest

PARTING WORDS
by Traude Ailinger

When sassy Edinburgh journalist Amy Thornton infiltrates
an environmental activist group, little does she know that
one of its members, stalked by an ex-boyfriend, will soon
be murdered. Thus she will collide once again with
bumbling cop DI Russell McCord. Anyone would think it's
their destiny to be ever entwined, whether they like it or not!

FREE with Kindle Unlimited and available in paperback!

CATFISH
by Sadie Norman

It is not without some malice that rookie detective Anna McArthur is called "crazy" by her colleagues. She certainly tends to act first and think later. But when Anna discovers the body of a murdered woman who has "catfish" carved into her chest, she feels a personal duty to do everything she can to up her game and find the killer.

FREE with Kindle Unlimited and available in paperback!

Sign up to our mailing list to find out about new releases and special offers!

www.thebookfolks.com